W9-CFG-248

THE

ABSENCE OF

EVELYN

Also by Jackie Townsend

FICTION

Reel Life: A Novel

Imperfect Pairings: A Novel

THE

ABSENCE OF

EVELYN

A NOVEL

JACKIE TOWNSEND

Copyright © 2017 Jackie Townsend
All rights reserved, including the right to reproduce this book orpor-
tions thereof in any form whatsoever.

Published by SparkPress, a BookSparks imprint,
A division of SparkPoint Studio, LLC
Tempe, Arizona, USA, 85281
www.gosparkpress.com

Published 2017
Printed in the United States of America
ISBN: 978-1-943006-21-2 (pbk)
ISBN: 978-1-943006-23-6 (e-bk)

Library of Congress Control Number: 2016958801

Cover design © Julie Metz, Ltd./metzdesign.com
Author photo © Ron Goodman
Formatting by Kiran Spees

All company and/or product names may be trade names, logos,
trademarks, and/or registered trademarks and are the property of their
respective owners.

This is a work of fiction. Names, characters, places, and incidents either
are the product of the author's imagination or are used fictitiously. Any
resemblance to actual persons, living or dead, is entirely coincidental.

For Mom

"I closed the box and put it in the closet.
There is no real way to deal with everything we lose."

—Joan Didion, *Where I Was From*

1

At least that *is over*, Rhonda thought, falling into bed. What was supposed to have been Rhonda's forty-seventh-birthday celebration had turned into something else once the ladies had gotten wind that her divorce was final. Who were these friends? There must have been more than thirty of them, these women of the Sonoran desert, ascending in their golf carts and SUVs to reach the sprawling house that clung to the highest peak of the Catalina mountainside, bearing gift baskets of Grey Goose, chocolates, and all that silly lingerie, as if Rhonda were some cliché. And yes, she had humored them, these friends for whom she'd done so much over the years, these friends whom she might not call friends in another life, because in that other life there had been no real need for such friends. But her sister was no longer of this earth, and so perhaps Rhonda had gotten a little carried away with it all tonight, regrettably now, letting loose in the name of solidarity, of womanhood, a "we will not be beaten" kind of thing.

It might not have been so regrettable had Rhonda's daughter, Olivia, not chosen to walk into the Great Room at exactly the wrong moment— Rhonda parading around in that powder-blue silk robe (over her clothes), having just guffawed to her friends some irrelevantly snide comment, "A half of a lot is a lot," what was followed by a cacophony of hyena-like laughter, the pop of another bottle, and Rhonda turning around to see Olivia marching out of the room.

1

Rhonda, buzzed and drifting off, woke herself with a start. It was just before 10:00 p.m. and she'd not said good night to Olivia, the last of her three children to still need her, even if she didn't know it. Rhonda forced herself from bed. Olivia, well into her second year at the University of Arizona, had been popping in of late, surprising Rhonda at all hours of the day and night. Little forewarning. She could no longer concentrate at the sorority or at the college library, she had assured her mother, which was actually code for her daughter wasn't getting along with anyone. Code for her daughter, who couldn't seem to be anyone but herself, had said the wrong thing to the wrong person, again.

Black from the inside out was the desert this time of night, and Rhonda had to feel her way along the walls of her bedroom in order to get to the hallway, where a light beamed via sensor. A few yards farther, another light beamed, then another, as if the world came to life only as Rhonda walked through it. And so it went along the *endless* corridor, as Rhonda liked to call it. She'd clocked it once: thirty-six seconds exactly to walk from her bedroom, past her office, the formal living and dining rooms, the wine cellar and guest suite, to reach the Great Room ("Great," as christened by the architect because it was the place in the house where great times were to be had by all at all times), where cathedral ceilings stretched out over an expansive living area and kitchen, with a fireplace big enough to camp out in.

From the Great Room, where Rhonda stood now, a wall of French doors opened up onto an indoor-outdoor patio, where plush couches sat large gatherings comfortably under a timed spray of cool mist. An infinity pool poured water over the edge of a jutting cliff, where manicured fairways sloped and curved. In the distance, a saguaro-studded valley.

Daniel, Rhonda's newly crowned ex, had designed the house himself, sparing no expense to ensure that it exuded the aura of its natural desert surroundings. Wood beams from an old Sonoran ranch, corrugated-steel walls from an Aztec Indian reserve, arched windows from a burned-down adobe church—most of the fixtures and furniture were sourced from antique salvage shops. Rhonda was never quite sure whether the result was gaudy or sublime.

Certainly now, she looked around and thought, *I have my answer.*

The ashes in the wood-burning stove were still smoldering. The caterers had cleaned up after the party, but there were stray pieces of lingerie draped over chairs, ravaged boxes of chocolates splayed about the kitchen island, a few empty bottles of wine exhumed from the depths of Daniel's cellar, errant glasses left here and there. Among them she spotted some water, which she grabbed and guzzled.

She gasped when she was done, the water gone. It took her a minute to catch her breath. What remained was a tomb of silence that always unnerved her. Never would she get used to the stillness of these late hours. And, just like clockwork, the curtains began motoring to their closed position. What shouldn't be startling always was.

After the curtains came the shades.

Ten o'clock, every night, the house went into lockdown. Daniel used to go to bed at nine thirty without fail, Rhonda being "Just a few steps behind, dear!" In actuality, she never went to bed before midnight. She hadn't had the heart to tell Daniel this when he'd programmed the various timers to accommodate everyone's living patterns, because that would mean pointing out the fact that he'd not even missed her in bed beside him; she didn't want him to miss her. Her timer had never been in sync with his, and vice versa—a fact made so evident by his departure, that timer having been up for some time. He'd not salvaged one antique on his way out the door. He took a few trinkets from his world travels, the framed blueprints of his first golf club designs, but the rest? Who ever wanted all of it anyway? He'd moved into one of those cookie-cutter fairway villas scattered about the base of the craggy mountainside, temporarily, he said, until he and Brie figured out what they wanted to do.

Rhonda plucked a black thong off the floor and stuffed it under a couch cushion, then began treading lightly down the opposite hall, toward the beam of orange light she'd spotted outside the theater room, which signified a warm body. This side of the house was considered the children's wing; the "treading lightly" was an old habit Rhonda had been unable to break even after the "children" had grown up and moved out. Mostly moved out, that is.

Once there, Rhonda took a moment to study her daughter through the double-glass doors of the room where no movie was playing, just Olivia, sitting there in the dark, swallowed up by an oversize leather chair, knees up, her hair looking more platinum than it a had a week ago, and longer, snaking down the sides of her face (forbidding anybody to see the tiny birthmark under her lip) and over her breasts, pooling on her belly, where she studied her iPhone.

A deep breath, and Rhonda pushed open the door and stood there. How best to start, when your daughter was not speaking to you? She finally just slid into a seat in the second row, released the recliner, plopped her feet on the rest, and spoke to the back of her daughter's head. "You didn't tell me you were coming home, Olivia."

"Next time I'll send out an alert."

"I wish you would use the front door like I asked."

"I have to ring the bell to enter my own home?" She looked back at her mother and, with no small amount of horror, said, "Mom, why are you still wearing that?"

Rhonda looked down. Bit her lip. She'd forgotten. "Oh, it's that silly movie," she said, waving it off with a hand.

Olivia faced forward again and said nothing.

"That movie with Joan Allen and Kevin Costner. I forget the name." She paused a moment to think of it. "Joan Allen's husband abandons her, just takes off with his secretary one day and doesn't come back, doesn't call. Nothing. Anyway, she takes to drinking Grey Goose for breakfast and wandering around at all hours of the day in a long, powder-blue silk robe not unlike this one." Rhonda gave herself another once-over. "Joan wore it better, as you can imagine."

"I can imagine," Olivia said, which Rhonda interpreted as an opening. She slid forward and draped her arms over the seat in front of her. "You'll never see a more pissed-off housewife in your life as you will Joan Allen in this movie. A cliché, perhaps. But hilarious, nonetheless."

She let go a little laugh, and Olivia said, "I have no idea what you are talking about."

"Maybe you need to see it."

"Maybe I do."

"*Upside of Anger.* That's the name of it."

"But that's the thing, Mom. What I've finally figured out. You're *not* angry."

No. Not angry, Rhonda thought. *Embarrassed, perhaps, but not angry.* "I will be no cliché, Olivia," Rhonda said in a voice of dead calm. "You must know that I was humoring those women tonight. And while I loved Joan Allen in that movie, that woman is not me."

"And here I was feeling all sorry for you," Olivia mumbled. And then she said something Rhonda didn't catch.

"What did you say?"

"I said you're happier with him gone."

Rhonda sat back and sighed.

"It's like you wanted him to meet Brie and leave."

They sat in silence for some time, until it occurred to Rhonda, "You're not worried about me, are you?"

Olivia didn't say anything.

"This isn't why you've been coming home, is it?"

Some kind of strangled huff.

Rhonda got up and went and stood before the projection screen. All this time she'd assumed that Olivia had been having problems at the sorority. Well, this wouldn't do. She cleared her throat. "Olivia. Honey. You absolutely do not need to worry about me. What happens to your father and me is irrelevant. *You* are what's relevant. You need to keep focused on yourself and your dreams and your future. Nothing changes, Olivia. Your father and I both love you, and we will continue to be there for you, no matter what. You do not need to worry about anything but yourself."

"Did you ever love Dad?"

After a pause, "What?"

"Did. You. Ever. Love. Dad?"

Rhonda, thrown by the question (which was *so* not the point), not to mention her daughter sitting there waiting, and so innocently, for an answer, could barely pretend to give it thought. "Your father and I have always respected each other, Olivia."

"I get that people fall out of love, or whatever, but you must have loved him in the beginning? I mean, right?"

She smiled, tightly, "Like I said, Olivia, our relationship has nothing to do with anything that you need to worry about."

"But—"

"Oh, does it really matter?"

"Holy crap, of course it matters!" Olivia jumped out of her chair, startling Rhonda, who stumbled backward against a wall speaker. The way her daughter's eyes were bearing down on Rhonda suddenly, well, it might as well have been Evelyn there, swimming around in that sea of deep green. Love, above all else. "God, you remind me of her sometimes."

"Who? What?" And then, "Oh, please. Mom. Don't . . ."

"Your aunt Evelyn asked me that same question once, point-blank and knowing the answer."

Olivia fell back down into her chair, looking defeated, pushed aside, what happened whenever Rhonda chose these rare moments to exhume her sister's ghost.

"So you never loved Dad." Olivia's was not a question this time, but an answer. "Not even in the beginning."

"I don't believe in that kind of love," Rhonda responded, in a tone so even and empty that Olivia's face drained of color, then turned red when Rhonda didn't waver, couldn't waver, not about this. It was the hard, cold truth, and if her daughter was going to ask the question, well, then fine—she needed to be ready to hear the answer.

And she'd heard it. Shoulders up, chin down, phone out, Olivia was back in lockdown mode.

A minute went by. "So what? Now you're never going to look at me again?"

Olivia looked at Rhonda, but from so far away it was like she was hardly there.

"Oh, come on, Olivia. You really think it works like that?"

No response.

"*You*, Olivia," came barreling out of Rhonda's depths. "*You* are living proof that it doesn't work like that."

Olivia looked up, alarmed.

"If your biological parents had been remotely responsible adults, instead of acting like high school sweethearts, they wouldn't have had to give you up!"

Olivia's mouth fell open, while Rhonda had to keep from visibly shaking.

A moment passed.

"I thought you said my birth parents *were* high school sweethearts."

Never have a conversation with your daughter half-drunk, Rhonda reminded herself. "Isn't that what I said?"

2

After the exchange with Rhonda, Olivia went and grabbed a bottle of Grey Goose from the stack that now sat behind the bar and took it with her to the study nook, a horseshoe-shaped room framed by windows that wrapped around a giant, hundred-year-old saguaro cactus looming in the front drive. Olivia never could stand the sight of that prickly beast—massive, stark, and illuminated by a single flood-light. When all the other lights timed off, this one timed on—a rebellion of sorts.

Her criminal law book lay open before her, but she couldn't focus. The word *respect* kept swirling around in her mind alongside the two vodka shots she'd downed in quick succession, and the pathetic image of her mother wandering around all tangled up in that silk robe. Over her clothes, of course, Olivia would have expected no less of her mother who had likely never worn a piece of lingerie in her life.

I don't believe in that kind of love.

Olivia's biological parents had been in *that* kind of love, so she'd been told—and as far as Olivia was concerned, if there wasn't *that* kind of love, then what was there?

Even Olivia's father had figured it out. "I'm fifty-five, Olivia. I want a real marriage. I want to be *in* love." Olivia flushed now just thinking of how she had flushed then, when her father had told her this, for she'd never heard him say the word *love* with such, well, vigor, for love was something never spoken of in their house, not in any real context anyway, beyond "Love you, hon," which her father would say using the same inflection to whomever he was speaking. In fact, he'd use the same inflection for most everything he said, including, "You're adopted, Liv," said matter-of-factly on Olivia's eighth birthday and while scooping a spoonful of Chinese takeout onto Olivia's plate. "I just thought you should know."

But ever since her dad found Brie, he couldn't speak to Olivia without his eyes tearing up. His voice maintained its uncompromising tone, just this incessant need to wipe tears from his cheeks. He would then frown at his hand, as if it were some aberration. As if he'd woken up from some long sleep and now had to go to *his people*.

And Olivia? Where were *her people*?

Olivia bit her cuticles. It was as if her parents' divorce had left a big, gaping hole in the fabric of her being. She'd never put serious thought into her adoption other than what her mother had relayed to her, which was that, according to the agency, Olivia's birth parents were love-struck high school kids in no way prepared to care for a baby. Olivia had no interest in knowing more. In her mind, her mom and dad were her birth parents. Oh, sure, Olivia might have used her adoption against her mother every so often, as a way to hurt her, or elicit a reaction from her, but even in those moments Olivia had never really *felt* adopted, just lonely, wanting different things from those around her. Feeling different. However much she might have hated her parents at times, she never stopped loving them because she knew they loved her. She'd only ever felt safe, coddled, and, ultimately, proud to be the daughter of such an esteemed pair. As Rhonda liked to phrase it, they'd chosen *her*.

But pair they were no longer. And so now, lately, all these doubts, rumblings, this sense that her mother wasn't telling Olivia the truth about, well, anything.

She logged into Skype. An array of contacts popped up, many of them sorority sisters whose statuses were either *offline* or *away*. It was Saturday night, after all; she moaned, low and long. *Hello? Anybody out there?*

Words, swallowed into the desert night.

It wasn't like she didn't want to be out having fun. Hadn't given it her all, as she tended to do when entering new social situations. Throwing everything she had at it. She'd rushed six sororities her freshman year. Gotten accepted by only one. It was her third choice, but still, she'd put her heart and soul into it. Attended every last event. Threw her parents' money at whatever cause or need. The scavenger hunts, costume parties, keg fests, fundraisers, marches, and walks; she'd slept around when it was required, done some drugs, passed out on the lawn, thrown up in the quad. She'd given all of herself and then some, and for what? Overzealous, someone had said about her; desperate, said another. Her reputation now preceded her, and now, not unlike high school, she was being ostracized. Ignored.

Her brother Stevie was online, she now noticed. They'd connected on Skype some time ago but had yet to actually call each other. They rarely communicated at all, in fact. Both of her brothers were much older than Olivia; Rhonda had driven them into sports at young ages, Chase the golf protégé and Stevie the soccer phenom, and by the time Olivia had come along, their lives had already been worlds apart from hers.

Olivia, too, had once had a sport, that sport being inherent, assumed, being the daughter of an Olympic champion. Sometimes Olivia wondered if she'd been adopted for just this purpose—following in her mom's footsteps. Club volleyball at age ten so that by fifteen she'd be starting varsity as a high school freshman. And she was. Had been. Ironically, she wasn't bad. The sport wasn't bad. The whole thing just felt wrong—practice, the sweating, the grinding pain of it all. Not to mention the fact that Olivia was five foot two, while everyone else in her family had to duck through doorways, including Rhonda.

"I quit." Olivia hadn't done this to hurt her mother. She had wanted to make her mother proud, but it just couldn't be *this*. After five minutes of scoffing, after Rhonda had realized Olivia was serious, they proceeded to argue for a good hour to no avail. Then Rhonda went into panic mode. She'd corralled the girls on the team. God knows what she'd paid them because for the most part they, to this point, had put up with Olivia rather than befriend her. But there they were, one by one, standing on her doorstep with home-baked sweets piled on wobbly paper plates and telling Olivia how much the team needed her. How it was no fun without her. Then came the athletic director. Even Chase and Stevie took time out from their adult lives, those that, ironically, had nothing to do with sports. "You're gonna get fat," Chase had said. Looking back on it now, she knew that statement wasn't far from the truth.

"But what will you do after school?" Rhonda had wanted to know, which was when Olivia dropped the theater bomb. "I'm a kid, Mom. I need to explore my passions." If there were a word that made her mom's skin crawl, *passions* was it.

But Rhonda was Rhonda, a woman who got with the program. There she was, seated front and center of every single theater production her daughter had subsequently participated in (even when Olivia's role was backstage), whooping and hollering when the curtain came down as if Olivia had just won a big game because she didn't know what else to do, for once the shock that her daughter wasn't going to be an Olympic champion like her settled in, she'd bucked up and supported Olivia—many checks were written for private singing, acting, and dancing lessons—in this orthogonal direction in which she'd taken her life.

But even after all that, even as Olivia headed off to the University of Arizona to study, not drama because one couldn't have a future in drama and Olivia so wanted to grasp the reins of her own future, but prelaw, as someone—she can't remember who now—had suggested, she got the feeling her mother still looked at her and saw an athlete.

Am I just a reflection in my mother's eyes?

Hadn't Olivia had dreams once? Of escaping this barren wasteland of a desert suburb that had sucked her parents dry of whatever love they'd apparently never felt for each other? Hadn't her plan been to go to an *out-of-state* university, one with a reputed dramatic arts program? Why had she so quickly settled on an in-state school? To be close to home? Some gravitational force beyond her control?

What was she still doing here?

Olivia dialed Stevie on Skype without thinking. She needed to talk to someone, someone who understood at least something about her, and like Olivia, her brothers were raised by Rhonda but were not of her flesh and blood (they were Dad's kids from his first marriage). Stevie had played D-league soccer in England for a few years, before Rhonda found him a job at the local private banking branch of UBS. Chase, who'd gone to Stanford on a golf scholarship, ended up quitting the team, and then the school, six months before graduating. He'd bummed around for a while, and then, out of left field, moved to Tucson to cofound a medical device company in which his parents were major investors. But he spent holidays in Alaska with his real mother now, with whom he'd recently reconciled. Olivia rarely saw him anymore. Neither did her mom.

At least Olivia wasn't Rhonda's only disappointment.

Meanwhile, Olivia's computer rang on into oblivion. No Stevie. No surprise. She pressed *end*, and then proceeded to sit there, feeling the weight of her heart pull her body down into her chair. She didn't know what was coming over her. She'd gotten used to being alone, hadn't she?

Her computer made a sound just then. It was the sound Skype made each time one of her contacts came online, though who cared. Not her anymore. Still, Olivia's eyes darted to it, if absently, the name barely registering; *it doesn't matter anyway*, she kept telling herself as she sat there blinking at it, her focus homing in—that inexhaustible last bastion of hope—and then she sat up abruptly.

She blinked at the name a few times, but before she could give that name more thought, that name began calling her. The shrill Skype ring sent Olivia flying back in her chair. It was a particularly unnerving ring, always catching her off guard, probably because it rarely rang. She glanced behind her as if someone might be there. She took a deep breath and turned back, coming forward again, closer to the screen, her heart beating through her chest.

Evelyn calling, the call box said.

3

The mouse pulsated beneath Olivia's fingers. Her eyes fixated on the name EVELYN. Aunt Evelyn? Was she calling Olivia from heaven? Olivia swallowed and clicked.

After a delay, a man's voice, deep and sonorous, "Olivia?"

She pulled back as his picture swallowed her screen. Dark, piercing eyes, chiseled face.

"You're not Aunt Evelyn," she managed finally, her first instinct being to hang up, but then he said, "Don't hang up."

There was a pause.

"I'm your aunt Evelyn's friend. Marco."

Her throat tightened. "I saw her name in the Skype box and . . ." And nothing. Aunt Evelyn's death came at Olivia again, all at once, this strange absence.

For a moment they sat there staring at each other. *Marco*—his name echoed, a whisper in Olivia's memory. *Marco*—the man Aunt Evelyn had been living with in Asia or Italy or somewhere, it wasn't exactly known. The man Olivia's mother seemed to despise for no reason other than that he was married, and not to Aunt Evelyn.

"I don't think I was expecting you to answer," he said. He spoke with an accent—Italian, perhaps. A guess, for Olivia had never met him. Never even seen a picture of him. Knew absolutely nothing about him. Her mother certainly didn't talk about him. But Italy is where the letter announcing Aunt Evelyn's death had come from. Two years ago. Thin, soft, Italia. Italy. Air Mail. Par Avion. There was an elaborate wax emblem seal on the back fold, which her mother contemplated for a painfully long moment before at last breaking it open. Her face set in stone as she read, and then she sat down in the nearest chair and stared out the windows into the scorched and barren desert.

"I have some of your aunt's things," Marco said. He sat almost regal-like, not moving or flinching, in a crisp, white button-down, as if he'd dressed for the occasion, though he forgot to shave, perhaps even shower; he was the kind of man, seemingly, that came with a scent. "I know this is an immense request, but I need you to come and get them."

Some kind of sound escaped her.

"I will arrange you a plane ticket to Hanoi."

"Hanoi?" Olivia frowned. "The letter came from Italy." The letter now floating to the floor in Olivia's memory, it having fallen from her mother's trembling hands. "She was not supposed to leave us in the first place," Rhonda had cried while Olivia grabbed the letter and read it. The English was broken and difficult to decipher. It didn't say how Evelyn had died, exactly, some kind of accident or illness, Olivia couldn't remember, which was odd, she thought now. All she knew was that there were no ashes, no body, no nothing—just a request to come and get Aunt Evelyn's things, which Rhonda never did.

"Her things are with me, here," Marco said. A vein bulged down the middle of his forehead.

Olivia thought back. It was so long ago when Evelyn had left. Olivia was seven or eight, she didn't remember exactly, just that they were still living in their old house on Darning Court, her aunt with them. Evelyn had just finished her medical residency and was getting ready to start a private practice in Scottsdale. Her mom and dad were putting up the money. It was all set, and then . . . well, those towers fell. Though Evelyn insisted that it wasn't the towers, she simply needed to go, she was joining Doctors without Borders and heading off to . . .

Olivia couldn't remember where, exactly. Asia. Perhaps Hanoi. Sure, it could have been Hanoi. She proceeded to travel all over, Olivia never knew exactly where she was.

Her mom and Evelyn fought about her decision to leave, but still, they remained as close as ever, talking by phone once a week without fail, no matter where Evelyn was in the world. They'd go on until the line dropped, sometimes a minute, sometimes an hour. (If the line hadn't dropped, would they have talked forever?) Evelyn would still visit during Christmases and never missed Olivia's birthday. But then Evelyn met this man named Marco and the calls stopped. From then on, when Olivia would ask her mom about Evelyn—where was she in the world, was she coming for Olivia's birthday that year—instead of answering Rhonda got quiet, as if she didn't know to whom Olivia was referring.

"She blames you for Evelyn's death," Olivia said, when it occurred to her why this call had not gone to her mother.

He looked straight at her, unblinking. "As well she should."

And if Rhonda hadn't gone to Italy to get Evelyn's things, she certainly wasn't going to go to Hanoi. She wouldn't let Olivia go to Hanoi either, a thought that gave Olivia a moment's pause.

"Evelyn spoke fondly of you."

Olivia blinked at the screen, at the tiny box that reflected her image. The image he was seeing. Was that her? She had this sense, suddenly, of being very far away, as if she were an abstraction of herself, some other girl there, trapped inside that box. "We'd been close, once," she said finally, tucking her bra straps behind her tank. Her gaze fell downward. It wasn't only Olivia's mother who'd let Evelyn slip away, Olivia had too.

"Do you have a passport?"

She looked up again. "I have a passport," she said, though her brow furrowed as she considered where it was. With her mother, no doubt, bringing her back to why this was so ridiculous. "Look. I can't fly all the way to Asia by myself."

"You are nineteen, are you not? In your country this means you are an adult, yes?"

She sensed a slight disdain in his voice, as if where he lived people weren't defined by an age. More importantly, Olivia wondered how he knew she was nineteen. And what else had Evelyn told him about her? Olivia's relationship with her aunt, after she'd left, was reduced to a Skype call here and there, a handful of visits. What did her aunt really know of Olivia to tell?

And what did Olivia really know of her aunt other than the ideal she'd created in her mind—nomad, seeker, a woman who lived by her passions and heart. Her affair with Marco had only fueled this ideal, sordid and thus glamorous, as opposed to her mother's conviction that disaster loomed, that this man would destroy Evelyn's heart. And in the end, Olivia supposed, her mother had been right.

"It must be soon, if you are to come at all."

Was he not hearing her?

A curtain billowed in the wind behind him.

"Classes just started," she said. What she was ruminating over was the upcoming October break. "Can't you just send her things?"

His silence seemed to say this was not an option.

But what if . . . She peered at him now. "How do I know you're you?"

He reached for something and held it up to the camera, as if he was prepared for this question.

Olivia narrowed her eyes. It was a composition notebook, one with the familiar marble cover; her aunt used to keep her journal in books like these. He moved the notebook closer to the camera. Olivia's name was scrawled at the top, the loop-di-loop of the *O* and the curlicue of the *a* not to be mistaken. She blinked at it a moment. "That's mine," she said.

"I know," he said.

What is my journal doing there? she wondered, the vision of where it *should be* still so indelible in Olivia's mind. After Olivia's aunt had told her that she was leaving for Doctors without Borders, after Olivia had assured her of how proud and excited she was for her, after her aunt had left Olivia's bedroom teary-eyed with remorse, perhaps Olivia had been in a state of shock, possessed by some inexplicable loss, and she went over to her dresser and retrieved the notebook from its sacred buried spot, and went and threw it in the trash.

"Open it," she said to Marco now.

He set it aside, looking unsettled from even having touched it.

Silly, eight-year-old stories about crushes and butterflies and streams, and now, another vision: Olivia tucked into her childhood bed, her aunt a silhouette beside her, the soft drone of her voice filling the blackness with a story. *A prince falls in love with a girl from a far-off land. . . .* Even now, Olivia could see the moon through the window, big and bold and bathing the room in blue light. *They don't speak the same language, so they communicate with expressions, gestures, and sensations. . . .* Olivia had once interrupted her aunt to ask what *sensations* meant, at which point Evelyn took Olivia's hand in hers, her eyes that soul-searching green. "Feel that?" she had said, squeezing, and Olivia had. She had felt that.

The girl knew that she could not have the prince, for he was betrothed to a princess, but loving him had changed her, and she could never go back to her home, she could never be the same. She travelled the world, figuring that if she circled the globe enough times, their circles might overlap and he would find her again.

"I want to travel the world," Olivia would always say.

"Then you will."

Olivia's face flushed horribly now, so embarrassed was she to have remembered every word of her aunt's story, and then hearing her child's voice, "But did he find her again?" Olivia had made her aunt tell her the story so many times that she finally bought Olivia a journal of her own and made her write the story down so that she could tell it to herself whenever she wanted.

"You're right. Don't open it," Olivia said to Marco.

"I wasn't planning to."

For a few moments they stared off in other directions.

"As I said, I will be leaving soon," he said finally.

"But where are you going?"

Their eyes met and held. The sudden urgency in her tone had startled them both, as if their futures were now connected somehow, which was silly.

"It doesn't matter where I am going. What matters is that you do Evelyn's memory this great favor and come."

4

The next morning, Rhonda was up, showered, and dressed by seven o'clock. After tossing and turning all night with that ache in her chest, that wave in her dreams building across some sea, going over every aspect of Olivia's body language the previous night in response to what Rhonda had so stupidly blurted out in a fit of . . . rage, bitterness, jealously? Had Olivia accepted Rhonda's excuse about being drunk and not knowing what she was saying, or had Oliva only pretended to accept Rhonda's excuse about being drunk without knowing what she was saying, etc.—six hours back and forth like that, and Rhonda at last ripped off the covers and started her day.

The only way to end the battle in her head, the question hovering in the air, was to take action. Rhonda was nothing if not a woman who took action. Option one: create a diversionary tactic. Option two: *do* something, something she should have done years ago. And since she was in no way prepared for Option two, she got busy with Option one, which meant getting a serious move on selling this mausoleum of a house—why should she be the one stuck living in this tomb?—and finding a new one. House hunting! Just the thing to get Olivia focused away from what *wasn't* and toward what *was*! Like using all that idle creativity of hers to help decorate their new home! And if that didn't work, well, then, there was that dog she'd always wanted . . .

Rhonda spent an hour on the phone with her real estate agent, then some time with a clerk at the animal shelter, and still, it was only 8:00 a.m. Rhonda couldn't wake Olivia until at least eleven, another three hours, so she distracted herself with foundation business. She exchanged emails back and forth with Peggy, her executive director, regarding the fund's annual returns, which were negative for the third year in a row. Knight, Inc., would have to cut some grants, but which ones? Not Chase's certainly. Though his wasn't a grant. His was a Series B investment. He'd emailed Rhonda the paperwork a few days ago and had sent a follow-up that morning. They were on the brink of something big, Chase had assured her (she'd participated in the prior two rounds of funding). No assurances necessary, she didn't need to say, *I just want you to be happy.* She got on the phone with her accountant and had him wire the funds. That's all she had ever wanted, for her children to be happy, fulfilled so that she'd at least done something right.

Speaking of which, she glanced at her watch. Ten o'clock. She sighed. She'd waited long enough. It wouldn't kill Olivia to wake up before eleven, Rhonda thought, heading down the hall to her daughter's bedroom. "Rise and shine," Rhonda said, standing at the door, mustering as much energy and vigor into her voice as possible.

No response.

"Come on, Olivia, I thought we could go check out some open houses today. I've got some places picked out. One even has a built-in dog park! She put her ear to the door listening for a latent squeal about that dog. Nothing came back. No squeal. Just silence. Rhonda turned the door handle, surprised to find it unlocked, and pushed it open. Clothes were strewn on the bed, floor, and desk chair. "Olivia?" Rhonda went to the adjoining bathroom, where she found the aftermath of a makeup tornado, but no Olivia.

Rhonda got out her phone and sat on the bed. *Think first*, she pleaded with herself. *Think before you text. Give a minute of thought to the situation in order not to come across as meddling and intrusive, not to mention panicked. Maybe Olivia went to work out at the gym, or drove to Starbucks to get her morning Frappuccino, a drug store run?*

But Rhonda's pleas with herself rarely worked, and certainly not now, after what she had said last night. Only sixty seconds passed before her fingers got busy. *Where are you?* She sat there, staring at her phone, waiting for a response. For whatever Rhonda and Olivia's differences, whatever their fights or moods, whatever their opposing worldviews (according to Olivia), they still texted ten times a day. It was the phone's fault, Rhonda lamented now, throwing it on the bed. She was helpless against its power. And just like that it beeped, as if to remind her of its power. She picked it up. *Heading back to school early*, read Olivia's text. *I forgot I have a study group.*

Rhonda got a vision of her daughter flying down Interstate-10 steering with her knees so that she could text with both hands.

Please don't text and drive. Call me from speaker.

She did, twenty agonizing minutes later. Rhonda suggested house hunting next weekend, but Olivia said that she wouldn't be coming home next weekend because of Greek Week.

There was a moment of dead silence before Rhonda said "Great!" too enthusiastically. *Where had that come from?* Olivia had made it clear that she had no intention of participating in Greek Week this year; once had been enough.

"Then I guess I'll see you the week after, for semester break?"

"I'm going hiking in Taos with a friend," she said.

Rhonda pulled the phone away from her ear. Stared at it. Put it back.

"I told you, Mom."

Rhonda was certain her daughter had not told her.

"I told you last week."

Silence ensued while this news settled in.

"I thought you'd be glad for me."

"I am. I was just . . ." *What friend? And since when did Olivia hike?*

"She's in my international relations class," Olivia said. She was remaining unusually obtuse and low-key about this girl. Normally, Olivia would be unable to hide her excitement upon making a new friend. "She's the sister I never had, Mom!" How many times had Rhonda heard this desperately childish claim from her daughter? The claim with the sardonic undertone, as if she were blaming Rhonda for not giving her a sister, having witnessed so intimately how much Rhonda had, once, relied on her sister, for all the times Olivia had listened to Rhonda and Evelyn gab on about nothing and everything as if Olivia weren't there—sisterhood, the kind of solidarity you didn't get with anybody else. "Is this about last night? What I said . . ."

"Mom." Deadpan. "I'm just going on a trip."

"Right. And how will you get there?"

"Dad gave me the M3, remember?"

"All that way, in the M3?"

"We'll take turns driving."

After a pause, "How are you on money?"

"Well, if you want to give me some, I won't say no."

Rhonda jotted something down. "I'll move some cash into your account."

"You're the best, Mom," she said, with an undertone that implied the opposite.

The silence grew awkward. Rhonda wasn't sure how to get off the phone, and Olivia wasn't making any moves even though she was likely dying to hang up. If this were a competition of who could *not* say goodbye first, Olivia would win. She had once wanted to be an actress, after all.

"Well, I should let you go," Rhonda said.

"Okay."

"Call me when you get to Taos so that I know you arrived safe."

"I will."

"And you'll text me."

"Like always."

After hanging up, Rhonda sat there, staring out the window, seething at Daniel. *Daniel and his quest for love, what had he set in motion?* It was a question that stayed with Rhonda throughout the day and left her sleepless most of the night, until the first light of dawn, when she could take it no more and she got out of bed already dressed in sweats. She brushed her teeth, found flip-flops in the mudroom. A few minutes later she was winding her way down the mountainside in her golf cart. It was still mostly dark out. She had the cart lights on, as well as her hoodie because the air was still frozen. Dew was all over everything, sliding off the rocks and dripping from the bramble, the fairways ice. Not a soul in sight, too early for even golfers, but not Daniel.

Around the other side of the clubhouse, next to the tennis courts, Rhonda slipped her cart silently into a slot before the club's Olympic-size swimming pool. Every morning at six o'clock, ever since Rhonda had known Daniel, he swam laps. And if he was no longer swimming them in their infinity pool, he had to swim them somewhere.

She entered through a side gate.

He was alone in the pool. Rhonda went over and stood at the end of the lane he was swimming in; he cut through the water with cool, clean, methodical strokes. To infinity and back, Daniel used to joke— no fewer than fifty times.

When he didn't notice her, she went and got the Styrofoam life preserver and tossed it into his lane. He stood up and looked around. "How long have you been standing there?" he asked, pulling off his goggles.

"Too long," she responded.

Daniel came over and climbed out of the pool. Steam poured off him. In his Speedo he might as well be naked, and yet nothing. As ever, not one stir below her belly, which was odd, really, because she'd always found him attractive. His hair more strawberry than gray, his arms and legs bristly but taut, naturally, never was he out of shape, though it wasn't about vanity. It was about dedication and passion. He swam because he loved to.

She handed him his towel. "We need to talk about Olivia."

He began drying off his legs. "Is this about the M3? I told her you'd have to okay it."

"Like I was going to say no after you'd already given it to her."

He smiled: that gleam of pride, he and Olivia and their little secret.

"The M3 is not why I'm here, Daniel. I'm here because . . ." She cleared her throat. "You know . . ." She paused, thinking that he might be able to fill in the rest, but he just blinked at her.

Rhonda peered back at him. Of course he wouldn't be able to fill in the rest. When was the last time they'd spoken of this with each other? Ten years ago? When Evelyn had left for Doctors without Borders and Rhonda and Daniel had gotten into that fight?

"I want you to promise me, Daniel, that you won't say anything to Olivia about Evelyn being her real mother."

He wrapped the towel around his waist.

"Why would I do that?"

"I don't know. Let's say she asked you?"

"Has she asked you?"

"No. Not directly. But . . . well, I might have said something." She paused so he could ask what. He didn't. "I made some idiotic reference. Our divorce has unraveled her a bit, and now I'm just worried she's starting to wonder about her origins."

"Well, you had to imagine she was going to ask about her birth parents at some point."

"Sure. Yeah." No. Not really.

"So just tell her the truth."

Her jaw dropped.

He sat down on a lounge chair.

As if it were that simple.

"It *is* that simple, Rhonda."

She stood blinking down at him, Mr. Enlightened. Though, to be honest, Daniel had always hated this business between Rhonda and

Evelyn. He was a man who spoke the truth—straight, direct, and irrespective of consequences.

"We're her *real* parents, Daniel."

"I never said we weren't."

"It would be different if Evelyn were alive, but . . ." she paused. "I just don't see what the point is of telling her if Evelyn's dead."

"He's alive, isn't he?"

She met his gaze. A moment passed. "I don't know, presumably."

"Does he know?"

She gasped and huffed. An interrogation was not what she'd anticipated. Daniel had never probed about Olivia's real father. He preferred to remain oblivious, practically, to the whole thing. He would take Evelyn's baby in as their own, no questions asked.

"Who knows?" she said, resignedly, staring beyond Daniel, at their house clinging to the mountainside in the distance. Her sister had been so intent on *never* telling Marco about Olivia. But that was before Evelyn and Marco got back together years later, when Rhonda was sure she'd at long last get *the* call. One day. Or that they'd just show up, Evelyn and Marco, to claim Olivia as their own. But nothing. No one showed up. Rhonda got nothing. "He has no rights."

"Doesn't he?"

Fucking Daniel. She stood up abruptly. "This is not why I came here, Daniel." She paced over to the far edge of the pool and stared up at the waking sky. This was not supposed to be happening. This had not been the plan. None of this had been the plan. The plan had been for Evelyn to participate in her daughter's life. To be there and watch her grow up and that someday, maybe when Olivia was eighteen, they'd tell her the truth.

Rhonda paced back to Daniel. "Look," she said. "I know you've had some kind of rebirth, that you've awakened or whatever, but you are still you, Daniel. So, please promise me that you won't blurt out anything that could damage our daughter for life."

His eyes receded. His expression drew closed. "Fine. I'll do whatever you want."

"What I want, Daniel, is for you to take this with you to your grave." She stood there shaking in the aftermath of that request, feeling like the bad guy that she was.

She wasn't sure what to do next. Finally, she just said, "Thank you."

He looked down at his hands.

For everything, she wanted to add. *For taking care of us. All of us.*

5

Rhonda drove the golf cart back to the house in a daze. *Just tell her?* She flew over a speed bump without even feeling it. Then another. When she reached the great vertical climb the cart slowed to a crawl with the gravitational pull. Hell, she could walk it faster, if she weren't so out of shape. So out of touch with the world. This world she'd created for herself, the last threads of which she'd do anything to hold on to.

Maybe Daniel was right. Telling Olivia *was* that simple.

Or, perhaps it was time for Option two?

She arrived home, birds screaming everywhere, all that fluttering and flapping in the morning light, woodpeckers hacking at the chimney and her mind as she walked methodically and without thought down the endless corridor to her office, straight to the file cabinet, the bottom drawer, way in back. She wasn't even sure if she had saved the letters, in her rage, sadness, and desperation at the time, if she'd not simply burned them. But no, they were there, in a brown paper bag next to Olivia's adoption papers. ITALIA. ITALY. AIR MAIL. PAR AVION. She had never told Olivia about the letters that came after the one announcing Evelyn's death. What was the point? The news had not changed. Or that's what Rhonda had convinced herself. In reality she had been afraid to open them, so sure was she that in them would be a request from Marco to see his daughter.

She opened them now, scanning the pages, but no such request was there. Not one reference to Olivia, just the same phone number to contact about Evelyn's things.

Rhonda got out her cell phone. Her hands were shaking. It took her a few tries to get the number dialed right and make a connection. Her heart pounded with each ring. This went on for some time. The ringing. *Would it ring on forever?* she wondered. Yes, after two more minutes, she surmised that it possibly would. She hung up.

She sat there, stunned. She had not anticipated how much she had wanted someone to answer, to be on the other end—Marco, this man who'd stolen her sister's life. It had been a fluke, Evelyn and Marco's meeting. Chance. Rhonda was twenty-seven at the time, Evelyn twenty-five and in the midst of med school, when they'd dropped everything to fly to Italy so that Rhonda could chase after Bill. It was Evelyn who had insisted Rhonda go, that she fight for Bill, her fiancé at the time, who'd decided to postpone their marriage to play professional basketball in Rome, of all places. Rhonda had rashly broken off the engagement only to regret it later. When at last she did go to Italy, bringing Evelyn along for courage, it was too late.

Italy was like a bad dream. It's where Rhonda had lost not only her heart, but her sister's heart too. For while Rhonda had left Italy abruptly, Evelyn had decided to stay, so taken was she by the decaying, old, ancient city. The next thing Rhonda knew she was getting a call from Evelyn saying that she had met someone, that she wasn't coming home as planned, the irony of which was too disconcerting to fathom.

"Don't worry," Evelyn had told Rhonda. "It's going nowhere because he's going to be married," and then, in response to Rhonda's silence, "It's not like that, Rhonda. He doesn't love her."

"Then why is he marrying her?"

"He's a prince."

"A what?"

"A prince."

"I don't really understand what that means."

"He has obligations."

"And that means he can cheat on her?"

"She doesn't love him either. They're like brother and sister."

"So this is just a fling?"

"I knew you wouldn't understand."

Evelyn returned from Italy a year later, the affair over. *What was there not to understand?* "I told you it wouldn't last."

"You're missing the point," Evelyn had said. She carried with her no resentment, for Marco anyway. She had loved, and that was enough. "It's not about whether *it* lasts, Rhonda. It's about that *it* exists. Please, just tell me you believe that *it* exists."

"*It* doesn't mean anything."

"*It* means everything!"

Her sister was referring to intimacy, the kind of intimacy that lived on even in absence. Rhonda and Daniel had been married for less than a year by then, and they were still intimate, but even in the beginning it had not been pleasurable for Rhonda. She had had pleasure before Daniel, perhaps not the kind her sister was talking about, but she had had pleasure with Bill.

"It's not sex that I'm talking about." Evelyn used to get so frustrated with Rhonda, who now wanted to laugh at these dialogues with her sister that kept playing out in her mind. Evelyn knew that Rhonda had married Daniel as a safety net, a way to escape the pain of Bill, and she would never let Rhonda forget it.

Rhonda gathered up the letters, plus the adoption papers and took them with her to her bedroom. Into her closet, the size of a small bedroom, she went to the back, pushed over a pile of laundry, and felt around the wall for the groove where the child-size door was hidden, clicked it open, and crawled in.

Why Daniel had built the panic room in Rhonda's closet and not his was a wonder. The only thing they kept in it was a safe and Daniel's skeet shooting rifle, which he'd taken with him, thank God. Evelyn was always so livid about that gun, as had been Olivia, she who lived unknowingly on in her mother's image.

An eight-by-eight-square-foot space, enough room for five people to stand in, uncomfortably, while awaiting rescue. But from what, Rhonda sighed, leaning back against the wall. For "just in case," that's what. Daniel was nothing if not dedicated to his family's well-being. This was his Plan D. This was the kind of respect Rhonda had been talking about when Olivia's face had twisted up in disgust: *Your father and I respect each other.*

Rhonda didn't understand why Olivia had been so shocked to hear this. It was not like Rhonda and Daniel had ever portrayed their union as some magical force of fate. In fact, quite the opposite, it was something Daniel liked to boast about, how Rhonda had looked him up in the UCLA alumni directory. That she'd come searching for *him*.

Daniel had been in the graduate physics program there while Rhonda had been an undergrad majoring in "Olympic hopeful"; studies not her priority, she had tutors for everything. For physics that meant Daniel, who was not shy about wanting to sleep with her. She'd been, for all intents and purposes, in her mind anyway, engaged to Bill at the time, but Daniel didn't care. He was wired for sex, not love. When the time came years later, Rhonda having returned from Italy, slapped awake, Daniel was the first man who came to her mind, a man who wouldn't want what she couldn't give him.

Rhonda was surprised to find him landlocked in Arizona (he'd been an avid surfer), well into his doctorate, divorced, and raising two sons, Stevie and Chase, ages three and five. He had put emotional value into a committed relationship when she'd known him as a guy who went from one woman to the next.

She moved to Arizona, shut the door on sand and salt and her mother's deteriorating dementia. She and Daniel married within a year. Evelyn showed up not long after with what she thought was a stomach virus, her body's reaction to an ended affair, but what they soon discovered was no virus at all. After recovering from the shock (for Rhonda this took one minute, her sister was another story), Rhonda kicked into gear and convinced Evelyn that it was possible. Rhonda and Daniel would adopt the baby and they could be a family. All of them. A real family. Evelyn would finish med school while Rhonda raised the kids. They were what mattered now. The kids, Olivia, she would be their champion now. The first toy Rhonda bought Olivia was a volleyball, not stuffed but real. And Stevie was already excelling at soccer by then, and Chase was a natural on the golf course. Daniel had already begun tinkering with golf club design, applying his intuition and his knowledge of physics to several aspects of the club—materials, aerodynamics, size and shape of the cavity back, and the redesign of the sweet spot for tour irons, gaining an optimal balance between forgiveness and control. Daniel, brilliant but an introvert and oblivious to business matters, received several patents thanks to Rhonda, who encouraged him to hire a patent lawyer, as well as a business consultant. Rhonda didn't know what Callaway was at the time, just that suddenly she and Daniel had so much money they didn't know what to do with it, and she was on a first name basis with the professional golfer Phil Mickelson.

They bought a lot of stuff.

Everything their children needed to be the best.

They hired a financial advisor.

They began designing the mausoleum, bought more stuff.

Hired help.

But then those towers fell. Evelyn left for Asia. Nothing was ever the same again. Rhonda and Evelyn talked by phone once a week. Evelyn visited at Christmas and for Olivia's birthdays. Then, by some magical force of fate, years later, Evelyn and Marco reunited. Rhonda had no interest in knowing how or why, having been struck dumb by her visions—two lovers walking off hand in hand into some sunset—eating away at her mind. Coincidentally, it was around this same time that everything about Rhonda's life seemed to grow old, as if she had aged five years for every one year that passed. Olivia quit the volleyball team to go off in some orthogonal direction. Chase and Stevie were grown and gone. There were no more games to go to. It was as if her children's passion for sports had never existed. Chase had reconciled with his estranged mother, and Stevie went from one serious girlfriend to another. It was love that everyone wanted now, living and breathing in the air all around her. Even Daniel wanted "more."

Daniel. Poor Daniel. Suddenly, he was just there, at every turn, wanting to do things with Rhonda, Olivia, wanting to go places together as a family. He'd been planning this one particular African safari adventure, but the boys certainly didn't want to go—they were off living their own lives—and Olivia was busy with yet another school play. He'd finally come to Rhonda, out of the blue, and asked her to go away with him, alone, just the two of them, to reconnect.

Alone? No kids? What might be a normal question to ask one's wife of fifteen years had been shocking coming from Daniel, from either of them. Rhonda had stood there blushing, then she laughed like it was a joke, and when that didn't deter him she mumbled something about the charity event next month and got busy with whatever disparate task awaited her attention.

Had Rhonda no control over anything?

Thus, The Knight Foundation was born. Rhonda appointed herself board president, hired a top-notch executive director, and, the way Rhonda had captained her teams, she captained this fund. She was certain Daniel's midlife crisis would pass, that he would get back to focusing on his designs, his tinkering. Meanwhile, Rhonda discovered that she had a knack for management. She was scrupulous. Meticulous. Always hedging disaster, a good trait for a CEO, which was how people began referring to her, if only facetiously. Basically, she was good at writing checks.

She'd married Daniel to get as far away from the name Stevenson as

possible, what everyone from her past had called her, the name emblazoned on the back of her jersey, her last name being her signature, the
symbol of her. And she'd achieved that—Knight, Daniel's last name,
had become her symbol now. Rhonda, "Knight" in shining armor.

Then came Evelyn's death, which, rather than securing the lid on the
Stevenson coffin, exhumed it.

It wasn't long after that that Daniel told Rhonda that he'd met someone else.

Oh, how could she have not seen this coming, Rhonda lamented
again now, dialing open the safe (Olivia's birthday). She reached far into
the back. She kept no treasures in here, no precious family heirlooms,
but this one. She brought out the blue velvet case with the Olympic seal
engraved on the lid. She opened it, and sat squinting into the glare of
that beaming, bold medal, waiting for the heat of it to embroil her as it
always did when she stole this secret moment for herself. Those times
when she might have been in need of a little courage. Daniel thought
it was ridiculous that she kept it hidden away in here. He'd designed
a cabinet in the grand foyer to display it for all who entered, which
she'd scoffed at, though her modesty was feigned. She was proud of her
medal. But the memories were too precious. She didn't want Daniel
thinking that it in any way belonged to him, nor the woman she was
when she'd won it.

She pulled the medallion from its casing. Felt the weight of it in her
hand. Heavy, solid, steady. This medal was her. The essence of her. She
placed the medal around her neck so that its warmth could permeate
her chest, its power could radiate all the way into her heart. Courage.
Courage to do what she should have done, a long time ago.

6

"Mom?"

"Olivia?"

There was static on the other end. "This reception is horrible." It didn't help that Rhonda was riding in the golf cart. "Where are you? Did you make it?"

Perhaps Olivia had said something, but the open wind, the intermittent whooshing, was making it hard to hear. "Are you okay? Do you need something?"

"You said to call when I arrived. So I'm calling."

The signal went away, and then came back.

"So, how is it?"

"I can't hear you, Mom; are you in the golf cart?"

A logical question, for why would anyone drive around in a golf cart if they didn't even golf? Why would someone have a golf cart configured for street driving when one could simply drive on the street in their car?

"Where are you going in the golf cart?"

The phone store, passport office, last minute details. Hadn't there been a time when she refused to drive in the golf cart? "I'm doing what I'm always doing. Missing you." Then, after a short silence, "Sorry. I couldn't help myself."

"Mom, you need to get a life."

"You called all the way from Taos just to tell me that?"

Lots of background noise.

"You girls at a bar already?"

There was a long, almost fateful pause.

"Olivia?"

"Yes, Mom. You called it. Wild amounts of fun being had by all."

Sarcasm, not unexpected, but still, her daughter sounded distant, farther away than normal, a touch of loneliness in her voice, and Rhonda wondered again what might be going through her daughter's mind—if she was, in fact, ruminating on what Rhonda had so rashly said, and oh why couldn't Rhonda just ask her. Why couldn't she just be up front with her daughter? With anybody?

Or perhaps her daughter had simply found, as she always did inevitably, an uncompromising character flaw in this new friend and wished no longer to be with said friend. "It's freezing there at night; did you bring a jacket?"

"Yes, Mom," Olivia responded dully.

"I mean a winter jacket."

She let out a moan.

"Sorry. I'll stop."

"I've got to go," Olivia said suddenly.

Don't go. "If you want to come home, Olivia. Just tell me. I can fly you back, and we'll get someone to take care of the car."

Silence.

"Olivia?"

"I'm not coming home, Mom."

"Well, of course you're not. Just do me a favor and have a blast, will you? And stay warm?" Rhonda spoke it as a question, a tentative, hopeful question, because the other thought she kept having was that Olivia had not made a new friend at all and was lying to her mother about being in Taos. But what was Rhonda to say? For she was lying too, wasn't she?

7

"*Bella Roma, no?*"

Rhonda woke as if from a trance, and blinked dully at the bell-man, who said it again, "*Bella Roma, no?*" Like a romance novel was Rhonda's sardonic mental response. He'd been gesticulating at her for the past five minutes under the heat of the beating sun, ever since she had stored her luggage with him and inquired about directions to Palazzo Rossellini. It was 11:00 a.m. and her hotel room was not yet ready. She had selected this hotel because of its proximity to the palace, situated on Via del Corso, a main thoroughfare that split Rome's ancient city center. According to the map, the palazzo was right up the street and, yet, all this hand waving.

One last, final wave and she was off, falling in line with the swarms of tourists he had assured her would not exist this time of year, early October, the weather at its glorious best. But there they all were, with their cameras and maps, marching toward some massive, sprawling, ancient structure. It looked like a typewriter; the bellman had been very proud to share with Rhonda this little secret about the great monument. Rhonda squinted at the structure now in the distance as she plodded on, not getting the imagery, but oh well. It didn't matter. She was not here to see the sights.

Though twenty minutes later, there she was before it, the type-writer that didn't look like a typewriter as much as a giant staircase into heaven—perhaps its gaudiest, grandest entrance. She turned around and doubled back. She'd missed it, the palazzo, its entrance being opposite of the typewriter—narrow, identified by only a small crest carved into the stone, two swords crossing over an *R*, the same crest melted into the seal on the envelopes she carried around. She stepped back to get a better look at the regal, intricate façade, it was crammed between two modern, ugly buildings. *New money*, as someone had once referred to her and Daniel's wealth, meaning she was the ugly modern building. Or at least that's how she felt presently, passing through the gate, the heels of her boots clunking obnoxiously along the stones as she walked along the shade of a portico in the otherwise quiet and peaceful interior. Both palatial and unassuming, she came upon an elegant, verdant courtyard surrounded by statuesque fountains and stopped to gaze at them, lulled by the shaded tranquility, this walled fortress protecting her from the chaos outside.

"*Chiude all'una*," came at her from behind, and she spun around. Behind a small window sat a man with a tiny head and darting eyes. "We close at one o'clock for lunch."

"Is this Palazzo Rossellini?"

He handed her a brochure.

She looked at it, confused. "I am looking for Marco Rossellini." She pulled out the letter from her purse and slid it through the window. "He has asked me to come."

He looked at the letter.

She looked at the brochure. A museum of some sort. This couldn't be right. "Perhaps you can tell me where he lives now."

"You can wait inside," he said, passing back the letter. "But you will need to buy a ticket."

She bought a ticket and went inside. The entrance was past a door that she had to duck through and up a narrow flight of stairs. At the top sat a bored-looking woman behind a register next to a turnstile. Rhonda handed her the ticket and entered. *If this was a museum, it*

must not be in any guidebook, Rhonda thought, looking around. She
did not see one other patron as she proceeded down a long corridor
whose thick, dank, tapestry-lined walls stretched high up into a ceiling of arched stone. Her allergies immediately kicked in. Her sneezes
echoed. A security guard at the end of the hall eyed her suspiciously.
She quickly passed by him and into a tiny, square room with a vaulted
ceiling, completely frescoed so as to make her feel as if she were in the
fresco, floating among the clouds and Gods and angels. From there,
another series of corridors housed heavy, dark oil paintings, some massive, some the size of postage stamps, consuming every inch of wall
space. Faces, stark and weary, proud, composed, a world of pain behind
blackened eyes. She wondered if Marco painted any of these. "He's an
artist," Evelyn had told Rhonda at one point, or that he dealt in art or
some such thing, by that point of their phone conversation Rhonda
had stopped listening; it was too much to bear, this vision of her sister
posing for her artist prince with nothing on but a crowned jewel. It
had been Rhonda's imagined version of events back then and apparently was still now, and Rhonda stepped back from whatever dark and
dreary painting she'd been staring at, dizzy suddenly.

She found a nearby chair and sat down. Just for a moment. A minute
or two. She closed her eyes.

"*Tutto bene?*"

She opened them, startled to see the ticket man, short and taut, discerning the chair she was sitting on. She promptly stood and looked
back at it—gold inlaid legs, intricately woven silk. She put a hand over
her mouth. "I am so sorry about that."

He said nothing and motioned for her to follow.

They went through a series of other corridors, then down a wide
switchback of marble stairs leading to an underground cavern. Naked
men, busts of kings and governors, lined the walls. Glass cases filled
with armor and swords. In the middle of the room, strangely and as if
she'd entered another dimension, was a fencer. A wide strip of marble

lay imbedded in the parquet floor and he was darting up and down it as if he were filleting some imaginary beast.

The ticket man deposited Rhonda into a chair (hard, cold, metal), told her to wait there, and left.

She wasn't sure what to do. The fencer didn't take notice of her. Tall, sharp-edged and graceful, disguised by mask and fencing suit—Marco, she assumed, though she wasn't sure why and certainly wasn't going to interrupt him and ask. She continued waiting. A few minutes later the ticket man came back dressed in a fencing suit of his own, the jacket hanging down by his waist. He went over to the man she presumed to be Marco and proceeded to take notes in a worn leather journal. "*Footwork*," he yelled sharply. Marco darted to the left.

"Nothing is more important than footwork!"

This barking and note-taking continued for some time, and Rhonda, who'd just gotten off a ten-hour flight, had to stand up at one point to stretch her back. She wandered over to the sword collection, a glittering array of sharp objects of all sizes, shapes, and antiquities, gilded with emblems or stones or engravings written in languages she couldn't interpret. There were cases filled with trophies and medals and old black-and-white photos. Olympic fencing teams going back to—she looked at one of the dates—'42! Wow.

"Lighter, *adagio, dai!*"

Rhonda spun around, startled. The words had come so sharply that the display cases rattled. The ticket man was shaking his head and pinching his nose at his protégé, what went on for a good solid minute before at last he fastened up his suit and slipped on his gloves. He marched back over to Rhonda, passing her to get to one of the cases, where he retrieved one of the swords, this one pencil thin and dulled at the end and who knew how many millions of years old. On his way back he paused before Rhonda and said, "This was once one of the greatest *salles* in Rome."

Yes, that's what she figured.

"Fifty of the 112 Olympic medalists going back to the games of 1912 were produced on that strip. I was hoping my cousin would make it fifty-one, but alas . . ." He slid on his mask and strutted back over to Marco.

The two fencers stood facing each other, erect and motionless. They brought their swords to their chins, and then dropped them to their sides. "En garde!" one of them called out, and before Rhonda knew it the ticket guy, whom she could distinguish because of his stunted height, was in full attack. It was startling and somewhat disconcerting to watch him lunge directly at Marco, striking at his chest and groin, with full force, it seemed, their blades clashing and bulging, and yet it was only a matter of minutes before he'd backed Marco up ten paces. Lackluster, tentative, Marco was no match for his teacher and finally just fell down on his butt.

Rhonda stood up.

The ticket guy ripped off his mask. Using his foil, he flicked the sword from Marco's hand. It dribbled a few paces on the floor and settled; the ticket man stomped out of the room.

Marco sat up and rested on his knees.

When he slid off his mask, a tumble of raven hair fell out.

He wasn't Marco. He wasn't even a he. He was a she.

8

The girl could be no older than Olivia, Rhonda guessed, though she was much taller than Olivia, too tall, perhaps, a sight Rhonda was still contemplating as the girl tucked the sword beneath an arm and pulled off her glove and strode over with an outstretched hand, "You have come all the way from America?"

Rhonda took a step backward and smiled tentatively at the dull tip of the sword pointing in her direction. *Yes. I have come all the way from America*, she thought, still unable to form words.

"I am told you know my father?"

The surprise must have shown on Rhonda's face.

"*Mi scusi*," the girl said, apologetically. Then she bowed her head and introduced herself properly. "*Sono* Carlotta. I am Carlotta, the daughter of Marco." She rattled off a last name that seemed to go on forever, long enough for her to unbutton her suit jacket to reveal a sweat-through L.A. Lakers T-shirt. "I am so sorry for my appearance, but I was in the middle of practice, and Grand Master will not compromise on my lessons."

"Marco is your father?" It still wasn't processing.

There was a buzz, and the girl pulled her phone out from a pocket on her thigh, answering as if in mid-sentence. "*Zia, si, okay, va bene*," she said, flashing Rhonda a tight smile. She put her phone away, stored her sword in its case. "Come," she said, leaving Rhonda no option but to follow.

42

They exited the hall through a different passage, up some steps and through a back door that led to an alley, or perhaps it was a street, for they had to splay against a wall to allow for a sudden passing car. The girl proceeded, as light as a feather, along the decaying cobblestones while Rhonda followed along, trying not to twist an ankle. Twenty paces later they were laboring up two flights of stairs to a rather drab and unremarkable second-story flat where a woman was waiting—in contrast to her surroundings, a very beautiful, elegant woman wearing a stylish scarf and a graying version of Carlotta's raven hair fastened in a loose bun.

She took Rhonda's hand into both of hers, "È *come se la conoscessimo gia'*."

Rhonda looked to Carlotta for translation.

"It is as if we already know you," Carlotta said, and Rhonda returned a smile of utter confusion.

"This is my aunt, Isabella. My mother's sister."

Isabella moved in and kissed Rhonda's cheeks, then she stood back to examine Rhonda. Carlotta followed her aunt's gaze, up and down, down and up. They exchanged some words in Italian.

"*Zia* can speak English," Carlotta said to Rhonda. "But she is too embarrassed." The girl flashed a smile of resign at her aunt, who nodded in agreement.

"She wants me to tell you that you look just like her."

Rhonda's mind was swirling. "Her?"

"Evelyn."

First of all, Rhonda reflected, she and Evelyn had different mothers and didn't look alike at all, and second, *you know of Evelyn?*

"My aunt says that she is very sorry for your loss."

Blood rushed to Rhonda's face. Pounded between her ears, and Isabella quickly led her into a parlor room off the hall, cramped yet cozy and dimly lit.

"We have been waiting for you," Carlotta said, following.

She had no idea what they were talking about. The letters were from Marco, who had asked Rhonda to come, which she had not done because . . .

"I didn't want—" Rhonda gasped suddenly. Her hands were shaking. She had just wanted it all to go away. And now, well, it wasn't going to *go* away, until that is, she did something about it.

"*Per favore*, please," Isabella paused, unable to find the word for *sit*, so she simply deposited Rhonda on the couch, and then nestled beside her with Carlotta on the other side. "You have heard from *papà*?" Carlotta asked, all their shoulders touching.

Rhonda looked at Carlotta, then back to Isabella.

"Grand Master said that you had a letter from *papà*."

A moment to connect Grand Master to the ticket guy, Rhonda pulled the letters from her bag. "Well, yes," she said, handing them to Carlotta, who handed them to Isabella.

"Ah, *le mie lettere*," Isabella said after taking a moment to look at them.

"My letters," Carlotta translated, her face suddenly ashen.

"Your letters?"

"I write these letters," Carlotta said, her eyes still on them. "As *zia* asked that I do because *papà* was . . . how do you say . . . not well?"

Rhonda took the letters back and reexamined them. They were signed with a stamped surname. "I just assumed they were from Marco." She looked up again. "I am very confused."

"It is time change, no?" Isabella offered, in a sudden burst of English. "It is very difficult."

"Where is Marco?"

"We don't know," Isabella responded, as Carlotta got up and paced to the other side of the tiny room. Isabella frowned after her, and then she turned back at Rhonda. "We hope . . ." Isabella tried, but ultimately she could not find the words in English. Carlotta, arms crossed, looked past Rhonda and said, "We hoped that *papà* had contacted you. That you came here to tell us news of him."

Rhonda looked from one of them to the other. Only now could she sense the deep sorrow on their faces, the lost hope in their eyes, what they had thought Rhonda was bringing them.

9

Isabella fed Rhonda pasta with pesto because, Carlotta explained, in Italy, food could solve any problem. Rhonda took one bite and almost cried; she literally had to pinch the bridge of her nose to stay the stinging. Warm, earthy, soul-soothing flavors that seemed to only make the problem worse, leaving Rhonda to feel even more vulnerable, which might have been their subliminal objective. *Dai, mangia*. You must eat. *Ancora*. More. Eat more.

Now Rhonda was stuffed. And empty. The three of them were back seated in the parlor room (so far the only time the two women had left Rhonda's side was to let her go to the bathroom) and Isabella was insisting that Rhonda stay the night. Rhonda, for her part, was slowly trying to extract herself from the clutches of this clawed couch. She thought that now might be a good time to go back to her hotel and check into her room.

"But it will be easier if you stay here," Carlotta said. "Tomorrow we must leave early."

"Where are we going?"

She made a look, *don't you know?* "To the cottage, of course."

Rhonda narrowed her eyes, ever so slightly.

"Certainly, you will not want to wait one more minute. Certainly, you are anxious to arrive there."

Isabella cut in and she and Carlotta exchanged words in Italian.

Rhonda, meanwhile, was thinking, *Cottage? What cottage?* She was desperate to ask, but got the feeling from the way they spoke that she was supposed to know about the cottage, this being an intimate detail of her sister's life here. Rhonda was too mortified to admit that she knew nothing of her sister's life here, that she and Evelyn had not spoken in . . . her mind wouldn't calculate the number. Five years before her death? And at that point her sister was . . . where was she? Myanmar? Laos? It didn't seem possible, even to Rhonda, that it had been that long, for she had spoken with Evelyn so often during that time, in her mind anyway, she'd managed to convince herself that they *had* spoken. It was what she had told people anyway; with Evelyn dead, the history was Rhonda's to recreate now.

"There is no point in trying to dissuade *zia*," Carlotta continued. "It will just be easier if you sleep here." Suddenly, Rhonda had no more energy to argue. All this talk about sleep was making her, well, sleepy, if not hallucinatory, because if she wasn't mistaken she was seeing Evelyn now, her pained smile reflecting Rhonda's from across the room (Evelyn hated being photographed) sitting on a credenza, in a frame that was draped in beads and flowers.

Rhonda reached out to hold onto something.

"Are you all right?"

The armrest would do.

Isabella went and got her some water. "I will send Grand Master to retrieve your luggage. And then tomorrow you and Carlotta will take the early train."

Train? Where is this place?

Later that night, lying on Carlotta's bed, Carlotta on the trundle, their feet dangling off the ends, Rhonda's exhaustion felt mildly like a dream, one in which she was falling. Though her limbs wouldn't relent, nor her mind, for she was getting caught up in Carlotta's emotion, as the younger woman explained to Rhonda the hard road to becoming an Olympic champion.

What sort of weird dream had Rhonda walked into?

"My day starts at 5:00 a.m. with a three-kilometer run. Then, before the palace opens to the public, I work with Grand Master in the *salle* on attack, lunge, and defense. I do my university courses with *zia* until one o'clock, which is when Grand Master and I meet in the *salle* again to spar." She paused and looked at Rhonda. "At this point you arrived today."

Today, Rhonda thought, trying to maintain a grasp on reality. It seemed like years ago. In fact, she might as well have been tucked into her own childhood bed. It could have been Rhonda waxing on about her Olympic dreams to Evelyn, who lay below her, all caught up in them. Rhonda had never been able to see her sister's face—and how nice it had been to be able to say this new word, sister. At the age of eleven, Rhonda had come to live with her father and his second wife and their seven-year-old daughter, Evelyn, whose room Rhonda would now share until Rhonda's mother "got back on her feet." They could have hated each other, rivals for their shared father's attention, but it hadn't been like that. There was this instant connection, this bond of trust, not to mention this overwhelming obligation, for the girl hung onto Rhonda's every word. What had been Rhonda's dream morphed into both their dreams because Evelyn didn't have a dream of her own. Becoming a doctor wasn't a dream. It was a given.

"Rhonda, *dormi?* Are you asleep?"

Of course not.

The girl went on with her schedule. "After my late lunch with *zia*, I have ballet and language lessons. Then, after the museum closes, Grand Master and I go through strategy, and then, sometimes, if Grand Master is angry at me, like he was today, more *footwork*!" She mimicked his dictatorial accent from earlier, and Rhonda couldn't help but laugh.

"Does he always teach in English?"

"Italian, sometimes French. According to Grand Master a great fencer must know the workings of his opponent's mind. And the World Cup qualifiers are in America next year. So now we focus on English in the *salle*."

"What is a *salle*, Carlotta?"

"Maybe it is like university, no? A school, a place where fencers live and study and learn from a grand master, only second to Pope." Carlotta crossed herself to make the point. "But today, as you see, the *salle* is a museum. *Zia* works in accounts, Grand Master sells tickets, the security guard is my second cousin, and Grand Master and I steal time there when the museum closes."

She sighed then. "Poor Grand Master. I am the only student he has left. And I fail him."

"Is he always so impassioned? Or was it because I was there."

"Oh, no. It is not you. It is *papà*. Grand Master is very jealous of *papà*, and so when you come saying the name of Marco, well, Grand Master *impazzisce*."

"Impa . . . ?"

"He go crazy. We do not say *papà's* name in the *salle*."

"I'll remember that for next time."

"You see, Grand Master, *papà's* cousin, became in love with *mamma* when *papà* left. And while I think *mamma* may have loved Grand Master back in this way, she stayed true to *papà* until her death, and so Grand Master feels that *papà* did not deserve her, that *papà* never loved her the way that he did because *papà* loved Evelyn. Anyway, this is just the way it has always been." She made a gesture with her hands. "It would be easier if people love who they were supposed to love."

Rhonda glanced at Carlotta sidelong. *Is she for real?*

"Anyway, Grand Master says that I have lost my edge."

"He was purposefully trying to humiliate you."

"I was once the best." It came with a long sigh. "In Milan last weekend I placed fifth. Now I must place first in both Torino *and* Florence or I do not make the World Cup qualifiers in New York next year, and if I do not make the World Cup qualifiers I lose my sponsorships. And without sponsorships, well, I cannot fence."

"Then you must stay here, Carlotta. You cannot miss practice. I can go to the cottage by myself."

"Oh, no, *zia* would never let you go to the cottage alone. Plus, she and Grand Master say that I must go. That your coming here is a sign; it is time I come to terms with my . . ." She paused to search for the word. "Ghosts?" With that the girl's gaze drifted to a tiny frame on the bedside table, a photo, cracked and faded, of a bride and groom, the kind you might see on the top of a wedding cake.

Rhonda had never met Marco, and Evelyn had never kept any photos of him around. But somehow Rhonda knew that this dark, brooding man must be him, and that the dazzling, tiara-wearing beauty next to him must be his fated princess. As if she were standing in a pool of golden light, and he, with a dark cloud over his head, just like Evelyn had said.

"She is very beautiful, no?"

Rhonda nodded. "You have her hair."

"She died when I was thirteen."

"I'm so sorry, Carlotta."

"She had a weak heart."

More like her heart was broken.

"*È cosi,*" Carlotta said finally. Then she yawned and rolled over. "*Che sonno.*" A minute later Rhonda could hear the girl's deep breaths of sleep.

10

The mood had shifted the next morning, Rhonda sensed. Where yesterday she represented hope, today she was the memory, an empty reminder. Isabella skirted in and out of horrific traffic and around the errant ruin to get them to the train station on time, all the while speaking passionately to her niece, who sat in the passenger seat rolling her eyes and nodding her head, knees slammed against the dashboard.

Isabella couldn't stop crying on the station platform. Something dire was taking place that Rhonda was not privy to because they were speaking in Italian, and it wasn't until Rhonda and Carlotta boarded the train and Isabella did not, that Rhonda understood—this was where Isabella and her family's participation ended, had always ended, and the tragic tears, well, they were just her way of saying, "Good-bye, I'll see you in three days."

Those tears stayed on Rhonda's mind long after the train left the station, as well as the image of Isabella trailing alongside their compartment as it moved away, waving. Rhonda and Olivia's good-byes were the opposite, a surface hug to mask any evidence of desperation, a low-key, "Go get 'um, girl." Certainly, no tears. A latent stinging between the eyes, but not . . . one . . . tear. Rhonda didn't believe in tears, the tears that would have taken Olivia's moment and turned it into her own.

In Rhonda's view, tears were self-serving.

For Carlotta too, apparently, for once on the train at last separated from Isabella, Rome, and the Palace, Carlotta ripped off her Italy sweatshirt as if it were strangling her. Underneath, she wore a rather revealing, army-green tank top that said THAILAND. Her bikini was already on beneath it. She jammed open the window, which wasn't easy, and lit a cigarette. Her hair flapped angrily against her skin as she smoked it.

"Have you been to Thailand?" Rhonda asked.

Carlotta glanced at Rhonda, and then down at the shirt as though she'd only just remembered she had it on. She shook her head no.

Rhonda wondered if their bedtime conversation had put her in a foul mood.

"How long until we arrive?" Rhonda asked, if only to break the silence.

"Not long," was all she said. Then she threw her cigarette out the window, and promptly fell asleep.

Rhonda, seated across from Carlotta, took this opportunity to get a good look at the girl, for she had noticed it right off, something foreign in the eyes, Olivia had it too. Rhonda wasn't sure how long she'd been staring at the girl whose head was like a rag doll's and whose mouth now leaked drool. Rhonda was about to reach over and wipe the girl's chin with a tissue when she startled awake. She blinked around. "*Cazzo*," she said suddenly, jumping up and gathering their stuff. "*Dai, veloce.*"

Rhonda gathered up her things and they hurried to the exit, where they stood awaiting the train to roll to a stop. It was an afterthought of a station, Rhonda could see. In fact, she wasn't sure the train was even going to stop, if they weren't going to have to jump. But at last it did stop, they clambered off, and five seconds later the train moved on. Rhonda stood watching it go, as if it might be the last train she'd ever see. Carlotta, meanwhile, well into some routine, headed straight for the lone bar. Rhonda went and found her at the counter, where they took a *caffè* and *cornetto*, and where the handsome barista seemed very pleased to see Carlotta. There was gesturing and arm waving and an agreement of some kind after what looked like some persuasion and, again, arguing.

"What was that about?" Rhonda asked, after they left.

"*Mah*," She waved a hand in the air as if to say it was nothing. "Ricki. He says that the sun shines now that I have returned . . . a great wave of heat, something like this; I don't think it can be translated. . . ."

"It seemed like you were arguing."

Carlotta frowned, as if she were thinking, *Why would Rhonda think this?*

They took a bus from the station for another twenty minutes along a road that edged pure sapphire. Nestled in the rocky shore were villas and mansions, *pensioni*, half-finished hotels, pizzerias, cafés, and touristy trinket shops—an odd mixture of the sublime and chaotic, imposing and rustic, charming and tacky.

From the village, where the bus dropped them, they bought groceries and cigarettes, and began walking with all their stuff. "I suppose there are no taxis around here?" Rhonda paused after a while and asked.

The girl kept walking.

After a couple more blocks, "A car service?"

Carlotta dropped her things.

Thank God, Rhonda thought, doing the same.

The girl was staring out over a low retaining wall at the Tyrrhenian Sea spreading stunningly on the horizon.

Some minutes went by.

"It's breathtaking," Rhonda said.

"Soon it will be gone."

Rhonda glanced at her.

"Yes, the government will soon take this too." With that she turned left and confronted a green metal gate, and Rhonda thought, *The sea? The government is taking the sea?*

No, the cottage. It sat directly behind the gate, which the girl was now fumbling to unlock with a key. She had to use all her weight to slide it open. They maneuvered their rolling suitcases down an impossibly steep driveway, at the bottom of which was parked an even smaller car than Isabella's, underneath a trellis of dead ivy. It made the cottage look like a dollhouse—a single-story white stucco structure with green-shuttered doors and windows all locked and battened down.

Carlotta disappeared.

Rhonda took in the salty, nostalgic breeze. Ever since Rhonda could walk, the sea (or, in her case, the ocean) was home. It pulled at her, from all directions, and soon she was standing at the backside of the cottage where a graveled patio terrace sat directly over the rocks twenty yards from the water. The world stood still for this moment, or so it seemed, so that Rhonda could take in the presence she so overwhelmingly felt: her sister as she must have stood exactly here, beneath the same sky and before the same sea, searching for something beyond it.

There was a loud, startling bang, and Rhonda whipped around to see Carlotta emerge from the cottage's French doors, waving away a cloud of dust.

Rhonda fell into a sneeze and coughing fit as she followed the girl inside, into the veil of haze and disarray, the stench of loss and abandonment that Carlotta, as best as she could, wore with an air of nonchalance. Sheets covering the furniture looked like odd-shaped ghosts. Carlotta began frantically ripping them off to reveal, one by one, the artifacts on which these ghosts had sat or lingered or touched. It wasn't much, two worn easy chairs with accompanying footstools, a long wood table framed with a bench. A television on a wobbly tray. Carlotta pointed to a door off the living area, where she informed Rhonda she would sleep, and then took her bag to the opposite bedroom, where she would sleep, presumably.

She returned a minute later with a towel, cigarettes, and cell phone. "I'm dying for a swim," she said. Not so much dying for a swim, Rhonda got the idea, but dying to be anywhere but where she was. It became clear to Rhonda then, with no small amount of concern, that the girl hadn't been back to the cottage since Evelyn's death. That this place, in all its abandonment, represented the hour of Evelyn's death. And so then Marco's, his disappearance anyway. This had been *their* cottage.

This was where she had died.

Hence, the acerbic mood.

Shit, Rhonda thought, wishing someone had told her. She ran after the girl, who had already fled down the steps that tunneled beneath the wall to the beach. Rhonda stood squinting into the sun, trying to see where the girl had disappeared. A minute later her figure reappeared, heading down the shore. She crawled over a cluster of boulders, where she met up with two boys, or were they men, wearing Speedos. One looked like the barista from earlier. They chatted and smoked and kicked at the water with their feet. Then they headed inland, disappearing from Rhonda's view.

Rhonda sat down on the low wall right there, disoriented.

A shift in the wind, perhaps. A feeling she couldn't pinpoint. She wasn't sure, exactly, what life she had presumed her sister had lived after reuniting with Marco—exile in Siberia . . . new identities in Mexico . . . an exotic island off the African coast? What Rhonda hadn't pictured was this: her sister living a quietly idyllic life on the edge of a seascape not so unlike the one she and Evelyn had grown up in.

How long she sat there contemplating this she did not know, just that the need to pee became pressing, which reminded Rhonda that the groceries were still sitting outside. She went and got them, plus her luggage, and dragged everything inside. She wasn't sure where to set things, what with the thick layer of sand caked over everything. She'd need to call someone to come and clean. When Carlotta got back she would talk to her about how they could get this place in shape, cleaned out, and packed up, whatever it was that needed to happen before . . . What was with the government taking everything?

In the kitchen now, Rhonda stared at the fridge, afraid to open it. Would animals jump from the cupboard?

She left the grocery bag, still packed, on the wobbly wood table, noting a bottle of clear liquid on a high shelf before going to find a bathroom. The toilet had a pull chain, and the shower consisted of a nozzle and a drain, no doors or stall. No hand towels, so she went looking for a linen closet. What she came upon was a small room stacked with oil paintings, an easel in its center holding a half-finished portrait of an elderly woman. The scorned pride in the woman's eyes was disconcerting, as was the steep crest of her jaw. Her face, pencil drawn with wrinkles, looked ghostly in its unfinished flesh.

A gust of wind.

The scent of dripping sea. "She died with nothing." The girl's breath brushed the back of Rhonda's neck.

"Who is she?"

Carlotta, wrapped in a wet towel, moved in closer. "Duchess Irene of Greece and Denmark," she said. "My father's grandmother."

There was a pause.

"*Papà* had been painting this portrait before Evelyn died. It was a requisite from the museum in honor of what would have been *nonna* Irene's hundredth birthday. I believe it was torturing him. They were very close."

"Are those the . . ." she began, stepping in closer, "the Pyramids?"

The girl shrugged. "They couldn't live in Italy, so they lived in Egypt. Something about taxes, the monarchy, I don't know, no one ever talks about it. Anyway, *papà* was born there, and his grandmother practically raised him."

Rhonda stepped in closer. There was a medallion around the duchess's neck.

"She is the reason that I fence," Carlotta said, and Rhonda had to steady herself. The medallion was in fact an Olympic medal, but that wasn't what was making Rhonda dizzy momentarily, it was the small

speck below the woman's lower lip, the one she wore with all the grace
and pride that such a mark might mean to a woman of her stature.
Rhonda quickly moved away from the painting, keeping her back to
Carlotta while perusing the others standing stacked against the walls—
portraitures—men, women, children—solemn faces, proud, imposing,
austere—if only to recompose herself.

"He'd close himself up in this room for hours."

"The faces, they stare back at you," Rhonda cleared her throat and
said.

"Evelyn thought it was his way of seeing into his past, of finding the
people he'd lost."

They stood wordless for a minute longer, and then the girl scooted
Rhonda from the room. "He'd be mortified to know we were in here.
I'm not sure why the door was even open. He must have been working
when—" she stopped herself. Then she shut the door, locked it with the
ancient key that was already in the lock, and said she was going to take
a shower.

Rhonda found a rag under the sink in the kitchen and began dust-
ing any and all surface areas. Carlotta reappeared twenty minutes later,
dressed in the same miniskirt and tank top from earlier, her hair had
dried and she smelled like coconut; her skin was glowing. "I'm going
out with some friends," she said, rummaging through her purse.

"I can't imagine how hard it must be for you here," Rhonda finally
found words to say; banal words, she realized, as the girl stepped slowly
backward and then turned and hurried out.

A flock of seagulls shrieked with her departure. Rhonda went to the
terrace doors, wanting to flee with them. But she knew that that was
impossible, that there was no escape from whatever it was crushing
her chest.

Dusk.

The inevitability.

The door to the bedroom Rhonda would be staying in was swollen.

She had to shove hard to get it open, and then it took a moment for her heartbeat to settle. More sheets, more oddly shaped ghosts. She pulled them off, one by one, delicately, so as not to disturb the dust. A small vanity, a brass bed, and, the most wrenching sight of all, linens disheveled from a lovers' last sleep, on which Rhonda's eyes became fixed. She wanted to turn away but couldn't, the sight of them there, tangled in each other's limbs.

Suddenly, there was no air in the room to breathe. She grabbed her chest and glanced around. A tall window stood behind the wooden writing desk. It looked out onto the sea, presumably, though the shutters were closed. Rhonda opened them, behind those were another set of doors; she opened those too, a cumbersome task that sent her spiraling into a state of anxiety and frustration because she was desperate for fresh air, to wash away this dank, molded stench.

Breathless from the task, she sat at the desk and stared into the falling darkness. The birds had quieted, consumed by crickets now, the beginnings of a moonlit sea. She switched on the desk lamp. A stack of paperbacks, all in Italian. Had her sister learned Italian? *Yoga for Dummies*? Rhonda stood and perused the walls on which hung prints of ancient ruins, maps. A credenza held some clothes. Not much. Evelyn was always giving away her clothes. Not because of altruistic reasons, but because she despised clutter. Nothing pissed her off more than a drawer too stuffed to close. She was just as happy to wear scrubs.

The sundresses hanging in the closet made Rhonda pause. She ran a hand over the delicate fabrics. When had her sister ever worn clothes that hung?

She pulled down a box from a high shelf and set it on the floor. Beneath a bundle of moth-eaten sweaters were some papers, Evelyn's visas, a medical certificate, hospital badges, and photos of the deprived, starved, sick and dying. *Ugh.* Rhonda chucked the photos into the air and watched them rain down like confetti. She hated her sister for leaving them, for all the good she'd gone and done for the world when the world, according to Rhonda, was right at home where she'd left it.

This was it, her remains?

No. This wasn't it. There was another box behind the first. She pulled it down and slid off the lid. Underneath another bundle of moth-eaten sweaters (her sister was always cold), there they were, and Rhonda fell down onto her butt, surprised and then not, staring at what she saw. A dozen or so notebooks holding her sister's most intimate thoughts, tied together with cooking string in that funky knot that only her sister could untie. Or tie, for that matter.

She went to the kitchen and got a knife. Something struck her—the need for courage—and she stood on a chair to get the bottle of clear liquid, which she brought back with her to the bedroom, locking the door behind her. She pressed her back to the wood for a moment, cradling the bottle and knife to her chest. Then she took the journals and bottle and knife with her to the unmade bed.

She took a sniff from the bottle, which emitted a murderous, acrid scent. A swig made her cringe. She slipped the knife through the string. Flipped to a random page. A village in Burma, facing an outbreak of dengue fever and other infectious diseases; they were running out of medicine. Another swig, another book, another page. Cambodia: tuberculosis and HIV. In another book, the Thai border: famine, futility. Refugees. *He's lost his parents, his siblings. He is ten. He is starving. I feed him. Bathe him. But he does not want to live.* Another swig burned a hole in her stomach.

Another book. Then another, every place Evelyn had been, every person she'd not saved, every sensation she'd felt, every sight that enlightened her, every temple and tomb, was written here. *The day felt softer, a lighter shade of gray. This is my third time back to the base of the upper sanctum, dizzying enough with its labyrinth of stone stairs and corridors and courtyards in this valley of the gods. But it's the pinnacle*

I'm after, the highest of the five lotus-shaped towers, where the Buddha sits in meditation, where once only kings and monks had wandered.

Everything Rhonda had never asked and Evelyn had never told her. On all those phone calls, for there had been many in the beginning.

The drink was settling in, the pressing reality.

There was no reference to a child, just her presence felt, beneath the purpose of every word.

This last book had ramblings mostly, if not all out delusions. Malaria? Rhonda went still at this word. It couldn't be right, and it took her eyes a while to adjust to it there, scribbled on the page, the fact that her sister had spent all these months in misery, thinking she might die, without Rhonda knowing it.

Burn them. Burn them all, Evelyn had written, as if she knew Rhonda would be the only one dispassionate enough to read what were meant to be private thoughts. *I don't believe in posterity, Rhonda. There will be nothing of me left when I go. Olivia will have to live with that*—Rhonda looked up at the cracked and peeling ceiling, and thought, *Finally. A note. Something.* Anything that might give Rhonda some bearing on what to do. Her chin trembled. She continued reading . . . *that's if she ever comes asking and you choose to tell her. I know that we once agreed on this, to tell her if she came asking. But if I were dead, what would be the point? I've never been a mother to her. In my imagination, maybe, but the reality is that if I had wanted to be a mother I would have. What I'm saying, Rhonda, is lie to her. Lie to her if she asks. There is truth in lies. You are her mother. You will always be her mother. Believe that and she'll believe it too. She wouldn't be alive if not for you. Please, Rhonda, burn the notebooks, all the useless, self-serving words. I'd burn them myself if I had the energy, or the courage. If I don't live past tomorrow, I'll know that I lived life in the only way I could. I won't miss it. But I will miss you.*

Rhonda sat there, stunned and shaking.

No. It was the illness that made her sister write those things.

She closed the notebook and then scoured the room for more. There had to be more. This couldn't be it. She must have written something to Olivia, things Evelyn would want to say to her daughter, but there was nothing. There were no more journals. Her sister had survived the malaria somehow; she'd found Marco again. What more she had to say belonged to him, apparently. *Burn them. Burn them all.*

The room was a swirl.

Rhonda gathered up the notebooks.

Why couldn't you be more like Evelyn? Daniel's voice came at her now, even though he'd never actually said the words to Rhonda, she could see them in his eyes. *Why can't you love me so much that you'd even give up your own child?*

She wobbled her way to the door with the notebooks. Fumbled with the lock. The thing was, in Rhonda's own way, she did love Daniel. She juggled the books to the terrace, grabbing matches from the living room fireplace as she did. Daniel had brought Olivia into his life as if she were his own, never one question, and Rhonda loved him for that, was willing to stay devoted to him until the end for that. This was *her* way. Being loyal. Dependable. Having integrity. Down the tunneled steps, she stumbled across the pebbly shore. But Rhonda's *way* never seemed to be enough. She stacked the journals into a pyramid. Never enough. She threw a lit match on them. She watched them burn.

11

The crickets screeched so loudly that Rhonda woke up. She'd left the doors open, and now the stars were drilling holes in her head. Her mouth was dry. There was a faint stench of ash in the air, her fingers smelled burnt, then, a vision, fiery and bleak, and she sat up, suddenly, in a pool of sweat.

Had there been some kind of bonfire?

She stumbled to the living room, and almost fell over her suitcase, which still sat by the French doors leading out to the terrace. She hobbled over to the floor lamp and switched it on. A depressing orange hue infused the room, framing the blackness of Carlotta's open bedroom doorway. Rhonda went and peeked inside. The sheets were still covering the furniture, the girl's bag sat barely opened on the bed beneath the shadow of a painting, bleak and hazy. A wall clock read 1:00 a.m. Where was Carlotta?

Rhonda was too disoriented, not to mention starving, to know if she should be alarmed about the girl's absence. She went to the kitchen and emptied the grocery bag. Two boxes of pasta, cheese, bread, anchovies. A bag of what had been frozen octopus, which Rhonda contemplated absently for a moment, was now laid out on the wobbly wood table.

She opened the cheese, which she quickly wrapped back up because it released a foul stench. She thought idly of the pasta, trying to remember the last time she'd boiled a pot of water. The anchovies were thoroughly confusing, not to mention the octopus that she now realized should have been in the freezer. She finally just tore off a hunk of baguette and sat down in a chair right there, feeling helpless, as she always did when the task of cooking was presented to her. It reminded her of all the motherly things she was inept at, and for which she had paid help on her speed dial—catering, laundry, tutoring, personal shoppers, drivers, the school principal, his key administrators, and most importantly, Pizza Hut . . . which led her down a spiral of dark thoughts, those that always led Rhonda to the same place: she wasn't meant to be a mother.

She closed her eyes, the words burning in her mind. *You are her mother. You are her mother,* and without thinking she got out her phone and began dialing Olivia. She hadn't come here with this intention, had she? To lie? No. She had planned to tell Marco the truth, and then the two of them would tell Olivia together.

And yet, *there is truth in lies.*

Rhonda's cell had no bars, so she went outside and held the phone up to the stars. One bar, two, then back to one again. She tried anyway. The ring sounded weird, and then it clicked off. She sent a text: *Checking in. Give me a status update on Taos.*

Nothing came back. Which is when she realized nothing had been sent. Her text remained "undelivered." She checked her phone settings. Before leaving she'd gone to the AT&T store and purchased the premium international package to ensure there was no disruption in her lifeline home. Seamless. Her life was to remain seamless—divorce or no divorce, mausoleum or no mausoleum. But she'd not figured on bad reception. No Wi-Fi. But then what would one need it for here in the land of Gods and lovers? Why communicate with anyone else at all, when you had tangled limbs . . .

She slammed shut her eyes. A slow rumbling of panic . . . what if Chase was trying to get a hold of her? Had he received her wire, had he closed the funding round? What if Stevie was trying to contact her about a bond maturing in their endowment? What if Olivia was upset and on her way home from Taos right now to find her mother not there? Rhonda pressed her fingers to her lids. These were the exact kinds of situations she made sure she was never in. It's why she had stayed home all those years. It's called *being there*. When was the last time someone couldn't get a hold of her within three minutes? Even when she was in a meeting, she had her phone prominently displayed on the table so that she could read every new text. Daniel used to chastise her about how rude she was being to the person she was with, often that person being him. Until finally some last straw broke and she seethed back at him like a rabid animal. "They're my *kids*, Daniel."

He gave up after that.

She stared at her phone now, blinking at it. Then the word "Facebook" flashed like a neon sign in her mind. When all else failed, there was Facebook. Although Olivia had *unfriended* Rhonda last year, Rhonda was still Facebook friends with most of Olivia's old friends, the ones that had come and gone. There were many. Perhaps Rhonda could get a sense of Olivia's activities through one of them. She would have Carlotta take her to an Internet café when she returned. Rhonda looked at her watch. Well, perhaps tomorrow.

She stood still in the piercing silence.

Now what?

Pasta. She headed back to the kitchen. Pasta would soothe her grappa-scorched stomach. A pot was already on the stove, full of dust and moths. She cleaned it, filled it with water, and turned on the burner; the flame ticked but wouldn't catch. She turned it off, afraid the house might explode, which it then did, sort of, in the form of Carlotta bursting through the back kitchen door, accompanied by a waft of pastry and cigarette fumes.

"There's a bakery in the village," she said, throwing a bag on the table. "My friends must always have the first *cornetti* out of the oven."

Rhonda had to restrain herself from groping at the bag. "Those friends you were with at the beach?"

Carlotta, noticing the pot of water, came over to the stove to help. "You were watching?"

"I recognized the barista."

"*Riki e' una testa di cazzo,*" Carlotta grumbled, igniting the burner with her cigarette lighter.

"Isn't he a little old for you?"

"Not me . . . you. He is insisting to meet you."

Rhonda wasn't sure she'd heard the girl correctly. Luckily, she went off in Italian then. What was becoming a pattern when she got passionate about something, or pissed off for that matter, as good as her English was, Carlotta could only express certain sentiments in her native tongue.

Rhonda reached into the bag and pulled out a *cornetto.* Thankfully, the girl's back was to her because Rhonda folded the entire melting pastry into her mouth at once—it was just easier. Consequently, it slid down her throat in one big lump. The flavor was overwhelming, and painful, and in lieu of being able to speak, she sat back and watched Carlotta rummage around in the cupboards. "There is a bottle around here somewhere."

"It's in the living room," Rhonda managed to speak finally, and the girl went and retrieved the bottle, flashing a devilish look at Rhonda, who, for her part, thought she might be sick if she so much as smelled it.

Carlotta poured two tiny glasses. "*Cin cin,*" she said, holding up hers.

Rhonda held her breath and brought the glass to her lips but quickly removed it. "How old are you?" she asked.

"Eighteen."

"What is the drinking age here anyway?"

The girl's brow knitted. "Drinking age?"

The water was boiling, and when Carlotta turned around to add the pasta, Rhonda poured her grappa into the sink. She took a cigarette from the pack right there, inducing the memory of the ash and burn, the blazing fire of guilt she now harbored for having torched her sister's notebooks in a fit, of what, drunkenness? And what did that solve? The truth was still staring at Rhonda in the face. Or the lie. *You're her mother.*

But there was still Marco to consider, and whether he knew that he had not one daughter, but two.

Carlotta took a cigarette from the pack. "My mother does not know that I smoke." She held out her lighter for Rhonda, who inhaled, the smoke reaching far into her lungs.

"Neither does mine," she said.

"In Italy, we are often two different people."

"It is not so different in America."

"I love my aunt but she keeps me in a glass jar. And Grand Master, *mamma mia . . .*" She went off in Italian again, gesturing and shrugging as if Rhonda were understanding, until Rhonda asked for a translation, and Carlotta shot her a confused glance, as if to say, *Oh, that's right, you're not Evelyn.*

"At the cottage I have always been free," she said finally. "But now the cottage is prison. I do not want to stay here. I cannot stand it here. How can I possibly . . . ?" Her voice dropped off, as if over a cliff, and she turned away from Rhonda to check on the pasta.

"Tell me what it was like, Carlotta. Here, with them?"

The girl didn't say anything.

"What would you all do?"

She shrugged. "*Boh.* I don't know. Not much."

"But tell me something. Anything."

"Just stuff, I don't know!" Carlotta yelled out suddenly. Then she let out a long breath, her back still to Rhonda. "We ate, we slept, we dreamt. . . ." Her voice tapered off in frustration. At last she turned around, and, gazing absently past Rhonda, began to describe the rapport her father and Evelyn had had, a language all their own that made Carlotta feel, at times, as if she were intruding. And yet she felt welcome, a part of her father's life as never before.

"Never before?"

"You must understand, as a child, I lived with this black cloud hanging over *papà*. My family does not talk about this. But when I asked *mamma* once about it, she said some men were just sad. And that *papà* was one of them."

Evelyn. It was Evelyn, Rhonda couldn't say.

"The cloud followed him around until one day it swallowed him up. He went away—I was eleven, I think. He did not return."

"But then he did return," Rhonda said.

"Two years later. *Mamma* was ill. *Papà* came home." She paused, as if thinking back. "And there was this woman. This doctor woman named Evelyn."

Carlotta turned back to the stove. The pasta was done. "I didn't want to like Evelyn," she said finally to the blackened kitchen window. Then she dumped the pasta into the strainer in the sink.

The steam rose into her face. "*Mamma* would be so happy to know that I was cooking." She turned around suddenly. "*Mamma* hated fencing. She thought it was not ladylike." She shook her head then, fighting a teary smile, fighting the desire to say what she couldn't help but say. "Evelyn didn't miss one of my competitions."

Rhonda put her head into her palms and squeezed.

12

The notebooks were ash. But what of Evelyn? According to Carlotta her ashes had disappeared with Marco, who was perhaps dead. Certainly unstable. Depressed, erratic. Sad, Carlotta had said. A man to stay away from, Rhonda was sure. Rhonda's trip to Italy had not been futile; rather, it had been an attestation. The only thing left to do now was clear out this cottage, take what memories Rhonda wanted of her sister and return home, where Rhonda would find a way to go on with Olivia as before.

There is truth in lies.

When Carlotta awoke, Rhonda sat her down and together they made a list of everything that needed to be done—cleaners, packers, shippers. They were going to need a storage space. The girl stared back at Rhonda doe-eyed. *Papá*'s paintings in storage? *Assolutamente no!* And this idea of hiring people to help them was entirely confusing to her. Just buying boxes was cumbersome. The post office closed at will. Three times Rhonda had walked there only to find a sign that said they'd be right back. It was the barista who stole boxes from the café for them. They didn't need many; there wasn't much. And Rhonda was swift about it. First thing to go were those moth-eaten sweaters, which sent Carlotta to her knees as if bludgeoned.

"But this belonged to *nonna*!"

"*Nonna?*"

"My grandmother." She reached for another sweater from Rhonda's pile. "Luisa knitted this for *mamma!*" she cried.

"Luisa?"

"*Mamma's* wet nurse. She died just after *nonna* did."

It went on like this for some time, Carlotta applying a name and face to each sweater, while Rhonda stood there guilty with disbelief, *Evelyn wore your mother's sweater?*

After that it was decided that Rhonda would do the packing, and Carlotta would go to wherever it was she went with her friends down the shore each morning, that place from where she'd return smelling of the sea and all its intoxications. Each day her skin would be a deeper shade of bronze, her hair more tawny than black. Rhonda might forget what she was doing momentarily, taken in by the sight of the girl, out on the terrace drying her long waves with a towel in the fading light.

What possessions Marco and Evelyn owned consumed little space. The photo frames were the size of postage stamps, a few porcelain vases and figurines, again tiny, the books in the shelves were pencil thin. The TV was the size of a hatbox, and the footstools reminded Rhonda of a fancy restaurant she'd once been to. How Carlotta, in all her amazon glory, managed to fit into those slim wooden easy chairs was a wonder.

Luckily, the furniture would stay for the new owners (another fact that Carlotta could not bear, for each piece dated back to some Baron or King). Who these new owners were, exactly, other than *sto cazzo di governo*, was not clear. It didn't matter. Three days later Evelyn's possessions amounted to one box, Marco's paintings were in storage, the neighbor's gardener's wife had come and scoured the place clean, and the cottage was ready for its next iteration. And Rhonda was ready to go home.

She sat on the terrace wall waiting for Carlotta, antsy for her return, making mental to-dos regarding their trip back to Rome in order to stay the sinking sensation in her chest. For the beach had this horribly lonely feel. Even the air had changed textures, the sun having seemingly just risen was about to begin its descent back down. Dusk would come early tonight, she thought. With it, that feeling of abandonment early October always brought her, the last residues of summer having vanished, as if everything had long started, and without her, again. She hopped off the wall suddenly, as if out of her own skin. *Forget it*, she thought. Grimy, smelly, a mess—her shorts were ripped on one side, and her T-shirt was stained with sweat. She'd just go find her.

Down the steps and through the tunnel and out over the rocks, Rhonda reached the boulders where Carlotta and her friends had their cigarettes each day. She cobbled over the rocks to the other side. Just around the bend, inland a few yards was, of all things, a beach volleyball court on which Carlotta was in the midst of a doubles match with the barista as her partner. She was just going up for a serve, a jump-serve, and Rhonda almost slipped off the rock on which she was balanced.

As if things hadn't been strange enough already, Rhonda thought, righting herself. She sat on her knees, feeling almost violated, unable to move. That was herself out there, wasn't it? Rhonda? Five-eleven, she guessed, and there was a time when Rhonda looked like that in her bikini too. Taller. Lean and strong, her limbs effortlessly springing from the sand every time she went up for a spike down the line, or lunged to dig a ball far from reach. The girl was no novice, Rhonda was sure. Trained, naturally skilled, her limbs shone, she barely broke a sweat while Rhonda was sweating just watching.

No breeze. Rhonda was squinting so hard she was tearing. And then it occurred to her that Carlotta, who had spotted Rhonda crouched there motionless in the sand, was now waving her over.

Rhonda wiped off her knees and made her way there, slightly embarrassed.

Carlotta stepped off the court to meet her, assuring Rhonda that it was she who was embarrassed, for she'd not played in a while.

Rhonda, breathlessly, said, "This is what you've been doing all day?"

Carlotta began setting herself the ball.

The barista came over. Rhonda wasn't sure, but he might have been gushing as he shook her hand, introducing himself. One of the other men came up and did the same thing. Carlotta, still setting herself the ball, explained that the guys played for Laverno, a club league nearby. Then the two men began conversing among themselves, incorporating a few words of childish English that Carlotta rolled her eyes at.

"What are they saying?" Rhonda wanted to know.

"They want to know if you play."

Not in the realm of what she'd guessed they were saying. "Well . . . once, yes . . ." she muttered.

"They mean now." There was mischief in her smile, and Rhonda took some steps backward. "Me?"

"They want to play with the Olympic gold medalist."

Rhonda stood there, stunned. She'd certainly not told Carlotta this. Rarely had she in twenty-five years spoke of it unless someone specifically asked her about it. And even then, she would find a way to change the subject.

"*Maschi contro femmine.*"

"Guys against girls."

Rhonda gazed at Carlotta, that ball she was setting herself rising higher and higher, and it slowly began to occur to Rhonda what was happening. She could tell just by the way the girl's elbows were tucked in just so, the W-formation of the hands, that Evelyn had something to do with this. Rhonda could even picture the moment in her mind, one day Evelyn passing the girl the ball, trying to find a way to make friends with her, and the girl perhaps resisting at first, but finally, one day, passing it back.

"You must play," said Carlotta.

I need to go home.

"Please play," the guys moaned, making prayer gestures.

Something screamed, the caw of an airborne seagull, and Rhonda shot her gaze toward the heavens. Her sister had left them. She'd gone on to make other people happy. To be a mother in other ways, and Rhonda didn't know if she was sad, relieved, or clinically depressed.

Or pissed.

Fuck it, she thought.

"It was a silver medal," she said, taking the ball from Carlotta and heading onto the court.

The barista gladly gave up his spot and went to the sidelines to watch. Rhonda and Carlotta rallied for a few minutes while the two men on the other side hassled them with trash talk (they spoke in Italian, but Rhonda could recognize trash talk in any language). Then Rhonda grabbed the ball and brought Carlotta into a huddle. "The strategy is this," she instructed to the girl. "You listen and do what I tell you." Forget about however many years it had been since she had played, Rhonda didn't step onto a volleyball court unless she was prepared to win. "I'll stand at the net, while you, in all your nimble glory, will return every serve to me right on target. This is the key: it has to be right into my hands at the net. Then I'll set you the ball, exactly where you want it, every time." As an outside hitter by training, Rhonda knew where Carlotta would want the ball before she did.

"Got it?"

"*Si, va bene*," the girl said, though she didn't look so sure, for the key to the whole plan was an unwavering confidence, something Carlotta had lost recently.

To a layman it might sound like a ridiculous plan because it left no room for error. To Rhonda, it was entirely executable.

Even after they lost the first game. "You're the heavy hitter," Carlotta said, waving her hands together in prayer. "*Mamma mia, per favore*, let me set *you*."

"We need to play to each other's strengths. Right now our strength is your youth."

"*Mah*, I hit it long five times."

"You can slam the ball. I get it. But the sand game is not about that. It's about placement. It's about me knowing where you're going to be three steps before you're there. Same with them for you. Just tap it where they're not. It doesn't have to be pretty."

"*Mah . . .*"

"You say you've lost your edge. Well, this is how you get it back."

"Edge?"

"Look, think of it as a conversation."

"*Che cosa*?"

"The kind you have in your head on the fencing strip. Only you'll be having it with me. Mine. Yours. I'm here, etc."

The girl said nothing.

"Do you trust me?"

"*Si, certo, mah . . .*"

"Because this won't work if you don't trust me."

After it was over, after they'd taken the guys three out of five games one hour later, after Rhonda had bent over catching her breath for a good five minutes, after she didn't remember the last time she'd felt this spent and invigorated at once. So many images, so many emotions—for one, how incredible muscles were not to forget, to know what's required of them, always, especially and unforgettably those muscles pumping blood to her heart. This game was who she was. This game was about her, and it had been so long since anything had been about her.

The cawing came again. To rid herself of the sound Rhonda fled to the sea and dove in. The others followed, and they all floated around in the water for a while, the guys peppering Rhonda with questions she barely understood, about the Olympics, America, in that gesticulating, flirtatious manner. She was sure they were humoring her, she couldn't quite tell, just that the attention felt nice. She chided back as best as she could, thankful that they couldn't understand her. She finally waved them off and limped her way back to the cottage, thinking that she might have pulled a shoulder muscle. She fell into bed, where her body shut down immediately into sleep, in which she remained conscious of nothing but the faint purr of her own snoring.

In her sleep there was a five-two rotation and she couldn't, no matter how hard she tried, spike the ball. She'd take her approach, but then her arm would turn to jelly and the ball would tumble off her chest and roll to the ground. This would happen over and over, the ball would roll flat off her arms and plop to the ground, crumpled, deflated. She was out of her mind with frustration. Tears were streaming down her face. She was crying hysterically and Carlotta was shaking her. She gasped and shook free. "Rhonda," the girl said.

Her eyes flew open. She didn't know where she was.

"I was dreaming," she gasped, looking around her. The terrace doors were opened. Sunlight filtered in with a breeze. The sea was a blinding glitter. "It was awful."

"Who's Bill?" the girl said, and Rhonda blinked at her.

"You were calling out his name."

She pushed her hand through her hair, which was wet. Her tank top was soaked and beads of sweat ran down her arms. "He's an old friend," she said, for what other Bill could she have been dreaming about?

Carlotta went to the desk, opened the pencil drawer that Rhonda had not noticed during her drunken search, nor her packing, and returned with a photo.

Rhonda stared at it, not moving.

Carlotta said something in Italian.

"Yes, we were quite the handsome couple," Rhonda said to the photo. Bill in his varsity jacket, Rhonda in her USA national team sweats. They'd just finished playing Italy, of all teams, in Atlanta, and Bill had flown in to watch. Rhonda passed the photo back to Carlotta, "I can't believe Evelyn kept this."

"She said you were high school sweethearts."

"She talked about me?"

Carlotta looked at her, astonished. "She always talked about you. She was so proud of you."

Rhonda crawled out of bed. She went and stood at the open terrace doors so that Carlotta could not see the pain in her eyes.

13

She had wanted to leave. Was going to. It was just a matter of . . . well, one more round, one more match, one more challenge. It was the guys who kept insisting, switching partners, recruiting ringers. Just one more match, and then. Then, she'd put the photo out of her mind. Stop all this reminiscing, as if the floodgates had been opened.

It was as if the Earth's rotation had stopped the moment Rhonda had touched that ball, and then began rotating again, but in the other direction. She was growing stronger. Leaner. If not purposeless (with each day that passed—three and counting—their departure became vaguer), she often found herself here seated on this terrace wall staring out at the shifting colors of the water and thinking of high school.

Their school was a mile from the beach, and often at lunchtime she would round up Bill and Evelyn and drag them there. Bill would want to lie on a blanket and sleep, preferably spooning Rhonda, or to do other things with Rhonda. . . . But Rhonda would always be pulling him over to the weather-worn volleyball net.

Bill had a decent, if not erratic and deadly, jump serve, and Rhonda liked to practice serve retrievals on the sand in preparation for gym practice that afternoon, which would feel effortless in comparison.

"Come on, Bill," she might chide. "My mother can hit it harder than that."

Inevitably, the next serve would hit the sand before her sprawled-out body could get to it.

"You're making me look bad, Stevenson," he'd yell back, never referring to Rhonda by anything other than her last name. Bill wasn't just the star basketball player of their division, but one of those gifted athletes who could pick up any kind of ball and know what to do with it, naturally, effortlessly. And he wasn't shy to tell you so. So went the trash talk.

Meanwhile, Evelyn would finish Bill's math homework, or write the last few paragraphs of his English paper, until she'd hear the inevitable calling, "Evelyn, why don't you get over here and show your sister how it's done," to which Evelyn's response would be, "If you could spell, this wouldn't take me so long."

"Spell this," he'd say, setting the ball high up in the air to himself, and then spiking it straight down on the other side of the net.

Finally, Rhonda would come and drag Evelyn over. "Stand here," she'd say, positioning Evelyn where she wanted her at the net, "and set me."

Rhonda had taught Evelyn how to set for this purpose.

And Evelyn had taught Carlotta. Rhonda now stood watching the girl from the sidelines, herself spent after three straight matches while Carlotta was just getting going, charged after each passing win, her confidence growing. Her plays savvier, subtler. Rarely did she go for the kill. Her opponents would die their own deaths after she'd land a ball delicately back left or pitched it high and right. Rhonda smiled to herself all the way down to the shore, having left to go take refuge in the sea.

"*Mah dai*, Rhonda. *Non andartene*," Giuseppe called after her.

She had bought a bathing suit from a local shop; it must have been a decade since she'd worn one. She got a vision of that exquisite infinity pool back home, unable to remember the last time she'd swam in it. The thought of putting on a suit depressed her. But something about these

Italians strutting about in all their gorgeous, Speedo-wearing glory, guts and cellulite and all, made Rhonda feel less inhibited about her body, which was changing, slowly. Even in her prime, with a shape not unlike Carlotta's, she had been ashamed of her body. Didn't understand it, or the looks men gave her, and then there had been Bill, constantly begging Rhonda to sleep with him. But she'd been adamant. Losing her virginity could wait.

"Wait for what?" Evelyn had wanted to know.

"Until I'm ready."

"Ready for what?" Her sister hadn't been one to relent.

Babies, Rhonda thought but didn't say. She knew her sister would not understand, nor feel the same way, but for Rhonda sex meant babies, of which she wanted many with Bill, but when the time came and no sooner. What Rhonda didn't know at the time was that Evelyn had already lost her virginity. It wasn't until they were in their twenties that Evelyn shared this little factoid about her life, that she had been sixteen, to be exact, when she'd lost it to one of the boys who went to the Catholic school, in the back of his hatchback. Their intimacy continued for six months until the boy's guilt got in the way, or his mother which Evelyn thought was more likely, and they broke up. Evelyn told Rhonda that she'd been heartbroken. They were halfway through a bottle of wine, and Rhonda could only stare back at Evelyn, shocked that she herself had had no clue. How could they have shared a room all that time and Rhonda have had no clue? "Oh, stop worrying about it," Evelyn had laughed it off and poured Rhonda more wine. Her sister seemed humored by Rhonda's horror-stricken reaction. "You were into your thing back then. We were all into our own thing." But Rhonda was mortified, and she quickly changed the subject, petrified that her sister would ask about her own virginity, and how she'd finally lost it.

With that thought, Rhonda, who had been floating on her back in the sea, succumbed to the weight of her body and sunk under. Her head, everything fully submerged. She stayed there as long as possible, listening to the silence. Then she pushed off the bottom and through the surface, gasping for air.

Back at the cottage, she retrieved the photo from the pencil drawer, as she often did upon her return from the beach, and stood there gazing at it. Sadly, Bill hadn't been her first. Her husband, ironically, had been her first. Daniel. Though this was long before they'd married. Back when Rhonda was in college. Bill had been on the road with his team, she'd not seen him in three months and now he hadn't returned one of her calls, and oh how Rhonda had regretted sleeping with Daniel. Sex with Daniel had not been tender, more like a test of her physical stamina and endurance (which was no test); she'd not been in love with Daniel. And she often wondered if this had ruined her, because the sex with Bill thereafter, while tender, felt tainted, like it was missing something. But still it was theirs, and they did love each other, but later she wondered if it wasn't the reason they'd broken up. If something hadn't been wrong with her.

That familiar sting crawled up her neck; she went to put the photo back in the drawer. Though it occurred to her that she couldn't leave it here. She laid it on the desk thinking that she'd give it to Carlotta, a souvenir of sorts. But a gust of wind billowed the curtain just then and swept the photo into the air. Rhonda tried to catch it, flailing her hands ridiculously about. It finally fluttered to the ground, landing on its backside. When she bent down to retrieve it, she saw BILLYSPIZZA.IT written in faint red pencil. Below that, his email. She blinked at it a few times. .IT? The hairs stood up on the back of her neck.

He was still here?

It was as if all those "one more day" looks she and Carlotta had been exchanging were simply a ruse until Rhonda turned over this photo. As if her life had been suspended until she turned over this photo. Everything was packed and they were ready to go, but they hadn't gone. Until she turned over this photo.

Ghosts. Carlotta had said. She needed to rid herself of the ghosts.

Rhonda had searched for Bill before, when she'd first joined Facebook years ago. In that initial rush of connecting with everyone in her golf community, the revelation of having this view into the world, specifically her kids' worlds, she being friends with many of their friends. Until friend requests started piling up from old teammates and peers, something she'd not counted on, and she began to realize the magnitude of social networking, as if it had been created for the sole purpose of tormenting her. Slowly, one by one, she accepted each request, "Did you fall off the face of the Earth, Stevenson?" and "I thought I'd never find you!" The memories came flooding back, and for a while, caught up in them, she searched for Bill, a variety of times. A hundred pages worth of Thompsons would inevitably pop up. She'd finally given up.

She tucked the photo in her purse and hurried down to the Internet café while Carlotta was still at the beach. She bought a glass of grappa from the bartender and took it with her to one of the computer nooks. She set the picture to one side, and sipped the drink. It took her a moment to recover from the scorch and burning. One more sip. Then she turned the picture over. She typed in the URL. His face popped right up, almost too quickly. She was not prepared to see that luminous, cocky smile of his. Not yet, and she almost knocked over the glass reaching for it again. He was dressed in his Lazio jersey, throwing pizza dough in the air.

It had never occurred to her to search for him in Italy. He had married an Italian, after all; it was not inconceivable to think that he would still be here twenty-five years later, though Rhonda had never thought it really possible that he'd move here at all, given how close Bill was to his family in Newport Beach, California, all of whom were shocked and stunned by what he'd done.

But the thing gnawing at her the most, what was causing the slow rise in her blood pressure—forget about the happy pictures of his wife and teenage sons on the "About" page, forget that it seemed he'd barely aged one bit—was the name BILLY's splayed behind him in the picture. It was the name of his restaurant, presumably, now stabbing at her heart. She closed her eyes, all those sleepless nights rushing back to her, she and Bill whispering into the darkness, planning their future together, postathletic careers, Bill's to start sooner than hers since he wasn't NBA material. She'd always cut him off when he spoke about opening a restaurant, assuring him that it was a ridiculous idea, and that he couldn't possibly be serious. He'd be much better off going to business school as they'd planned, while she pursued her spot on the national volleyball team and competed in the next Olympics, her ultimate dream. After that, she'd go back to school for her teaching credential and coach. Bill would go into sales, ultimately. He was a born salesman. They both wanted lots of kids, and they'd need a secure income for that.

Which was why, after she'd achieved her Olympic dream, she turned down her fourth-year spot on the national team. She was barely postprime, still had some solid years left. But she'd had her moment. She'd stood up for her country, proudly, on that podium, tears streaming down her face. She didn't see how more medals would help build her and Bill's future. The future they had planned together.

And then one day he came to her out of the blue and said that he'd signed up with *Lazio*.

Lazio?

Italy, he'd clarified, at the dumbfounded look on her face.

It was just something he wanted to do, he told her. He wanted to see the world.

"But what was there to see? Rhonda had demanded to know. This, after eight years together, in all their talk about building their future, in not one of their conversations did he talk about *seeing the world*.

He went.

She stayed.

And when she finally relented and went after him, Evelyn in tow for courage, it was too late. Three months was all it took for Bill to meet someone else.

Her heart was pounding. Somewhere in all that grappa-induced reminiscing she'd typed and sent an email to Bill at the address on the back of the photo. And now—exactly eight minutes and thirty-nine seconds after she'd pressed send—Bill had responded. His emboldened, unopened reply sat staring back at her now.

She clicked on it.

"Where you been, Stevenson?" it began.

14

"And he's been living here all this time?" Carlotta asked.

Rhonda gripped the wheel, trying to remain focused. It was a miracle that the car ran at all. They'd had the neighbor's gardener give it a jump start. And then Carlotta climbed into the passenger seat. Carlotta had taken a few driving lessons upon turning eighteen—the legal driving age in Italy—but wasn't yet comfortable with the idea of driving, having so rarely gotten the chance to practice, not to mention the fact that neither *zia* nor Grand Master could stand the idea of her behind a wheel.

"I don't know. I guess," Rhonda finally responded, struggling with the clutch.

"What about his wife?"

Rhonda hadn't meant to tell Carlotta everything about Bill (or most everything), but it all just spilled out. And yet the girl had remained pragmatic, as if this was Italy and these hopelessly romantic excursions happened all the time. *His wife?* Rhonda hadn't thought about his wife possibly being there. Would Rhonda have to meet those gorgeous sons? Was she prepared for that? She was already on the verge of heart failure. From the pictures she'd scoured on his website, he looked barely changed except for some graying around the temples and tiny crow's-feet around the eyes still that smoky green. He wore the same goofy grin, as if he were about to make you laugh—and most likely he was.

Would he even recognize Rhonda? Over the years her hair had shifted from blonde to brownish gray, then, finally, its current state as of that morning at the hair salon, a color-rinsed golden yellow. She'd gained thirty pounds and her skin was chafed from years without sunscreen. These past days spent in the Mediterranean had brought some life back to her, yes, but she was nothing of the girl she'd once been.

It took them a while to find parking around the corner of his restaurant, which sat on a busy thoroughfare on the outskirts of Rome, in some hilly suburb next to a church whose bells were ringing presently, so loudly that Rhonda could barely hear her own thoughts. The streets were nondescript, with rundown apartment buildings from which telephone wires dangled perilously and laundry draped from balconies. Neon-lit gas stations, minimarts, an Indian restaurant, Chinese.

And Billy's.

Rhonda turned off the engine but couldn't get out of the car. "I can't do it," she said.

"What?"

"I can't do it. Let's go."

"I have to use the restroom," Carlotta said.

"I've been thinking," Rhonda grabbed the girl's arm. "Maybe fencing shouldn't be your whole life."

The girl's face twisted up, as if to say, *What the hell are you talking about?*

"Take volleyball, for instance. You're good at it. Maybe you should diversify."

The girl's expression did not change.

"I don't know. I guess I've just been thinking a lot. Going over my past and how 'one track' I was, thinking how my life had to be this one way and I—"

"I would never play volleyball; are you crazy? Do you know what Grand Master would do if he knew I had played here this week?" She went into a low seething tirade in Italian. "Please, you must not tell them that I have played. *Zia* would never let me be alone again. I could hurt myself."

"I was just . . ." Rhonda paused. The look of horror on the girl's face was the exact same look Olivia had given Rhonda all those years ago when her daughter had said she wanted to quit volleyball for the theater and Rhonda had thought she was joking. "Oh, Olivia," Rhonda had waved as if she were batting away a fly, as if she knew more about Olivia than Olivia did. Then came that expression, the one emblazoned in Rhonda's mind because she received it so often. *Do you not understand me at all? Do you not know what makes me tick?*

"Fencing will always be my first love. Even if I lose my sponsorship, I don't care. I must always find a way to fence." Carlotta freed herself from Rhonda's grasp and ran toward the entrance.

Rhonda sat there motionless, her heart pounding. Why had she said that? She knew what made the girl tick just like she knew what made herself tick, and that's exactly what frightened her. To find something you want with every bit of your soul so early in your life, you must be prepared for what happens when this same calling abruptly ends, as it had for Rhonda. Twenty years ago. No. That can't be right. If someone were to ask Rhonda what the most important thing of her life was, she'd say her kids. Absolutely. Hands down. Her kids. But the best time? The best time in her life? Rhonda's shoulders sank now. The answer was always the same—not words but visions, visions Bill was always in— and she needed to get the hell out of here. Her first coherent thought in six days—she was making a fool of herself.

She looked out the window, trying to see through the candlelit glass into the restaurant, past the trees twinkling with a thousand tiny lights, for Carlotta, who was taking forever.

Some time went by. Cars and scooters zooming past rattled the windows and her nerves. What the hell was taking so long?

A knock at the window and she practically jumped out of her seat. It was Bill, his hand braced on the roof of the car, bent over, smiling that class-clown smile of his. She smiled back, awkwardly. He walked around and opened the passenger door, adjusted the seat all the way back, and got in. Still, his knees hit the dashboard. "*Mah che cazzo,* these Italian cars," he grumbled and she laughed, abruptly. The man was six feet, seven inches tall. He consumed the car. "You look ridiculous," she said.

"You look good," he said.

Rhonda pursed her lips.

"I'm serious."

"You're never serious." She glanced anywhere but at him. "Which is why you're still in Italy."

The silence was awkward, which he seemed to enjoy. In fact, in a flicker of panic, she thought that he might reach over and tickle her torso, not stopping until she cried Uncle.

"How is Evelyn?" he said finally. "I've called the cottage a couple of times. It just rings and rings."

"Uncle," she whispered.

"What?" he said.

It was all Rhonda could do to keep her face from contorting in agony. She had a variety of things she wanted to say to this man, things she'd been practicing over the years for when this occasion presented itself, for somehow she always knew that it would . . . but not this. "You were in touch?"

"She needed someone to talk to."

Rhonda felt the blood leaving her face.

"We both did. Someone from home, someone who knew the people we once were." He shifted in his seat.

"How did you find each other?"

"Evelyn found me, about five years ago. She and Marco had moved to the cottage, and she contacted me. She came here a few times. We had lunch. She told me about the estrangement between you two. At first I couldn't believe it. I'd never met sisters so close. After she visited a few more times, I began wondering what was up. I pushed her, I felt she wanted to tell me something, was trying to, but then, well, she never did."

Rhonda didn't move. Didn't flinch.

"She seemed tortured."

Rhonda's eyes darted past his shoulder. Where was Carlotta?

"My son is making her a pizza," Bill said, as if peering into Rhonda's mind.

"Oh." She tried to relax. "How old is your son?"

"Nineteen. He's got a knack for it."

"For what?"

"Making pizza. Though his mother is livid. She wants him to go to university in the states."

"No basketball?"

"Hates it."

"Olivia was the same with volleyball."

"But your son . . . I heard he was a golf pro."

"I pushed too hard. He is now a serial entrepreneur with the sole purpose of making more money than his father." Her voice was flat and emotionless.

Bill shrugged. "They say champions like us skip generations."

She glanced at him. "Same Bill."

"I still have the six-pack; want to see?"

"God no!"

He made as if he were going to pull up his shirt, and when she put an arm out to stop him their eyes met briefly, those amber flecks, and she averted her gaze, which happened to land on his biceps, the ones he used to flex for her entertainment because he was always as thin as a rail. He flexed them now, and she rolled her eyes as if she were sixteen again. *Be serious, Bill. For once,* she would say too often. She wasn't going to say it now.

"You ever go back to California?" she asked.

"Once a year I take one of the kids, or both, and go visit my mother."

"How is your mother?"

"She still asks about you." There was a twinkle in his eye. His mother had hated Rhonda. So jealous was she of Rhonda dating her number one son, and they burst out laughing now thinking about it.

"She came around, finally," he said, sobering.

"Yeah, when you abandoned her for Italy . . . suddenly I was her best friend." Rhonda began laughing again, which morphed into heaves and chokes. He waited for her to stop. She rolled down the window and put her head out.

"It took you a long time to show up," he said.

She jerked her head back. *This is how it's going to go down?* "I did show up, Bill. Remember?"

"You left before I could explain."

"What was there to explain? You were engaged."

"We could have talked."

"You're saying I'm the bad guy?"

"I didn't say you were the bad guy."

"You're the one who dumped me." She regretted it the minute she'd said it. It wasn't how she'd intended to say it; it wasn't even in the thread of what they'd been discussing. What had they been discussing?

"I asked you to move here with me, Rhonda."

"You said Italy was temporary."

"You never gave it a chance."

"We had a plan, Bill."

"Plans change. People change, dreams change. It doesn't mean we don't love each other."

Didn't love each other. She couldn't move.

"We're liquid beings, Rhonda, pliable; we discover new things. It's okay for things to change."

Her shoulders were so hunched that her neck began to ache. "I can't do this. No. It doesn't matter anymore. Let's change the subject. Your kids, tell me about them."

He did, after a resigned pause, and he seemed happy, which unnerved her slightly. "And you, Rhonda, are you happy?"

Could she pretend any longer? Yes, she could. "Terribly, terribly happy."

A minute passed. "Are you okay? You look pale."

"How is Evelyn anyway?" he added, when she didn't say anything. "I haven't heard from her. I've even tried her cell. Did she get a new number?"

Rhonda's body slumped forward.

"Is she all right?"

A wave of anguish, that sickening swell. "I think we should go inside."

15

Rhonda went to the bathroom and immediately threw up. Then she sat on her knees with her head in her hands. Outside she could hear Bill speaking in Italian with someone. He knocked, wanting to know if she was all right.

She got up and went to the sink and washed her face. She rinsed out her mouth and ran a hand through her hair. Her knees were wobbly when she finally came out. "I'm sorry." She looked around. "Can we . . . I'm just . . . I'm so hot." He led her through a narrow, arched hallway, down stone steps and into some kind of cellar. Wine crates were stacked along brick walls and drying appendages of all sizes and shapes hung from the ceiling. It smelled of musk and funk but at least it was cool. He sat her down on a crate and handed her a glass of water. "Sorry," he said. "This is the only place that my wife will not find me and if my wife finds me with you she will come at you with a butcher knife."

Rhonda looked at him with alarm. Then she glanced at the door, which he'd locked.

"I'm joking," he said. "My wife's in Calabria visiting her aunt."

"Evelyn's dead," she said.

He stood there for a moment. Then he sat down on another crate and stared hard into her eyes—yes, she was serious. He put his head in his hands.

"It was an accident."

He pushed at his temples. "When?"

"Two years ago," and before he could speak, "It was only now that I could bear the idea, to come here and deal with . . . her things. Their things." She looked up at the damp, darkened ceiling. "And now I feel like I'm lost in the labyrinth of Evelyn's life. I want to leave. But something keeps making me stay."

"That girl?"

"Carlotta."

"Evelyn told me about her."

Rhonda examined him for a long moment. "It never occurred to me that you were still in Italy."

"She was pregnant."

Rhonda had somehow lost the thread.

"My wife. She was pregnant. That's why I married her."

Something he'd never told Rhonda.

The irony.

"I've never really loved her."

She opened her mouth but nothing came out.

"It was you that I never stopped loving."

Rhonda adjusted herself on the crate, worrying that she might fall off and wondering if Bill had anything stronger to drink. *Why not tell me? Why make me wonder for twenty years? Is this what men do?*

Not all men.

Not Marco.

Bill looked down at this hands. Hands that could palm a basketball, her head, her neck. Shoulders. Strong, tender hands. "I wasn't going to have my baby out there flailing along without me."

As if he could read her mind.

"It was real between us, Rhonda. It still is real." He reached his hand for hers. She followed it with her eyes, watching while it enveloped her own, and the entirety of her being in the process. She wasn't sure she was hearing him right. Her ears seemed to be ringing.

"You're grieving over Evelyn," she assured him. "We both are." She felt her head gravitating toward his. His toward hers. The weight of their history.

"Come here," he said.

She looked into his eyes, startled.

It was a command. Something to obey and she did. She pressed her forehead into his chest, his build still hard and angular, his skin smooth and soft, the tender beating of his heart. She moved up into his neck, a swan's neck, and for the first time in a long time, she let herself be held.

Deep breaths followed.

So silly. So childish.

"You're shivering," he said. He went and found a tablecloth, checks of red and white, and covered her shoulders. Her whole body convulsed. *You have a wife and two sons, one still in middle school,* she didn't say as he held her inside the blanket. Nor did she tell him that she was divorced, free to love whomever, unlike him. But the moment had passed, and he was thinking about Evelyn.

"I think she had a crush on you," Rhonda said finally.

A wistful smile. It had been a source of pride. "You were jealous?"

"Evelyn had more to give than me. It was something I always knew. She had an ease with herself in a way in which I didn't."

He stayed silent.

"I wasn't very good at it, was I." It wasn't a question. "I always thought it was because we weren't married, this fear of getting pregnant even though we used protection."

"I couldn't be what you wanted me to be," Bill said.

It could have been the intimacy he was talking about; she wasn't going to ask. How does one know what one wants in that arena? If it were up to her, would she want anything to do with any of it?

His gaze moved from their hands to her eyes. They were diminished now, his eyes. If she gave him an out, would he take it?

"We're not those kinds of people, Bill," she said, removing her hand, and he seemed so entirely relieved. "The kind of people like Evelyn and Marco, people strong enough or brave enough or self-destructive enough to crush lives and hearts in the name of love."

"Well, when you put it like that . . ." He tried to make nothing of it but he was thinking, she could tell, the way his thick brows knitted together. He was thinking of his kids.

And what about Rhonda? What was she thinking?

She was thinking about Marco and Evelyn. She was thinking about what it would be like. To be loved like that.

"You're probably right," he said finally. "As I recall, you were always right."

She looked at Bill now and saw him, really saw him, for this first time, since she'd been imagining him all these years, as the one *not* meant for her. *We make things up in our mind*, she thought. *And these things comfort us. They keep us going. They allow us to live.* She stood. Her head hit a salami. "Ouch," she said.

He bit his lips, and they laughed, but it had hurt, really, really hurt. Holding her head she looked around now at all the delicacies so foreign to her—this world he'd made for himself. "You did it, Bill. What you always talked about."

He stood up, sort of—he had to stay partially bent so that his head wouldn't hit the ceiling. Who would have pictured this?

Carlotta drove home because Rhonda was incapable, jarred into blankness, unable to process. Dispossessed of even fear, for the girl was relatively new to this driving business, every so often a lurch, a stall. It took them a lifetime to get back to Rome's center. The girl drove at a harrowingly slow pace, yet she was pulsing with excitement, the thrill to be driving at last, while Rhonda sat staring into the chaos of zooming cars and scooters, numb. Hollowed out. Was that really it? After all the years of imaginings, ruminations filling her moments of idleness, pumping hope into her dried-up soul, the vision of her and

Bill's chance reunion, confrontation, his confession of enduring love and yet . . . here she was, and it all meant nothing.

Perhaps it had always meant nothing.

Her heart ached as if she'd lost him all over again. Only this time it was worse, finite, this knowledge that there might not have been anything there to begin with. *You've never been properly fucked, Evelyn* had told her once. This, in the middle of her marriage to Daniel, and Rhonda cringed now hearing her sister's words. Evelyn knew Rhonda hated to hear the word *fuck* used in that connotation. "You need to be taken," her sister had gone on, goading Rhonda, a wicked smile on her face (three margaritas in, the both of them). "You need to be ravaged." Rhonda had to put her hands to her ears. Oh, how she hated her sister sometimes. How she wished she had never existed.

And the few glorious days she'd had with Carlotta at the beach only made the reality more crippling. The Earth wasn't rotating backward; it was taunting her. The reality: Rhonda wasn't young and lean and strong anymore. She wasn't a player anymore. Her life had crested a long time ago, and everything since then, and everything to come, was simply the fall of all that was left.

"What is it?" Carlotta asked.

Rhonda looked at her. *I'm scared. I think I've always been scared.*

Carlotta pointed to Rhonda's chest, and Rhonda looked down. She'd been clutching her phone.

"Do you want to call her?"

Rhonda looked at her.

"Olivia."

With sudden, wide eyes, "Could we?"

Carlotta pulled over to the side of the road. "Call her."

Of course here there was reception. Four bars. Two tries and then Lillian answered. Rhonda gasped, instinctively. Why was Lillian answering Olivia's phone? Lillian was their Mexican nanny, hired by Daniel after his divorce to care for Chase and Stevie, and Rhonda had kept her on. She'd told Daniel it was out of obligation, but in reality she was petrified of instant motherhood. She'd never once, to this day, even though there was nothing for Lillian to do anymore, thought of letting her go. "What is it, Lillian?" Rhonda demanded. "What's happened?"

"All is fine," Lillian assured her. "Olivia is home and safe."

"Safe?"

"She's got a bacterial infection." Lillian went on to explain that they'd been to the doctor and he'd prescribed antibiotics and given her something for the pain. "It was something she ate." And here's where Lillian said something that Rhonda made her repeat a couple times. "Asia. Vietnam. Olivia went to Vietnam and didn't tell us."

"Put her on."

Lillian passed Olivia the phone but she was incoherent from the pain meds. Going on about dragons and caves. Lillian took the phone back and Rhonda had her repeat the doctor's every word, twice: hydration was the key, otherwise Olivia would be fine. "I'm on it," Lillian said, an American phrase that always sounded odd coming from Lillian's lips, a phrase she'd acquired working under Rhonda, the only phrase Rhonda wanted to hear when it came to her kids. And of course Lillian *was* "on it," but she was no Rhonda.

After hanging up Rhonda turned to Carlotta, who had lit a cigarette and was smoking it with her head resting on the seatback, her gaze fixed on something outside her window. The sight caught Rhonda for a moment. The girl's hand was trembling and she wouldn't turn this way. She'd heard the phone conversation. She knew what was coming. Rhonda took a few steady breaths, then one long deep exhale. "I'm sorry about what I said about playing volleyball, Carlotta. Of course I understand your love for fencing." Cars streamed by. Rhonda's impending departure, that's what was coming, had always been coming, but it was different now; something had happened between her and the girl, they'd grown close, and now perhaps Carlotta sensed that she was about to be abandoned by that closeness, once again. Rhonda reached out with her hand and directed the girl's chin to face hers. She latched onto those big, brown, unforgettable eyes. "You must look at me and know that, above all, I understand this." Beyond love, certainly, she didn't say. "And, I promise you, Carlotta, you will not lose your sponsorship. I will make sure of it. Just get me on the next plane home."

16

Had her mother really said *Stay warm*? Olivia had done nothing but sweat since her plane had touched down in Hanoi all of twenty minutes ago, when she'd had to deplane via stairway onto the tarmac and the steamy swelter hit her like a brick. *What the hell have I done?* came rushing at her in a moment of panic, and so once inside the chaotic terminal she'd found the first bathroom and shut herself into a stall and called her mother. A gut instinct Olivia hated herself for—had you really gone anyplace, or done anything, for that matter, if no one knew about it?—or perhaps it was a test. Would her mother know, inherently, upon hearing her daughter's far-end-of-the-earth voice, that Olivia was not in Taos? Or was her mother that out of touch? One minute into the call and Olivia had her answer. Yes, her mother was that out of touch. *Just have a blast, will you?* Olivia quickly got off the phone, her courage sufficiently refueled, and headed back out into the terminal to face whatever it was she'd gotten herself into.

In Marco's email, he told her that a man (not him) would be waiting for her outside of customs holding a sign with her name on it. But she wasn't expecting to have to distinguish this man in a mob of darkly clothed bodies pushing up against a low gate, frantic, waving signs with incomprehensible symbols and screaming out names in sharp foreign tongues. She stopped to scan the signs, but a luggage cart barreled into her from behind, almost knocking her over. She gasped and turned and shot a *what-the-fuck* look at the short, stalwart Asian woman whose cart was overflowing with suitcases. Olivia opened her mouth to complain, but then a man grabbed her and pulled her out of the rush.

"Jesus," she said.

"Olivia," he said, in that deep voice she now recognized.

He pointed to a man carrying a sign with her name on it. The sign that she'd missed.

"Did you see that woman?" she panted. "She almost ran right over me."

"Follow me," he said.

"Ouch," she said, at his grip.

His eyes were dialed into their destination, his face taut and intense. "This way," he said. A thin Asian man dressed in a black suit whisked away her luggage. "Hey!" she yelled, before realizing he was with them. He passed it off to someone else who was calling ahead to someone on his cell phone, their driver, presumably, because a slick, black Mercedes sped up to the curb just as she and Marco exited the terminal. A tall, dark-haired man, his face full of pockmarks, climbed out of the driver's seat, opened the passenger door, and they slid into the back seat, her luggage now in the trunk, presumably. It all happened smoothly and quickly, and before she knew it they'd exited the airport.

She turned and looked back at the frantic mess of travelers they had just escaped, wondering what could possibly be in all that luggage, when she was suddenly flung sideways in her seat. A hairpin turn into an alley, a "shortcut," Marco explained, and said she had better put on her seatbelt. There were more pitches and jolts; before she knew it they were speeding serenely along a six-lane highway as if none of that other stuff had happened.

"How was your flight?" he said, not looking at her.

She looked into the hollow of his pulsing cheek, thinking, *last row of coach, middle seat, next to the bathrooms, horrible,* but she bit her tongue. He would learn about her soon enough. "It was all right," she responded finally. "Except for the smell emanating from the guy next to me. I think he might have been dead. He didn't move once in the entire thirteen hours. Not even to go to the bathroom."

He smiled, as if to himself. "Welcome to Asia."

Welcome to Asia, words Olivia had to repeat in her mind. She looked around. "I can't believe I'm here," she said, unsure how exactly to start this conversation they would be having, presumably, for the next four days. "Can *you* believe I'm here?" She peered at him, quickly curbing her excitement, seeing the way he turned and examined her now, as if he might be regretting this already.

"It is, I suppose, somewhat disconcerting." He looked off again.

"It's just that . . ." she was flustered, unsure what he was referring to—*her* or *this place*. "My dad used to come here a lot." Her palms were sweating. She wiped them on her jeans. "Not Vietnam but China, where they manufacture his golf club designs. He'd always promised to take me with him one day. There was a time in my life when I had envisioned myself in foreign places. One too many *Sinbad* movies, I guess. *Aladdin*. I don't know where the visions came from, just this feeling that I was missing out on something. . . ." She'd gone on too long, she could sense, pressing her lips together, groaning inside at her tendency to do this. "Anyway, I'm here now."

"Vietnam is no China."

They could have been in China, for all Olivia knew of the world.

The light was fading into dusk, dissolving the landscape, which consisted of what looked like farmland. "Paddy fields," he told her. "I hope you like rice."

She did.

"And fish."

She did not. "Speaking of which, what was that foul beast they were trying to feed me on the plane?"

He smiled, knowingly, and she gave him a clandestine once-over—

handsome perhaps, slightly unkempt, except for the clothes, slacks, and a dress shirt, untucked. He reeked of tobacco.

Out the window beyond him, a parade of children in uniform caught Olivia's attention. Against the gray silhouettes of distant hills, they walked along the sides of the highway in twos or threes. In front of them marched young adults, also in uniform, all seemingly oblivious to the throngs of cars and scooters zooming dangerously past. It would be like walking along the shoulder of the 10 Freeway to Tempe, she thought, it just wasn't done. The walkers grew in numbers, and she wondered where they were going. She got her answer miles later as they sped past a massive, soot-stained ivory building that everyone was filing into only because, it seemed, that's what the person in front of them had done.

"That's a long walk," she said.

"Not when you don't know it," he said.

"They're going to work now?"

"This is the second shift. The first shift is going home, and there will be a third shift later. After everything they've been through, these people don't mess around."

She glanced back at them. "They don't seem unhappy."

"No," he said. "They don't." A world of undertone in that statement, for *they should be unhappy, shouldn't they?* Olivia wondered, having studied the history in school. She faced forward again only to see them approaching now from this direction as well. "What are they making?"

"*Boh*," he shrugged, as if it could be a variety of things. "Textiles. Plastic."

"For us, right? They've got people working round the clock for us?" She couldn't keep accusation from her tone.

"Not just us."

"My history teacher was a communist, or so Dad liked to call him when I'd come home and hassle him about the fact that he was giving away American jobs. He would just roll his eyes at me. Kind of like the way you are now."

"It's the future. There's no going back."

"Is that why you're here? Because there's no going back?"

He gave her a second look, as if there might be more to her than he'd originally thought.

"Like I said, I'll be leaving soon," he said.

"But you must *do* something here." "Do" came out sounding rather demanding. Olivia couldn't help it. She was curious to know what people she met *did*. How one day, she, too, might respond to such a question. *What did Aunt Evelyn do here?* So many questions she wasn't yet sure how to ask. Then their car jolted to a sudden stop—a traffic light that appeared out of nowhere, it seemed.

A flock of bicycles began pulling up, one by one, around their car. Some were loaded down with animals or appliances, some seemed to carry entire families. When the light turned green they all rode off together. No sputter or roar, as if the world had gone silent.

"They can ride on the highway like that?"

"It's strangely peaceful, isn't it?" he said.

"It seems dangerous," she said.

"Especially when we get to Hanoi. You'll see."

He was right: as the streets grew narrower and more congested, car sightings became more infrequent. No lanes and few signals and all those bicycles rolling along, their frames all synchronized in a graceful tilt to the right, then to the left, as they came around a wide bend.

"Where are we going?" she asked. They'd been driving for over an hour.

"The old city," he said.

"As opposed to the new city." She tried to be funny but he didn't laugh.

The silence grew awkward.

"I went to Europe once," she said, trying to make conversation.

"Scotland, with Dad, for my brother's golf tournament, and only after I'd begged and begged to go. Mom wouldn't go because God forbid she should want to leave the confines of our gated community, and Dad and I spent the entire time tracking my brother Chase, shot for shot, on the course. It was so boring I wanted to die. And cold. The wind was so strong we could barely stand up straight. We didn't see one tourist site." Her voice had reached a crescendo. She turned at him. "Can you believe it?"

"You have your aunt's eyes," he said.

The way he was staring at her.

She looked away.

"I'm adopted," she replied, turning back. It was a habit, a tic, something she did to shock people who might have come to some conclusion about her before even knowing her. But he didn't say anything. Thinking of Evelyn's eyes seemed to send him into darkness.

Hazel, Olivia remembered, sometimes green, a flash of amber, often black, depending on the light, when Aunt Evelyn's pupils grew all consuming.

The next thing Olivia knew their Mercedes was idling before a gated entrance while a security guard circled around examining the car's underbelly with a mirror attached to the base of a pole.

She asked what he was looking for.

"Bombs," Marco replied, with all the indifference in the world. "They're always looking for bombs."

"Bombs," she repeated.

"Don't worry, they've never once found one."

Her mouth dropped open, and then the guard saluted them through.

Thatched A-frame houses poked out from the jungle here and there, otherwise there was no sense of civilization. A canopy of dense foliage scraped the car as they proceeded up a road to where a woman stood waiting with a flashlight. After Marco made the introduction—Sue was her name—the woman took Olivia's luggage, and they followed her on foot down a trail that led into darkness. Olivia could hear the palms sweeping all around her in the warm wind, a rustling and scurrying. Eventually, they came upon a structure framed with wide wooden steps leading onto a veranda and into a softly lit, open-aired living area. The floors were polished, the furniture wicker and sparse. A fan twirled slowly overhead. He took off his shoes and indicated that Olivia should do the same.

He went to the other side of the living area and slid open the glass doors to the veranda. A balmy breeze swept through the curtains and Olivia stepped out and looked up at a sky of frothy grays. When she turned around he was gone.

She found him in the kitchen, pulling down a bottle of whiskey and a glass from a high cupboard. "Are you hungry?" he asked.

She eyed the bottle. "I'll have some of that."

He brought down another glass.

The alcohol singed her throat, her eyes watered.

"If you're not hungry, you should try to sleep," he said.

"I'm not tired," she said.

He pulled a tiny silver box out of his pocket. Took off the lid and held out a pill for her. "Take this."

"What is it?"

"Evelyn used to take them. To help her sleep."

The Aunt Evelyn Olivia had known slept like a rock, which came with being a medical intern pulling consecutive shifts at the hospital, the ability to sleep anywhere at any time, lips parted, head resting back on whatever surface was there. It could have been a brick wall and, still, Aunt Evelyn slept in peace. Or so Olivia had thought. "She had trouble sleeping?"

"Sometimes."

She stared at the pill. "No thanks."

"Very well."

He pointed to a door across the hall, and bowed his head. "That is your bedroom." He turned to go. "I'll see you in the morning."

She grabbed his arm. "Where are you going?"

He flinched, as if startled by her touch. Carefully, delicately, he unhooked her fingers. "I stay in the guest house," he replied.

"You're going to leave me here alone?"

"Toni, my driver, and Sue, his wife, sleep in that room over there. If you need anything, they will get it for you."

They didn't look like a Toni and Sue. "You're leaving me with strangers?"

"Technically, *I'm* a stranger."

She examined him. It was odd, but he looked familiar, or felt familiar.

He took the bottle and went out the back door, down the steps, then disappeared into the night.

A light switched off at the end of the hall.

She stood, listening to the silence, a silence so unlike the one she knew—the desert—dried up and hollowed out, empty. But this silence was different. Full and lush and alive. She felt strangely attuned to it, the soft wind, like a howling animal.

17

She blinked and stirred. There was a brief moment of alarm. The ceiling fan whirled overhead though the sweat still poured from her. She wasn't sure what time it was. She had gone to sleep listening to the music on her iPhone, whose battery was now dead. She got up and dug for the charger buried in the bottom of her suitcase. It took her a while to find an electrical socket, behind the bedframe, which she'd had to move, and then the charger wouldn't fit. She went out into the living room, pausing again, for the air was so thick and dense. She saw Sue out back sweeping the veranda, went to her, and asked what time it was. Sue smiled and nodded and bowed. Olivia smiled and nodded and bowed back, thinking, *well, this is awkward.*

A shimmer caught her attention through the trees, and she headed in that direction, pushing aside leaves bigger than her head. The ground felt like it was sinking beneath her feet as they moved into the foreign earth. She felt out of her body, her senses both dulled and heightened, jet lag perhaps. She looked up just before walking into a lake. Wide and vast, as placid as gray glass, with a pagoda floating in the center. And on the other side, veiled in silvery morning light, was an eclectic array of oddly shaped buildings, a mirage, a sleepy haze of vibrancy.

She turned to go back, but her foot dug into something sharp. She cried out. The sting made its way up her leg. She hopped around on one foot, then hobbled back to the house and sat down on the veranda steps, cursing under her breath. Something scurried up the wood column beside her and again she screamed, this time bloody murder. Marco came bursting out of the jungle, in boxers and slippers and no shirt, a cigar dangling from his mouth. Sue came running out of the house with her broom, and then started laughing when she saw what it was. Marco went over and tapped the wood, and the gecko, so he called it, scurried away. "You'll need to get used to that."

"I live in the desert with scorpions," she countered. "I can handle a little—" He took hold of her foot unexpectedly. "Gecko," he said, and Olivia gasped. Her foot was black with dirt, and he had pulled out the thorn with no warning. Blood oozed for some seconds, then dried out. "It might be good to wear shoes when you go out wandering," he said.

"I couldn't find my shoes."

He pointed behind her, in the vestibule, at two pairs of shoes neatly tucked under a bench.

Sue brought back a warm cloth and a first aid kit. Marco applied disinfectant while Olivia screamed, for the third time now, possibly her loudest yet. "Sorry," she said flatly, when he stared at her in alarm. "I've never been able to tolerate pain."

"Most people can't." His grip on her foot was firm, unwavering, gentle. Intense. She tried not to stare at the dark hairs on his chest while he spent some time applying ointment and then bandaging what was ultimately a surface wound.

"There's a lake right over there," she said, when he was done.

"I know," he replied slyly, as if they were sharing a little secret.

"All those buildings on the other side?"

"The old city."

"Oh, right, as opposed to the new city. Will you take me there?"

"Perhaps. Did you find your aunt's things?"

"Her things, no. Where are they?"

"They are in the room where you slept last night."

Olivia tried to picture the room where she had slept—bare, essential, the sheets like flower petals. She had cowered under them most of the night before falling into a delirious sleep just as the sun was coming up, and when she woke she was in a daze.

She stood up now to head back to the room, but then paused when he didn't follow. "Aren't you coming?"

He puffed on his cigar and studied her. Or something beyond her, and she gave up and went inside.

Sue must have snuck in after Olivia had left. The sheets were taut again, and the netting that had almost strangled her as she'd crawled into bed was now tied back. Sue had opened the blinds to let the sun filter in through the surrounding palms. The clothes Olivia had torn from her suitcase were refolded. Dewy purple flowers sat on the side table.

But no pictures, books, or trinkets—the closet was empty. The only artifact was a pinewood box that sat on a vanity table. Next to the box sat Olivia's journal, where her gaze fixed for some moments before she garnered the courage to pick it up. She brushed her palm over the cover, as if she could physically feel beneath it the words she'd once taken such care to write.

She was almost afraid to open it.

She wasn't ready to open it, to see herself as she was back then. All that hope and yearning, the story she'd read a thousand times of the girl who falls in love with a prince she can't have and so travels the world. Olivia had always thought it clairvoyant the way Aunt Evelyn told the story, as if she'd known about the love that she would have long before she'd had it.

Olivia blinked. A sting had caught her eyes, and she set down the notebook.

After a few deep breaths she lifted the latch of the pine box. She was thinking that in it were perhaps some jewelry, photos, letters, but then she never saw Aunt Evelyn wear jewelry or take a photo. She didn't believe in photos. "Why not just remember the moment as it came?" Evelyn would say, and Olivia would laugh because Aunt Evelyn was always saying the silliest things.

The inside of the box was lined in thick plastic, and without thinking

Olivia began to unseal it. A moment later she jerked back and gasped. An unconscious moment passed. She began moving away slowly, then not so slowly. Then she turned and stumbled out of the room.

He was no longer on the veranda. She fled past Sue through the jungle from where he'd emerged earlier. A small hut stood fifty yards away; she stopped and caught her breath and approached it slowly. A satellite dish was attached to the roof, which looked like it might lift off in the next monsoon. No walls, just a layer of thin curtains revealing a single bed in one corner and in the other a worn wicker chair in which he now sat with his feet up, studying the contents of an oversize book he had open on his lap. He'd not changed into clothes, and that foul cigar was still dangling from his lips.

She was at the steps now, a few paces from where he sat, and still panting from the fright. She opened her mouth to speak but he threw up his hand to indicate that she should hold her thoughts until he was done, which she would not.

"Are those her ashes?"

He kept reading, and rather intently, for another moment. He turned the page and jotted down a note. Then he closed the book, set it aside, and gave her his full attention.

"I said are those her ashes?"

"Yes," he said.

"You could have warned me."

"Can one be warned about such a thing?"

"Yes. They can," she said after some thought.

"Well, then, I'm sorry. I should have warned you."

There was an awkward silence.

"I thought her . . ." she gasped. "I thought her things were in there. Where are her things?"

"What things?"

"I don't know?" This was strange. "You two are the ones who lived here. Come to think of it, where are *your* things?"

"I never said we lived here."

She frowned. *Didn't he?*

"Vietnam was Evelyn's first assignment with Doctors without Borders. Hanoi was one of her favorite places, she always told me. And so, well, I brought her back."

Olivia edged herself backward, wondering if now might be a good time to turn and run, but then, well, he looked so lost suddenly. She squeezed her hands behind her back. "Aren't you supposed to, like, spread them or something?"

"You are."

Her mouth dropped open.

"It's what she wanted."

She stared at him, long and hard. "Are you crazy?"

He got up and disappeared somewhere.

She stared into the jungle. *Is he coming back?*

Yes, he was coming back, lighting a new cigar, whose cloud engulfed her. "How can you smoke those things?"

He sat back down examining the cigar in his hand, and then took another pull.

"Didn't Aunt Evelyn die of cancer?"

His eyes receded now. Another full minute passed before he said, as calmly as possible, "Evelyn was hit by a car."

Olivia shrunk back.

"You really don't know anything, do you?"

She looked down. "My mother won't talk about it. I just assumed . . ." She looked up at him.

There was no response. And she averted her eyes. There was that book he'd set aside, and she settled her gaze on it now. Thick, old, the page-ends leafed in gold. She reached over and opened it as a distraction from the heat of his discerning gaze. It was a book of maps of some kind, from the eighteenth century. "You find this interesting?"

"Yes, I do."

"And Evelyn? Did she find it interesting?"

He looked at her, this was an odd question.

"Please tell me," she said now. "I want to know. I want to know everything."

He took the book from her. "Evelyn would just as soon watch a Lakers game."

Olivia studied him with alarm for a long, hard minute, as if this were some kind of sign that she was, in fact, in the right place with the right person, and she wondered if he had any idea. She couldn't count the number of Lakers games her mother and Evelyn had forced Olivia to watch with them. Those two, who acted more like children in those times, so vastly different from one another yet strangely connected by this one single, solitary thing—the Lakers. Their father had been a fan, they had said. They shared him, the Lakers, and on some days, so it felt, Olivia. And Evelyn wasn't even a sports person! She and Olivia preferred the classics, in word or film, foreign flicks, indies, all of which Rhonda yawned at. But when it came to Lakers banter, their Kobe addiction, Olivia could find no place. She'd sit on the couch scrolling through Instagram posts while Rhonda and Evelyn would be screaming at the players with margaritas sloshing in their hands—which was the other thing, how could they drink that disgusting stuff? But the most unnerving thing of all was that sometimes, when the two of them might throw up a double high-five at some three-pointer from half court, no matter how hard Olivia might try to resist doing so, she couldn't help but smile at the both them, clandestinely.

"Don't mess with their Lakers," she grumbled back to Marco now, bringing her thoughts back from this place he'd managed to derail her off into. And it wasn't over.

"Evelyn used to watch the games live on Dish in the mornings, when we were living in Thailand," he said.

"You lived in Thailand?"

"For a time, yes," he said. "And once, when our electricity went out." He turned to Olivia. "It goes out here too, quite often," he said forebodingly. "Anyway, Evelyn missed a Kobe buzzer beater." He tapped the ash from his cigar into a tray. "She didn't talk to me for an entire day."

"Ha!"

"It was the playoffs."

"Double ha!"

"As if it was my fault."

Olivia burst out laughing. They laughed together, and it felt good, to have this little conspiracy between them. "Everyone in my family was some sort of athlete," she offered.

"And what sport do you play?"

"No, literally, my brother was on the amateur golf tour, and my mother was, no joke, an Olympic champion."

"So was mine," he said, and she looked at him oddly.

"I mean, my grandmother was."

"Really?" She didn't believe him.

"Fencing." He did some maneuver with an imaginary sword.

"That's a weird coincidence," Olivia said, after a pause.

"It is," he said.

As if it were an invitation to sit down, Olivia did, on the floor near where his feet were perched because there were no other chairs. "I'm not a sports person."

"Me either," he said, removing his feet from the ottoman as if to make room for her. She scooted in closer. "You know what I really want to be?" she said.

No, he didn't know.

"An actress." Why not say it again, and with conviction. This man knew nothing about her.

"I thought you said prelaw."

"The problem is, I can't act."

"Oh?"

"I can't sing either, or dance." It had been fun while it lasted, her conviction.

"I couldn't paint to save my life, but I painted anyway," he said.

Olivia glanced around but there were no paintings anywhere. No easel. "You're a painter?"

He seemed to regret what he'd said. "I deal in antique prints."

"Will you paint me?" She was already beaming in anticipation. "I've always wanted to be painted. You know, like that girl in the movie . . . but with her clothes on, of course." She felt her face flush, horribly.

He gave her a sidelong glance, and she blushed even more for having said such a childish thing. Or not so childish, perhaps the opposite of childish, if not overtly adult. . . . Either way, adult or child, she felt safe, cocooned, even here, one phone call away from her mother swooping down and taking care of everything. And perhaps that's what Olivia had been thinking about when she had said that, of her mother seeing a painting of her daughter in the nude. Her mother had grown so nervous about Olivia's body. When Olivia was a little girl, she and her mother used to take showers together, showers that abruptly stopped at the first sign of Olivia's breasts growing. And then they kept growing, and growing, and perhaps Olivia did like to show them off (she might have not liked her body, but she wasn't afraid of it), but it was as if her mother couldn't see her anymore, the she below her head that is.

"So, you will paint me?" she said to Marco.

"No," he said.

It hadn't been a question. "Why not?"

"A variety of reasons come to mind, but I suppose the most important one is that I don't paint anymore."

"Why don't you paint anymore?"

He looked off into the distance, and watching him in that moment she realized that she could not be a child, ever pretend to be a child, again. "Did you love her that much?"

He winced, ever so slightly, as if the words cut.

18

They would go north to spread her ashes; that was all he had told her. They would set out early in the morning by car and, with this news, Olivia propped her shoulders on his footstool, rested her chin in her hands, and looked up at him expectantly. The afternoon lay before them. *If he wasn't going to paint her then what were they going to do?* her eyes were asking.

He said, "If you like, I can show you some things."

She could taste the sweat on her upper lip and feel pools gathering in the folds of her belly. "Things Evelyn might have seen?"

"Yes," he said.

"The places she might have gone?"

"I have tried to resurrect them. Though, I'll never know but one place. This place up north."

Her stomach moaned just then, startling them both.

"Come," he said. And she followed him.

To the main house and into the kitchen where he took a mango from the immaculately clean counter and began peeling it with a knife. Expertly, first the skin and then the slices off the pit, the process seemed cumbersome.

Olivia picked one up and it slipped out of her fingers. She bit her lip and tried again.

"It tastes like soap," she said, but it slid down her throat before she could spit it out, and then, the sweet aftertaste. "Um."

"It takes some time," he said, sucking on the pit.

"Real food?" she said, devouring another piece.

"What would you like to eat?"

"Pizza?" she smiled, wide and mischievous. It was a silly thing to say, but she was feeling silly, suddenly, and nervous. There was a thrumming pace about this place, the hazy, luminous lake with that floating pagoda, the dusted-over city beyond that, all the tumultuous shades of gray in those unsmiling eyes of his, telling her things no one else could.

They crossed over the lake via a tiny footbridge, where a barrage of bicycle taxis confronted them. Marco haggled in Vietnamese with one of the drivers, emaciated and scorched, and after a few minutes they climbed in. The man pedaled barefoot, his slacks frayed at the ends, a cigarette dangling from his mouth, standing at first to get momentum going, and for a few minutes Olivia wondered if he would be able to do it. He weighed less than she did, certainly. At one point she wanted to get out and push. But soon they got going and he sat down and they fell in with the rhythmic mass of two- and three-wheelers swirling around the maze of streets and alleys, where store workers gathered crouched around makeshift kitchens, their heads in bowls, slurping and sucking.

Every so often Olivia would catch eyes with the odd tourist couple riding in a taxi like theirs, with mystified expressions that mirrored her own. What was this place? The hot breeze blew against her face.

The man pedaled the cart down a narrow back street and pulled up just before slamming into a slanted brick structure. The cart wobbled as they clamored to get out. She followed Marco through a side door and up some dark stairs, into a cramped, hole of a restaurant in which they were the only Westerners. This, sadly, was her first startling observation, though no one seemed aware of this fact but her. She grabbed his arm and stayed close. They crammed into seats at a communal wood picnic table, where everyone was eating from big steaming pots of bubbling broth.

Their food came in a matter of minutes, with beers. She wasn't sure when, exactly, he'd placed the order. Marco ladled the soup into smaller bowls and passed her one. It was unclear what was swimming underneath the broth, and then she saw an eye peeking up at her. She almost fell backward off the bench. "No way am I eating that." She looked furtively around, but no one seemed to notice her outburst.

"It's the best part." He picked the head out of the bowl with his hands. He began sucking on it.

Her mouth dropped open. The stench of sweat and heat and dead fish was overpowering. She thought she might be sick. And yet . . . her eyes remained glued to him, as he now was scraping the eye out of its socket with a spoon. He held it out for her.

"Evelyn eats this?"

"No," he said. "But I do." He popped it into his mouth. "It's good luck."

Olivia stared at the gold cross on his neck. "And you believe in luck?"

Perhaps understanding the implication, he did not respond. She glared at him a moment longer, then down at her food. Her idea of an authentic Asian meal was P.F. Chang.

And yet, she stared deep into the bowl, salivating. With one last peek around, everybody sucking and slurping and speaking in that frantic, hectic-sounding language, then one last glance at Marco, focused on what he was doing like everyone else, she took her first bite.

When the broth hit her stomach it burned. It was spicy as hell, and she ate until she couldn't feel her mouth anymore, until her beer was gone and, surprisingly, the fish too. Except the head, which he ate, as well as the other eye, a plate of tiny bones and carcass all that was left between them.

"I told you," he said.

Her face was on fire, greasy, but napkins were scarce; she wiped her hands on her shorts.

They left.

Their friend, the driver, was across the street smoking, his cart parked exactly where they'd left it. At the sight of them he threw down his cigarette and ran over with a wide, burnt-toothed smile, his expression: *I'm yours*. For life. They climbed back into the cart and Marco gave instructions and soon the warm wind was on her face again.

The quiet and whirling, it did something to her mind. Her eyes felt heavy. She could feel the heat of his upper arm pressing against her shoulder. She didn't mind, and when their bicycle taxi pulled up to their next destination, Olivia found herself disappointed because she didn't want to get out. "It looks old," she offered sleepily, squinting at the structure in the distance.

"A thousand years old."

He climbed out and helped Olivia do the same. They began walking toward the entrance.

He asked her if she knew Confucius.

"Not personally, no."

He gave her a sidelong glance. "This is one of his temples. A host of the Imperial Academy, Vietnam's first national university."

"Oh, cool." They were at the entrance, an elaborate white marble arch with tiered, red-tiled roofs that curled up at the ends.

Inside was a quiet courtyard with manicured grass and sculpted trees and shaded benches where people sat in contemplation. Three paths cut through the garden to a second, more provincial arch. The middle path was for the king, he explained, the one on the left for his staff, and the one on the right for his army. He headed down the center, and told Olivia that she might want to take the path on the left.

She took the path on the left, and then paused when it occurred to her that he might have been kidding. She continued walking, watching him from a distance, his posture regal, elegant, weighted, as if he *were* a king, one carrying the world on his shoulders. *And she, who had taken the left path, was his subject?*

Their paths made inward turns and they met up again. They stood facing one another, and Olivia thought to herself, *What would have happened if I'd taken the other path?*

He raised an eyebrow, and she got the feeling he was wondering the same thing. His humor was as dry as bone; he unnerved her in a way she'd not been unnerved before.

They proceeded through the second arch and into the next courtyard. A cobbled path framed on each side by more pristine gardens led to a grand-looking pavilion built on four whitewashed stone stilts. They climbed the steps and stood in its middle.

"She came here?" she asked.

"I like to imagine she did," he said.

They stepped through the pavilion and into the third courtyard.

"I see her here, on nice days, walking along the gardens and eating buttered baguettes in the shade of a tree."

"Was she a follower of Confucius?"

He laughed, and Olivia frowned. She didn't like to be laughed at.

They came upon a large rectangular pool of water framed by a low stoned wall. WELL OF HEAVENLY CLARITY, the sign read.

"She wasn't a follower of anything, really. But I know that she would like him, as I do, for his belief in the practical. There are no gods or higher power in his view, just the belief in us as humans, and the fact that we can learn and grow and get better. That we can create ourselves."

That sounds right, Olivia thought. Staring into the glass surface of the lake as they walked by, searching for clarity. Her own experience had been different; everything that she had sunk her heart into so far had failed. "I'm still searching for my calling," she said, pausing to take in a tree in the shape of an elephant.

"I thought you wanted to be an actress."

"Yes. But I can't act, remember?" She glowered at him. "Which is why I'm prelaw."

"That's right. I now recall our discussion."

"People say I have strong opinions, which means I should be a lawyer."

"Is that what they say?"

"Someone did. Once. People are always asking what you are going to be when you grow up, and well, when you say *actress*, their eyes glaze over with pity. So I started saying 'lawyer,' if for no other reason than to see my parents' faces beam with pride. And now, well, here I am. Two years into a prelaw degree and I'm miserable."

He didn't say anything.

And even she was shocked by what she'd said. The first time she'd said it. "Did you know what you wanted to be?" she asked.

"I come from a world where you are born into what you will be."

"And what was that?"

He glanced at her, assessing her in some way. "A son. A grandson. A husband. A father. A man of duty. Responsibility."

"But this is the fate of everyone, no?"

He didn't respond.

"But when did you first know you wanted to be a painter?"

"I'm not a painter."

"Right. You deal in antique prints. Oh, come on. Just humor me and answer the question."

He thought about it. "Ever since I can remember."

They walked a few paces in silence.

Along the side of the fourth courtyard there was a tall portico where large blue-stoned slabs hung. On them were inscriptions of all the men (presumably they were all men) who'd graduated from the institution as doctors.

They walked along quietly, perusing the slabs that rode on the backs of gigantic turtles—some kind of auspicious symbol, good luck or good fortune, he told her, and then he asked her if she still wrote.

This surprised her. She stopped walking.

"Evelyn said you were a talented writer."

Struck, somewhere deep. "What else did she say about me?"

"That you were smart. Creative."

Something she hadn't heard in a while and for some reason it irked her. She grabbed his arm so that he would look her in the eye and see what was there. "Evelyn was wrong," she said. The words came out bitter and harsh and she instantly regretted them.

He looked down at her hand gripping his arm.

She sighed. "Look," she said in a much softer tone and letting go. "She was encouraging, but I'm simply no good."

"Why do you say that?"

"I just know."

"You can't act, you can't sing, you can't dance, you can't write?"

"I can write. It's just that there are so many other people that can write better than I can."

"Where?"

Olivia grabbed her hair. "I don't know." She began twisting it around with her hands. "At school, in the theater, online, everywhere. They're everywhere." A twisted laugh escaped her. It went on, the evil Olivia surfacing, and she wanted him to laugh evilly with her. She didn't want to be alone. But he didn't laugh. He studied her, and with no small amount of disappointment. "There are different layers of talent," he said. "I worked at mine. Did you work at yours?"

"What do you mean?"

"I mean did you study your craft. Did you really work at it?"

She tossed her hair back over her shoulder. "Look. Like I said. I don't have a craft. I'm still searching for my calling. Something I'm really good at, that comes naturally, and that I can do for the rest of my life."

"Law?"

"It's concrete." Now she sounded like her mother. "You know what I mean?"

"I think so. You expect things to come to you easily. And when they don't you give up."

After a stunned pause, "Hey, I've put in my time. I know what it means to work hard."

"No. You don't."

Olivia was silent.

"You have a wicked scowl," he said after a moment.

"Mom used to say that you could light a fire with my scowl."

"You could light one now."

"You know nothing about me."

He didn't disagree.

"And look who's talking. You're the one who won't paint anymore."

"That's different."

"Giving up is giving up. Same thing."

He fell silent. She was right, of course, and feeling pretty smug about it.

"Forsaken might be a better way to describe it," he said. "For me painting has always been torture—the essence of feeling alive, and I don't want to feel alive."

"Well, that's really pathetic."

They walked on.

"Where I came from, the artist was the hired help," he said. "The blue collar stiff who painted the frescoes on the castle walls, and sculpted the gargoyles on the turrets, so to speak, like Michelangelo was, in a way." He paused. "There was always that undercurrent of disdain."

"But you *were* a painter."

"Was I?"

"I don't know, I thought you said so."

"I said that I paint."

"See! See how this is all going nowhere! Oh, you're driving me crazy." Still, Olivia thought more about it. "My parents have always supported me in whatever I've done, even something as foreign to them as drama. But even though they wouldn't say it, I knew they didn't want me to waste my life in this way. To them, drama was a hobby, like sports, a means to another end."

"What end?"

"I have no idea."

"To own the art I suppose."

She stopped walking to think about what he'd said. "Our house is full of expensive art that they buy from touristy art galleries. But do they really appreciate the work? The artists? Because when it comes to their daughter doing art, it would be like, well, like I was copping out."

There was some silence.

"It will take everything you have," he said finally. "At times, it will feel like you're groveling, like you're nothing. It will be humiliating."

"So then why will I do it?"

"Because there will be nothing else you can do."

As if the matter had already been decided.

19

Olivia was beholden. Enraptured, as if in a dream. And that night, in keeping with their dreams, Marco took her to the theater. She wore a flowery cotton dress that he bought her from a street vendor since all she had brought were shorts and jeans.

He wore a sports jacket.

They walked along a path circling the lake. The main thoroughfare, which they would at some point have to cross to reach the theater on the other side, was spinning with the life of a thousand bikes and scooters and the odd car. It was like trying to cross a rushing river, and Marco had been keeping an eye out for a break or a pause in the flow. But there was no break. Or pause. And he finally just stopped walking and stared intently into it.

He took her hand.

She took it back. "I can cross the street by myself."

"No, you can't."

She looked left, then right, for a stoplight or a crossing. There was none. In the whole time they'd been walking there had been none. They waited, for what she was not sure. They might as well have been trying to cross a six-lane freeway. "But how will we ever get across?"

"Trust me." He looked at her hard. "Do you trust me?"

She gave him back her hand. His palm was sweating. "I trust you."

He began walking, slowly, calmly, intently, as if into a fire, and at first she held back.

"I said you have to trust me."

"We just walk into a sea of traffic?"

"We just walk."

And that's what they did. It was the most terrifying experience for her, and the most thrilling. It was as if they were parting the sea; naturally, organically, they were changing the tide. The drivers remained as if unaffected even though they were affected, the flow of their vehicles forming new patterns to accommodate them. It was not in their nature to bowl you over. You were a part of them and they a part of you. They were all part of everything, and that was how Olivia felt in this moment. No lights, no lanes, and yet the world had this higher order. This purpose.

The theater was inside what looked like an office building. Still, Olivia entered with great anticipation, not to mention swagger. She had seen and studied her share of theater productions, mostly local stock in Phoenix, or the Scottsdale Community and Player's theaters. She'd read all the masters. This dream of hers having come to a crushing head on a trip to New York. She and her mother had tagged along with her father, who was there for business. They'd been strolling down some fancy street near their hotel, when Olivia saw a flyer for an off-Broadway production of *Talley's Folly*. She'd not let up until her mother had bought tickets. Somewhere downtown, where her mom insisted the hotel car service wait outside until the show was over. There had only been two actors, a thirty-something man and woman, barely any props, barely any audience, in fact. Unrequited love at last requited. Olivia had laughed; she'd cried; she'd sat leaning forward so as to not miss one word of the streaming dialogue. She didn't remember breathing until it was over, when she'd turned to her mother bursting with awe, not to mention anticipation, for she'd just discovered what she wanted to do with the rest of her life! And then the lights came on. "You know who would have liked this," her mother had said, forebodingly, and Olivia's face fell flat. Of course she knew who would have liked this. Evelyn. "You're like her, you know," her mother said then. "You could be a doctor like her."

She and Marco settled into their cushioned seats, but Olivia was in no way settled. *Tally's Folly* stayed with her, that deep yearning, how she had looked up the playwright on the Internet when she got home, wanting to know all about her, what kind of person she was.

A gong sounded, loud, resonating, and not at all what Olivia had expected. The lights dimmed. She set her gaze on the stage—a bright, lime-green lake before a massive red and purple pagoda. Sky-blue, mountainous terrain painted the background. An orchestra of strange and unusual instruments sat on a balcony to one side. Olivia wasn't sure what was going to happen. She certainly hadn't expected puppets to paddle out in electronic boats, singing in Vietnamese. Then hop out of their boats and hydroplane around the surface of the lake dancing to their puppet master's commands via sticks they held behind the pagoda. They acted out the scenes of historic battles, water spraying everywhere. It was a puppet show, a fact Marco had failed to mention.

"I'm not three," she leaned over and said to him, for many of the patrons were children she noticed.

"Just watch," he said with a smile, or Olivia thought it was a smile. It was hard to tell the way the corners of his lips turned downward like that. And he was right. The whole production became surreal, absurd, and hilarious if not beguiling. She tried not to laugh because she had no idea what she was laughing at. A boy meets a girl, but tradition gets in the way, cultures and classes. There was a fantastic battle, blood and death, fire, and, in the end, a baby.

"I'm not sure what just happened," she said to him when the show ended.

"I don't think you're supposed to think too hard about it."

"It was kind of fun."

"I know."

"Can we see it again?"

He looked at her. "It's never enough, is it?"

"No." She smiled. "It's not."

He may have even laughed, which made Olivia laugh. And in doing so she glanced down toward the front of the theater, where there was even more laughter from a group of children headed to the exit. Their lips were deformed, she noticed, and her face fell flat; it was as if they'd eaten all or parts of them. She had never seen anything like it, and she had to focus hard not to visibly wince. She buried her head in her English language program. IN VIETNAM, it read, THEATER WAS BORN IN THE PADDY FIELDS, WHERE THE PUPPET WIRES COULD BE HIDDEN UNDER THE WATER AND THE ACTORS IN THE PAGODA. She peeked up again. No one else seemed to notice the children. Just like other children. Smiling, happy, oblivious. But how could they smile with . . . oh, it was horrifying.

"Are you okay?" he asked.

"I think I need real food," she said.

He took her to the Sofitel, a grand old colonial hotel where people seemed to know him. They sat in a far corner of a lush inner courtyard, under the soft orange glow of torches.

The breeze was pleasant, the air cooler now. They were silent, and protected, like the foreigners all around them. People from all over, she noticed, looking around and overhearing the vast array of languages.

A waitress appeared and lit his cigar with what looked like a blowtorch. She knew what whiskey he drank, and brought a bottle without him having to tell her. He sipped from a round glass and watched Olivia devour a burger and two orders of fries. "I don't like to share my food," she told him, when he reached over for one.

"Neither did Evelyn," he said, taking the fry anyway.

A young, dark-skinned man with blue, slanted eyes who was swimming in a fine tailored suit came over and greeted Marco in Italian. Or was it French? He spoke in English when Marco introduced him to Olivia. Gilles was his name, but she accidentally called him Jiles, and then, even more ridiculously, Gil, all while he just stood there smiling at her. Then he took her hand in his, "Such a beautiful woman," he said, kissing it. Olivia stole a glance at Marco, her whole body blushing. Did he think she was beautiful too? And then she realized her hand was still in Gilles's. She blushed again and pulled it away.

Gilles and Marco began speaking in a different language now while Olivia's mind spiraled. *Beautiful?* Certainly she had wanted to be beautiful. She'd grown up in an aura of beauty, not in the traditional, glamourized sense. Evelyn wasn't tall, like Olivia's mom. She was lithe. Alluring. While Rhonda had the handsomeness of a champion. Michelangelo might have carved a statue of her. Olivia had always felt invisible around them. When they were together, there was no room for anyone else.

But the spotlight was on Olivia, for now anyway. "I'd like some," she said, pushing forward her glass when Marco poured Gilles some scotch.

"She's got taste, too," Gilles said.

"For whiskey anyway," Marco said, pouring her a finger full.

The men raised their glasses, as did she. "What are we toasting?" she asked.

"That we meet again someday," Gilles said, looking intently at her. Then, with a silent urging from Marco, Gilles took a sip of his scotch, set the glass on the table, bowed at her, and left.

She watched him wander off. "Who was that?" she asked finally.

Marco took a moment to think about it. "Well, I suppose he is my friend."

"Suppose?"

"The oldest of friends, perhaps, and yet we only met for the first time two years ago, when the last thing I was looking for was a friend."

Olivia had to cringe, slightly, to get the whiskey down.

"I'd been heads down, lost, wandering through the narrow streets of this fantastical city, when I came upon a print in a shop window. I could not take my eyes off this print. It was the print of a carving I had seen on the wall of a cave from where I had just returned. It *was* the same carving, I decided, upon a long deep study. I went inside the shop finally. Other prints caught my eye. Colorful. Sad. Rural. I was drawn to them. Then I turned and there was this very striking young man. His name was Gilles, and his first words to me were that I looked like I'd seen a ghost. He spoke in perfect English, and for a moment I had this strange feeling that Gilles had known Evelyn. That she'd been in this very shop, looking at these very prints."

Olivia held her eyes still on Marco, her entire body set, riveted. *Go on*, she was saying. And he did.

"I had a small picture of Evelyn in my front pocket. I pulled it out, gently, so as not to wear the edges any farther. I showed it to Gilles and asked if he knew her, had known her, and Gilles looked at the photo for a long, long time, or so it seemed, as if time had stopped. He gave the photo back. Yes, he had said. He remembered her distinctly. She had stayed in the shop for a very long time once. She had gone through every single print he owned, the maps being of particular interest. She had a friend, she'd told Gilles, a friend who collected maps. She hadn't wanted Gilles's help even though . . ." Marco paused here to sidebar. "Gilles made it clear to me that in his youthful innocence he had tried to ask Evelyn out, for, as you know, Evelyn was captivating. But she kindly refused him. She just wanted to spend time going through the stacks. Hours of searching later, according to Gilles, Evelyn left without buying anything."

"She was searching for something," Olivia said, but Marco didn't hear her.

"My knees became weak," he went on as if in a dream. "Gilles led me to a chair. He got out a bottle of whiskey and poured two glasses, and I explained to him that I'd been traveling for seventy-two hours in order to rid myself of the ashes of this woman in the photo that were still in my possession.

"Soon Gilles knew everything. We began talking about prints. I had been a collector, once, for my family's estate, and my conversation with Gilles as such took on a force of its own. Relentless, it would not stop. It was as if I was staring into a younger version of myself.

"Turns out, Gilles and I had similarly ignoble pasts. His grandfather was of French nobility, part of those who occupied Vietnam, and his mother was from a wealthy Vietnamese family. After the war his grandfather, for whatever reason Gilles wouldn't elaborate on, was afraid to return to France, where his wife and children lived, not so unlike my own father's exile, both noblemen displaced from their noble heritages, their homes. Gilles didn't have a profession per se—he and I weren't raised to have professions—he had a philosophy, a way of life, which was to enjoy it. A self-proclaimed philosopher with a penchant for whisky and an eye for Asian art, he'd been floundering along until he inherited this shop from a dead uncle, serendipitously, as with all of his endeavors."

Marco paused here. Perhaps realizing he'd gone on far too long, but Olivia didn't care. She thought that he could go on all night.

"*Mah*," he said, shrugging his shoulders as if none of it mattered.

She looked over at Gilles, on the other side of the terrace now sharing a cigarette with the bartender.

She turned back to Marco, "Was that Italian you were speaking?"

"French."

"How many languages do you know?"

"Five. Or seven. It depends on what you mean by *know*."

"Is this the ignoble past you were speaking of?"

He set down his glass, as if suddenly curious himself to know how many languages he spoke. "Let's see," he said. "My father was Italian, I was raised in Egypt, and my mother was Greek. In school I learned French, and of course English, and then, after being here, Vietnamese."

"That's six," she said, counting on her fingers.

He recounted in his head. "Yes, you are right."

With the espresso that Marco ordered came green ice cream in the shape of an egg with a rubbery powdered skin. It wasn't like regular ice cream.

"Just try it," he said.

She did, almost too quickly. How easily she responded to his commands, it occurred to her suddenly. Alarmingly. It wasn't like her. Even if she were, perhaps, developing a small crush on this man old enough to be her father. Normally, in Olivia's previous experiences with crushes, they'd be so intense that her protective walls would go up. She'd have to ignore her crush, or use biting sarcasm when speaking to him, so scared was she of being crushed, to the point that she came off bitchy and rude, when in fact she was just miserably shy and awkward, and so afraid. But with Marco it was different. And maybe that's what it meant to be an adult. To open yourself up, to turn yourself inside out.

"How could you not like it?" he said.

"Oh, but I do," she said. "I do." She took another bite, and perhaps it was the cool minty flavor soothing her lips, tongue, and throat, but for some reason she thought of those children she'd seen in the theater, and she asked him what had happened to them.

There was a moment before he made the connection. "Nothing, really."

"It didn't look like nothing."

"They're born with cleft palates."

"It's horrible."

"It's relatively easy to fix. It just requires an operation. Your aunt Evelyn used to perform them." He paused, and Olivia felt his gaze, the way he thought deeply before he spoke.

He pulled from his cigar. Smoke wafted in the air around her, but she no longer thought that it was killing her as much as cocooning her inside the breath of him.

"Working at the clinic here was her favorite of all her assignments. Above all, she loved Hanoi. Its people. She would eventually move on to tougher places, Laos, Cambodia. Heavy, hard, depressing work where most of the time she felt as if she made no difference. She admitted to me that what she had been doing with Doctors was selfish, some form of escape. I told her it was the malaria talking. We'd been living in Thailand at this time, during her recovery. . . ."

"Malaria?" Olivia interrupted him, and he looked at her, almost hopelessly now, which sent her into great despair. He wanted her help, yet she was helpless to give it to him. "She had malaria?"

"There were good days . . . normal days. . . ." His focus drifted, as if he were remembering one of those good days now. A glimmer of light that just as quickly faded. "But she never fully recovered."

They fell silent.

"Why didn't you just bring her home?" she asked finally.

"I did," he said.

"I mean to us."

"Her home was with me now."

20

The ashes sat between them in the back seat of the Mercedes. Toni drove, and not much was said. It was still dark when they left, and so Olivia slept mostly. Every so often she'd stir awake and find her head resting on Marco's shoulder and the box digging into her side. She'd scoot back over to her window and gaze out into the cascading grayness. Before them a vast wasteland, so ghostly that it almost made sense where they were headed—the Bay of Dragons, Marco had said. He might as well have said they were going the supermarket, or the moon. She didn't even flinch.

They had been driving for some time, and, awake now, perhaps bored, she began to study his jawline—so serious, so grim. This went on for some time, until he said, without looking, "What are you staring at?"

She looked away, unnerved. Then she turned back, in an attempt at dignity, and said, "I'm trying to figure out what Aunt Evelyn saw in you."

"She always told me I made her laugh."

"You've got to be kidding me," she said, after a pause. Then, she couldn't help it. She laughed.

"See?"

She bit her lip, and told him she needed to pee.

He told her to wait, that they were almost at the rest stop. Meanwhile, they passed three other rest stops.

"Trust me," he said.

It was a nice rest stop. The stalls were clean, as opposed to the previous rest stops they had passed according to him, though the toilets were holes in the ground, and there was this warm stench of digested garlic hovering in the air. He'd prepared her for this too. Still, the reality was jarring. One needed strength to squat, and with her lackluster exercise routine, she had little strength. Everything was sanitary; there was an attendant whom she tipped with the shiny foreign coin Marco had given her. Afterward, she met him at the Internet café, where he was waiting at a table with two tiny bowls of soupy rice. He had bought her a Coke as requested, for himself he was drinking something thick and black from a tiny cup.

"Who eats rice at nine in the morning?" she wanted to know.

"It's very healthy," he said.

"It's gross," she said.

"Look around you," he said. "Do you see any overweight people?"

She glared back at him, not liking the implication, and then just beyond his left shoulder her eyes caught sight of a display case of Pringles.

"Don't even think about it," he said.

She moved the porridge around with her spoon.

"You need to eat something."

"But it's cold," she said, barely setting the spoon to her lips.

He reached into a plastic bag of some things he'd bought at the convenience store, pulling out a triangle of rice wrapped in plastic. "You'll like this," he said, unwrapping it. It was a puzzle the way he unfolded it from the plastic so that the sheet of seaweed wrapped perfectly around the rice triangle without tearing.

Her stomach growled suddenly, ferociously, even he heard it, which was embarrassing. She took the triangle and ate it quickly, barely chewing. At one point she stopped because she'd bitten into something.

"I know, right?" His eyes lit up with a smile so wondrous and unexpected that she blushed. "It's the surprise."

She took another bite. "Tuna fish?"

With a glint in his eye, "It's the best part."

At last, they agreed on something about food.

After they were done, he led her over to an Internet station and told her that now would be a good time to check in with whomever she needed to check in with, her mother, presumably, and Olivia agreed that this was a good idea.

"She doesn't know you're here, does she?" he said.

"Do you care?" she asked.

"Not really."

"If she knew I was here, she'd send in the National Guard."

The look of alarm in his face made her laugh. "I'm not kidding," she said. "I'm not sure what you did to her, exactly. But my mother hates you."

"Oh?"

"Do you know why that is?"

"Some people are unhappy, I suppose," he said, and Olivia thought that was weird, how he knew that about her mom.

Olivia sat down to write her email, opening up Yahoo!, but then she just sat there. She had nothing to say. Had it really been two days since she'd called her mother from the bathroom stall, frightened like a child? She'd come here to hurt her mother, but also to prove to herself that she was not her mother, that she was, in fact, far from being anything like her mother, and her frustrating ambivalence about love. So now would be the moment, Olivia thought, staring at the blank email, to follow through with the plan to hurt her mother, to let her mother know where she in fact was, here, with Evelyn's lover. And yet, now that Olivia was actually here with Evelyn's lover, on this road to the Bay of Dragons, none of that mattered anymore.

Something else was taking form. Shape.

"I miss you, Mom," Olivia typed finally, which was not what she had expected to type. Would she always miss her mother? This big, looming, massive beast of a presence. Her lioness and protector? Perhaps. Though this missing she felt now was different. Distant. As if she were seeing into her future for the first time. A future her mother didn't own. So she wrote that she had lost her phone on a hike through the red rocks, which was why she hadn't texted or received her mother's texts (presumably her mother had sent texts, though of course later Olivia would learn that her mother had sent no texts). That she'd call her when she got back to campus. "I love you, Mom," she wrote. Again, not what she'd expected to write. She was feeling this weird sense of foreboding.

Outside, the heat was rising with the sun. She could feel it burning through her sandals and weighing down her shoulders. Back in the car, she asked, "How much longer?"

"Two hours."

Her mouth fell open. "You said we were almost there."

"To the rest stop."

She watched the necklace of fresh garlands swing off the rearview mirror. Its delicate little woven petals reminded her of corn on the cob. Sweet, juicy, it made her hungry again, ravenous, so she fell asleep— how she used to cope with tantrums as a child, her mother liked to remind her. Dreamless. She woke up. A watery incandescence slid into view. It began to stretch and expand. Rock masses grew up into the sky, formations of all shapes springing up majestically from the water's depths—a deep, silky green. They grew larger, lusher.

"Those rocks are said to be the dragon's descendants." It was Toni who had spoken, at last, in English that was very broken.

"The legend is that in ancient times," Marco went on, "Vietnam was under fierce attack from the north. The Jade Emperor sent the Mother Dragon here with her children, who unleashed fire and emeralds from their flaming mouths to form a barrier from the invaders, who were eventually swept away. Peace was restored. Over thousands of years, the jade barrier evolved into this archipelago."

He spoke as if he might actually believe it, and so then did she, as she stared out at the landscape trying to imagine the rocks as dragons, stomping around with their heads careening, tails sweeping, emeralds glittering down upon everything, as the highway slowly morphed from three lanes, to two, then one. At last, Toni turned off the road and pulled into a harbor whose parking lot was crowded with tourist buses. He parked. He and Marco got out and conferred for a minute. Then Toni went over to where a large group of Vietnamese men stood haggling and waving at each other. He began haggling and waving with them.

Marco lit a cigar and leaned up against the car smoking it.

"What's Toni doing?" Olivia asked.

"We will need a boat," he said.

Toni waved them over, and Marco put out his cigar. He put the box of ashes in a pack, swung it over his shoulder, and began walking in that direction.

Her feet wouldn't move. *Wait. Stop*, she tried to yell out to Marco, but no words came, just that weird sense she'd been having. "She can't be dead," Olivia called out to him at last.

He stopped. Turned.

"I know it's strange." She had to speak loudly so the words could reach him. "But ever since you first contacted me, when I saw her name on the Skype box . . ."

"Come on," he said, coming back for her.

"I thought it was her."

"We've got to go, or someone else will get our boat." He grabbed her arm and pulled her along. "If we don't take this boat, there'll be none until tomorrow."

She yanked herself free. Perhaps it was the heat. "You don't understand. She's not dead. She can't be." She was wild now. It was rushing at her.

"Then whose ashes are these in my bag? Who was the woman I watched roll into that blazing furnace?" He was breathing hard.

So was she.

He took her arm again. His grip hurt. There was anger inside him that she'd not detected before. Somewhere in all this she had managed to lose her sunglasses. She never thought an overcast sky could be so blinding. Water streamed from her eyes.

"I feel sick," she said.

He swept her up into his arms, unexpectedly. Olivia was so shocked that it didn't occur to her to resist. She fell limp in his arms as he carried her past the dense throng of tourists rushing toward the docks and clambering up onto any and whatever boat available; he maneuvered them toward a dock in the opposite direction, to their own, private boat. He stood before it briefly. She could feel the strength of his arms holding her as if she were weightless. *Who is this man?*

"Does it float?" she asked.

"They don't call it a junk boat for nothing."

That's exactly what it looked like, a big piece of junk floating on the water. They were now boarding it via a narrow, wobbly gangplank. Olivia squeezed shut her eyes, sure Marco could not handle her disproportionate heft, that he would stumble, and they would both fall overboard. But soon they were on the stern, he was setting her down, and Toni was climbing on board after them with more bags.

"How do you feel now?" he wanted to know.

"I can't believe you just did that."

Her balance was unsteady, not so much from being on the boat as from being carried like that. Swept away. She held onto the stern's railing while she got her bearings, and together they watched the boat putter away from the dock, its engine working hard, petrol fumes polluting the air in its wake. Asphyxiating them. But then the engine settled into a soft, rhythmic, hypnotic kind of ticking. The world they were leaving began to shrink.

Her stomach felt better after some sips of a Coke. They climbed a ladder to the rooftop, where two hard-backed, regal chairs fit for a king and queen were nailed to the deck that was otherwise empty. Marco set his backpack on one, then came and stood by Olivia at the railing. They looked out together, neither speaking. She thought she would never feel this far away again.

A slight breeze made the heat feel less oppressive. There were stretches of shade as they floated past rock formations. It kept things cool and ethereal. And as they moved farther out into the emptiness, the other boats seemed to disappear. The silence became profound.

"Sorry for what happened back there," she said.

"There's no reason to be sorry. This is all rather strange, I imagine."

"Something happened," she said. "Something I've never told anyone."

"And you feel the need to tell me?"

"When I was young—oh, I don't know how old, ten or so. Evelyn was home on a visit, and we had our palms read by a psychic." She paused for his reaction, for it sounded silly now. But he gave no indication that it was silly.

"It was my idea."

"Of course."

"I made her go."

"I see."

"It was only supposed to be me that got my palms read. But then, just before we left, the psychic told Evelyn that she shouldn't leave without getting her palms read too. And being the girl that I was . . . am, I begged her to do it even though I knew she didn't want to."

He listened.

"I don't remember what the woman said to Evelyn, exactly, something about losing someone she loved, and Evelyn's flippant response was, 'Who hasn't?' Still, I remember that as being weird because I'd never heard Aunt Evelyn talk about being in love, or losing a love, for that matter. I thought she was toying with the woman, which made me kind of angry, because I didn't think one should toy with fate. The woman went on a little bit longer and then, as her finale, she asked

Evelyn if she wanted to know how long she would live. Evelyn said sure, why not, and then the woman, without pause, said forty-five."

He didn't move, not his eyes, nothing.

"I know you think I'm making this up, but I'm not making this up. I can see Aunt Evelyn now, bounding down the steps afterward, howling with laughter because she *had* been toying with the woman, and so of course the woman had to get back at her. 'Oh, you know it's all a bunch of . . .' she threw her hands in the air in place of the curse word she wouldn't say. 'But what about my love in a foreign land?' I'd demanded back, for this is what the psychic had told me, that I'd have three loves, and one of them would be in a foreign land, and Evelyn said, seeing my excitement, that the woman was probably right about that. Then we went and got ice cream and forgot all about it.

"When Mom told me Aunt Evelyn had died, I never even thought about the palm reading. In fact, . . ." she paused. It hurt so much. "I hadn't thought about Evelyn in a long time by then." She looked away from him. "It never occurred to me . . . until I came here, and you said that thing about my eyes looking like her eyes and I saw her eyes, not Evelyn's but the psychic's, the grayest, most surreal eyes I'd ever seen, and this place—the water, the sky, the earth—reminds me of them. Is none of this real? My mother never even went to a funeral, after all. Was there even a funeral? Was Aunt Evelyn playing some trick on us? Was she getting back at my mother for something? For her death at this age was a horrible coincidence, was it not?" Olivia was breathless.

He said, "She was forty-four."

There was a pause.

"When she died. Evelyn was forty-four."

"Are you sure?" She squinted, hard.

"Three weeks, two days, and eight hours shy of her forty-fifth birthday. I'm sure," he said.

She said, after swallowing, "Oh."

As if those three weeks, two days, and eight hours made up for the horrible coincidence, his composure remained intact. But still, she could see it had jarred him. He stepped back from the railing, felt behind him for the chair, and lowered himself down.

21

Toni called them down to the galley for lunch. They sat across from one another in a lacquered booth while an array of fish was presented to them. Whole fish, fried fish, strange fish, raw fish, fish with eyes, fish with teeth, and then she saw the french fries and almost cried. Before she knew it, the plate was empty. She washed them down with a sweaty cup of white wine. Toni, who sat slouched nearby in a chair, jumped up and had the cook make her more. Marco drank beer, and for a long time they looked out the window and watched the towering, verdant islets float by.

"There are caves inside," Marco said, after Toni delivered the extra plate of fries she was too ashamed to order. They'd been gliding into never-never land for some time now, and she couldn't remember the last junk boat she'd seen, and though she knew vaguely that they were headed to a cave with drawings, she no longer really cared where they were going. She didn't want to know how all this was going to end. She wasn't sure she wanted it to end. She squared herself to him now, and waited for his eyes to find hers. For he'd not really looked directly at her for any amount of time since she'd arrived in Vietnam. And it was time now that he saw who she was. "You're the prince," she told him.

He looked at her.

"I don't know why it's taken me this long to figure it out. You're the prince in Aunt Evelyn's story. And she was the girl who couldn't have you."

There was a pause. "I think you've mistaken me for somebody else."

"No. I'm sure of it now. That ignoble past you spoke of? You're the prince."

"I am no prince."

"If you're not a prince, then what are you?"

"The son of someone who once was a prince."

"Still, you could have said something."

"I don't know if they teach you this in American schools, but the monarchy in Italy is dead. It doesn't mean anything."

"It means that you knew her before."

A moment passed.

"She began telling me that story when I was very young. So it must have been a long time ago."

"I've loved your aunt for a very long time."

"When? How?"

He looked through Olivia, at something far off beyond her, and then at last his eyes did settle on hers, like a jolt, that flint of yellow. "A basketball game."

"You can't possibly be serious."

"I'm serious."

"Were you in the States?"

"Italy, strangely enough."

"They have basketball in Italy?"

"My family had an ownership stake in the Lazio team. I had floor seats, though I rarely went because I wasn't a big fan of the sport, as you can imagine. Our seats were more for status than anything else, to give away as gestures, tokens. The one game I did attend, Evelyn was there, alone, an empty seat between us. She was harassing the ref, and at one point I thought he might kick her out." He shook his head. "I couldn't take my eyes off her. She was like no woman I'd ever seen." He paused.

"She was there with one of the American players Lazio had just signed. I thought he was her boyfriend, and was very happy, later, to find out that he was not."

"Who was he?"

"A family friend," he said, after a pause.

"Go on," she said finally.

"Go on about what?"

"The story."

"That is the story."

"That's it?"

"Our eyes met, we exchanged words in different languages. She was shy, if not sardonic. I was hitting on her, and she knew it. 'Don't destroy my heart,' she said, thinking I didn't speak English, and I'll admit I kind of pretended that I didn't. I was—how do you say it in English—a bit of a *playboy* back then. Anyway, there she was, rambling on, until something finally occurred to her, which was that I understood every last word of what she was saying. 'What are you smiling at?' she asked, suddenly scrutinizing me, and I knew right then."

Olivia waited, but he seemed to be done.

"Knew what?"

He looked at her, as if he'd lost his train of thought. "*Alea iacta est,*" he said finally.

"Translation?"

"I don't think it translates."

"Try."

"It means, literally, 'the die is cast.'"

"Die?"

"You roll the die, and there is your number. There is no other number but the one showing."

A shadow came over them. A rock formation so close Olivia felt as if she could reach out and touch it.

"Perhaps one day you will understand."

He returned to that deep thought. She could tell he was feeling the warmth of Evelyn, somewhere. Meanwhile, Olivia was picturing this pair of dice rolling across a table, two numbers popping up. Her numbers. What would they be? What would they mean? Especially if Marco had gone on to marry someone else, which Olivia was about to remind him of, but his eyes had turned to dark liquid, and so she didn't.

Do they find each other again? Olivia's child's voice asked in her mind, as it had asked Evelyn, so many times. Her aunt had never given Olivia an answer, and now Olivia knew why, because at that time, Marco had not come back into Evelyn's life. "But how had he?" Olivia was about to ask him now, but the boat lurched suddenly to one side. She looked out the window. A ripple was spreading out to infinity in the otherwise placid jade. An old woman in a tiny rowboat, a speck before the mountainous cliff, was waving them down. Toni ran outside and threw her a rope when she got close, and then the boat tugged her along. Olivia thought they might be giving her a ride somewhere, to one of those floating villages Marco had told her about, though from where the woman came remained a wonder.

They returned to the roof deck and sat in the high backs like the king and queen Olivia now thought they were, in respective states of post-lunch stupor. Speaking felt like sacrilege to the silence this place embodied and so they didn't speak. Some time went by, until a dark head poked up from the ladder, waiting for Marco's nod, which he gave. The old woman climbed up, her coned straw hat hanging down her back by a string around her neck. She had pearls to sell. She showed them to Olivia, strings of soft pinks and blues: simple, elegant, oddly shaped pearls only found in these waters. The woman, who didn't speak English, ran the beads along her decaying teeth and instructed Olivia to do the same so that she would know they were real. She did as the woman asked, scrunching her nose up at Marco, who bowed his head as if to say that the gritty feeling she was experiencing was a good thing. Olivia was ashamed not to know the difference. Her mother thought real jewelry was a waste of money.

"Pick what you want," he said.

"They're beautiful," Olivia replied, declining graciously. It felt too strange, taking something from him.

The woman left after Marco bought Olivia an anklet anyway, though no apparent money had been exchanged—as if real stone carried meaning that had nothing to do with money—and the woman had helped Olivia put it on.

Olivia was glad when the woman left, the world having returned to that unworldly place. There would never be any other place like this one, she knew, gazing down at the green-hued pearls and then back out at the horizon, which, again, stunned her. She was just settling back into the serenity when Marco stood up, abruptly. They were tracking toward one particular rock formation now, one with no dock or landing point that Olivia could see, and Marco went down to the lower deck to discuss something with the captain.

After some minutes he motioned for her to come down. He had the pack with the ashes strapped to his back now.

"It's a good a hike up," he said, handing her a pair of boots with socks tucked inside. "Whose are those?"

"Trust me, just put them on."

She took them. "You say 'trust me' a lot."

She was trying to remember the last time she had followed someone so blindly.

They climbed down the ladder that dropped into the sea and boarded the rowboat, which wobbled and stunk. The woman, her hat on again, stood and paddled with one long oar, slowly, gently, the paddle barely breaking the water's surface. Something moved inside a net on the floor from which Olivia kept her eyes averted. She hung onto the sides, breathing in the salt and kelp. The mountain grew. They pulled up to where there was a tiny crest of flat rock that the woman clung to with her bare leathery hand. While she held the boat steady, Marco and Olivia clambered up the rock's slippery surface. Once safely on land, she turned and watched the boat drift backward, the old woman's eyes emptying out into the distance, their junk boat dissolving in the haze behind her.

When Olivia turned back around he was already past the rocks and making his way up a dirt path. She caught up with him when he stopped to study a piece of paper he'd pulled from his pack. She looked over his shoulder. It was a hand-drawn map.

"I've been here a dozen times and I still get confused," he said.

"You're not making me feel warm and fuzzy," she said.

He turned and started walking again.

The path grew narrower, darker underneath a canopy of trees, steeper. He did not stop. At one point she asked him to stop but he did not. He wanted to make the return trip before it was dark, he told her. An hour later they reached a metal gate, passed through it, and just beyond it was the opening to a grotto. Olivia stopped to catch her breath, to consider the fact that she'd never been in a cave before. He, however, headed straight inside the yawning formation without so much as a pause, which left her no time to be afraid because she did not want to be left alone there.

Inside, the temperature dropped immediately and all natural light dissolved. Manmade lanterns lit the way. Some of the paths were lined with planks and ropes. The walls appeared as if melting, dripping a montage of colors, blues particularly, yellows, oranges. Carvings appeared as they made their way in deeper. He stopped to examine one, and so did she, standing beside him now. Elephants dancing, snakes entwined in trees, lions arched in battle, their manes blowing in the wind.

Farther on, the limestone stretched and grew until the cave felt miles high. The drawings became denser, more intricate. The elephants became fabulously decorated, a bride and groom at their side, people in their wake, singing and eating among genies and fairies, birds and fish.

"The legend is that a young lady caught the eye of a dragon prince," he said, staring at this particular drawing. "He fell in love with her. Their wedding lasted for seven days and seven nights in the very center of this grotto." He paused to listen for something. She did too.

"Hear that?"

A pounding and rushing.

A river. He headed off toward it, Olivia following, but they didn't come upon any water. He checked the map again and explained that the first few times he'd come with a guide, who drew him this map, the map he now realized was upside down.

He righted it.

They took a different path—there were many to choose from—where, farther on, they did find a series of small ponds in which Olivia could see her reflection. "It was in these ponds where the young woman bathed her one hundred children, bringing them up wisely and happily." One of the ponds bled over a bed of rock and into a stream that continued on to where Olivia couldn't see anymore. According to the legend, this stream was the path made by the wake of the woman when she left the grotto with half of those children, leaving the other half behind with their father. She left this stream so that the children she took with her could find their way back.

He kneeled now, and unzipped the pack.

Olivia could hear water dripping, everywhere.

Out came the bag of ashes, which he set down on the smooth surface of the cave floor. He was having difficulty unraveling the plastic, so she helped him. Her hair stuck to her face. Her pores felt like giant holes he could see into. At last, it lay open, a gray chalky pile, not a small pile.

"What do we do now?" she said.

He didn't seem to know, so they sat on the cold surface of the cave with their arms around their knees, staring at it.

"Why here?" she said.

"Evelyn had come here once, while she was working in Hanoi. She had always wanted to come back, to bring me with her, to show me this place that seemed to haunt her. I said we would go; now that we were together we had all the time in the world to go." He rested his chin on his knees, and after a moment of reflection said, "This was the only place for her, in my mind. It has been two years since I came to bury her ashes. I have traveled to this cave a dozen times with that intention—I know all the guides, the junk boat dealers, the pearlmongers, the fisherman—but I have as yet been unable to let go of her."

"And this is why you brought me here." Olivia understood everything now.

He went slack, as if he'd resigned to something a long time ago. "I couldn't do it alone."

"But why me?"

It seemed as if he'd already put a lot of thought into this question, as if he were still putting thought into it. "We sometimes talked, idly, Evelyn and I, about our respective mortalities. You see, my family has a big, magnificent tomb in Rome in which I shall ultimately be buried. I will lie there next to Victoria, my wife, next to my mother and father and their mothers and fathers before them. Evelyn always used to make jokes about this tomb, and how relieved she was not to have to lay in there with me. She wanted her ashes spread—anywhere. She wasn't picky, she just wanted them given back to the earth. 'But what if I'm already dead,' I asked one time. 'Who's going to spread your ashes if I'm not here?' Her response was, 'Olivia.' And I said, 'Who's Olivia?' We'd kept our previous lives separate for the most part, and so she spoke only after some hesitation. 'My niece,' she said."

With that he fell silent.

Olivia reached for his hands and brought them to the bag and helped him scoop some ashes into his palms and together they let them fall through their fingers. They watched the stream take them away and, eventually, after traveling intact much farther than she would have thought, pull them under.

"Should we say something?"

"If you want."

"I don't know what to say."

"Say good-bye."

She threw more in. "I can't picture her face," Olivia said, her gaze following the ashes, which traveled even farther this time, as if Evelyn were resisting this, her final and last departure. "I'm trying desperately, but I can't."

He got out a small drawing pad and pencil and started sketching. Olivia moved in closer, enveloped by the radiant warmth of his body. She felt connected to this man, as she'd never felt connected to anyone in her life. The psychic had been right, perhaps not exactly right, but right, nonetheless: she would find love in a far off land. And that love would smell of earth and sun and she would want to melt into him forever; she leaned her head on his shoulder and watched him sketch the woman who would forever remain between them, for Olivia knew that Marco could never love her the way he loved Evelyn, the woman appearing before them now, as if resurfacing from the water's depths where they had just laid her, alluringly, forever suspended in time, that gleam in her eyes.

He gave Olivia the sketch when he was done. She folded it carefully and slipped it into her pocket. So this is what it feels like to have your heart broken.

He spread more of the ashes, reserving a small handful for a tiny velvet pouch that he then slid into his front pocket. This would always be Olivia's secret. No one would take this moment, this place, away from her.

They stepped back slowly, finally turning and heading back up the path on which they'd come. They had a long walk ahead of them, even after they reached the cave's opening and she could breathe freely again.

The light had shifted, changed. She was exhausted and thirsty but she didn't say anything. She didn't complain. She'd complained her whole life, it seemed, for she'd wanted so much. Wanted and wanted and wanted.

She looked up at the sky. There was a small break in the clouds through which a beam of silvery light burst. It followed them along the trail back down to shore where it spilled out over the water. They'd been gone five hours, and so she was nothing less than ecstatic to see the old woman there, floating off in the distance, waiting. She came for them. Olivia got on and Marco pushed the boat back but did not get on with her. "What are you doing?" she said.

"I can't go back," he said.

"What do you mean you can't go back?"

"There is nothing for me to go back to."

"But I don't . . ." She thought about jumping off the boat and swimming back to him. She had this innate need to understand him. She felt as if she'd known him from another time and place. "Please come with me. Don't make me go alone."

"Toni will take you back to Hanoi; you can get your things. He will take you to the airport."

"But where will you go?"

He stood tall and looked around him. The boat drifted backward. It started rocking and Olivia had to sit down because the old woman was turning it around, slowly, and then they rowed off into the vast Bay of Dragons.

When she looked back, he was gone.

22

It took what felt like a lifetime for Rhonda to get home from Italy to find Olivia in the last stages of a fever that wouldn't relent. She had headaches and wasn't sleeping. She could barely eat and had lost weight. She'd been on the antibiotics for three days and while her fever was down, it still hovered at one hundred degrees. Rhonda took her to a variety of doctors for second and third opinions (the first opinion, "It was probably something she ate," being far too vague), demanding a battery of tests, each of which came back negative, alongside a doctor's derisive look: *You're only making it worse.*

She just wanted answers. Was that too much to ask?

Rhonda was resigned to sit by Olivia's bedside where she lay half asleep, her face aglow with sweat, staring off, detached, but in a dreamy way (it was hard to tell what was going on inside her), and Rhonda, on some last ditch effort to come up with an answer to *fix* this, wondered if Olivia hadn't fallen in love.

"I never went to Taos."

"I had a feeling."

Olivia's eyes found Rhonda's and stayed there.

"How did you find him?"

Olivia, looking confused, said, "He found me."

"Oh," Rhonda said. *But what did he tell you? Did he tell you?* There seemed to be no sign that he did in the girl's eyes. So Rhonda did her

best to remain silent, knowing that she must stay quiet and nonjudg-
mental if she wanted Olivia to tell her anything at all.

"We scattered Evelyn's ashes."

Rhonda clenched her jaw so tight that it hurt.

"He couldn't do it alone."

Rhonda searched her daughter's eyes—still nothing. She dropped
her head into her hands as Olivia began describing her journey with
Marco to the cave with the dragons that Rhonda had already dreamt
about so many times, the way her sister had described it in such vivid
detail in one of the journals Rhonda had burned. Olivia went on for
some time about this journey, meanwhile, the light in the room shifted
colors, and Rhonda remained silent wondering how it would end. If it
would ever end.

"Weren't you afraid?" Rhonda finally asked, when Olivia described
how she and Marco had at last parted ways.

Her daughter looked away. "I was angry at you. And it was that
anger that fueled my courage. Not to retrieve Evelyn's possessions as
he'd asked, but to find out about this man who lived in your whispers."
She looked back at Rhonda now. "Yes, I heard your and Dad's whispers,
Mom. What do you think I am, deaf? I wanted to see your face when I
told you I had been with Evelyn's lover."

Rhonda put a hand over her mouth.

"For that was how I'd planned to say it. *Lover*, a word I knew you
would despise. There's no *respect* in the word *lover*. And no, Mom, we
didn't have sex. That's not what I meant by *been with*. It wasn't like that.

"I suppose I wasn't prepared to actually *fall* in love with him, if that's
what I've done. I don't know. What I know is that I let myself trust him
instantly, the minute he pulled me out of the rush of bodies exiting
customs. . . ." She stopped talking, abruptly.

"What?"

"You wouldn't understand."

"Try me."

"I knew he would be part of my life forever."

With that Olivia fell back onto her pillow, as if some weight had been removed, while Rhonda sat there stunned. She had spent the entire plane ride back from Italy preparing herself for an onslaught of accusation, so certain was she that her judgment day had come, but this, falling in love? This had not flashed up on Rhonda's radar. "Please tell me the feeling is not mutual," she whispered to her daughter, but only because she had fallen asleep.

A deep sleep, one that lasted three days, while Rhonda sat glued to Olivia's bedside, afraid to lose sight of her. Even with her eyes closed there was still this mystic, far-off beating beneath the lids, a surging among the dragons and jade or whatever Olivia had called the watery incandescence where she and Marco had gone to bury Evelyn's ashes. Together. Rhonda's chest tightened now, a latent reaction to the irony of Marco and Olivia being together. Rhonda's greatest fear, one she'd gone all the way to Italy to rid herself of, and yet, there seemed to be no getting rid of it. After having each traveled to the far ends of the Earth, Rhonda and Olivia were right back where they'd started.

What do you want from me? Rhonda looked up and asked the heavens. *Do you realize your daughter has fallen for her father?*

The heavens didn't answer.

I bet you didn't anticipate that.

They were beyond forgiveness, Evelyn and Rhonda, and yet Rhonda couldn't get the words to form. Words like, *Olivia, you can't be in love with Marco because he is your father.* Not even in practice. Rhonda's mouth would open, but nothing would come out.

Did he know and choose not to say anything to Olivia? Or had Evelyn not told him. And, if she'd not told him, wouldn't he have seen the resemblance staring back at him in Olivia's eyes? Eyes he's now left hanging, having disappeared into the void because, as he says, he has nothing to come back to—Carlotta, what about her?

Rhonda unstuck a strand of hair from Olivia's moist cheek. *Oh, how to tell her, tell all of them, everything?* And with that the girl's eyes peeled open. She squinted into the stale light and Rhonda went and opened the shades, a window. Bands of light streamed into the room at odd angles with a cool desert breeze. Olivia blinked. She looked around at the four walls of her youth, as if she weren't sure where she was. She pushed her hair back and sat up while Rhonda gave her a glass of water. She sucked it down, some of it spilling on her chin. She wiped it with the back of her hand. "I feel so much better," she gasped.

"You look so much better." And she did—everything about her sharpened seemingly, in focus, illuminated—though her eyes began to recede now, slightly, perhaps remembering everything she had confessed, and then, at once, they widened in alarm.

"I'm not upset," Rhonda said.

Full of astonishment and wonder—*did any of it really happen?* (For some time while Olivia slept, Rhonda had wondered.)

"But what do I do now, Mom?" Olivia pleaded.

It was a question Rhonda was neither expecting nor prepared to answer.

"I can't go back there."

"Where?"

"School, the sorority, any of it."

"Oh, sweetheart. Give it some time."

"I don't have time."

"What do you mean? You've got the whole world in front of you."

Olivia looked at Rhonda, as if struck by something.

"You need to rest, Olivia. Let's talk about it tomorrow." *Tomorrow. There was always tomorrow to tell her.* But Olivia had stopped listening. She was gazing intently beyond Rhonda, as if into the near distance of her future. At tomorrow, perhaps. Tomorrow, when Olivia would rise out of bed as if levitating. "Stay in bed," both Rhonda and Lillian took turns insisting. Olivia went to her desk and opened her laptop, got out her notebooks, her textbooks, and went to work catching up on the studies she had missed.

Two days later she did, in fact, go back to school. "But I thought you said you couldn't go back to school?" Rhonda was so confused, not to mention concerned.

"I have to finish out the semester strong, Mom. Please understand." Her eyes were wild. She seemed to have forgotten about Asia, or she made no mention of it. When Rhonda brought it up, however lightly, Olivia would gasp and plead, "Don't, Mom, please! Or I'll regret having ever told you!"

So off Olivia went, back to college as if on a mission, one beyond Rhonda, who felt listless in the face of it, in the face of everything that had taken place in the last weeks—what was she to do now? She seemed incapable of focusing on a *right* course of action regarding Olivia, of action in general suddenly, as if Evelyn was the puppet master now, and all Rhonda could do was crawl into bed, pull the covers over her head, and wait for further instructions.

And so that's what she did.

Weeks came and went. Olivia stayed at the university, reportedly studying like a fiend, how it was supposed to be, Rhonda reminded herself, and that she could not interfere with that. She'd wait until Thanksgiving to have a talk with her. The only reason Rhonda knew Thanksgiving was approaching was because Lillian had put out the decorations early this year, as if they might inspire Rhonda out of bed, where she had been for some time now, what she thought had been days might have been weeks. A month or two. It was hard to tell. There were no seasons in the desert with which to chart time. The sun always shone. Day after day the sky was a perfect blue. The hundred-year-old owls still cooed to one another at dusk; the coyotes ravaged at 3:00 a.m. The house temperature moderated itself, the shades adjusted to the daylight. There might have been a monsoon; buckets of rain fell a few hours each afternoon for some days.

Thunder and lightning so hard Rhonda thought the house would come down.

Then Olivia called and announced that she was transferring from University of Arizona to NYU's drama program. Rhonda blinked slowly for a few moments, taking in her daughter's fast breaths. "I think mine was one of their last acceptance letters. So the dorms are full. I can't get a spot for spring semester. Not that I want to stay in a dorm. So I'll need an apartment, and they want the entire tuition up front."

Rhonda sat up in bed. "Wow," she managed finally. She cleared her throat. "I guess I'm just catching up here. Since when did you want to go to NYU?"

An ever-so-faint huff came through the line loud and clear, as if it were too painful for a daughter to tell her mother what she should have already inherently known about her daughter's deepest dreams.

"Oh, Olivia—"

"It doesn't matter," Olivia cut her off. "The point is I'm going. Will you help me?"

After a pause, "Help you with what?"

"Get an apartment, flights, paperwork, you know the drill, Mom. Classes start on January fifth."

There was a fog in Rhonda's head she couldn't quite see through. Was her daughter really moving to New York? She barely wanted to snap out of it. "Well, I guess you could call Tammy, our real estate agent, and have her recommend someone out there. When do you need it by?"

"I'd like to get out there as soon as possible after finals. I could just stay in a hotel, I suppose."

Rhonda heard herself laugh, but it seemed distant. Someone else's laugh.

"Are you all right, Mom? You sound weird."

"Sorry, I'm just . . ." And then she muttered some excuse. "Grant season . . . my inbox is inundated. I haven't made a dent."

"Okay," Olivia said evenly, as if she were really saying, *What does any of that have to do with this?* "I thought we could fly out for Thanksgiving and spend the weekend looking for an apartment."

"Oh, I can't go with you, Olivia."

There was a pause.

"What do you mean you can't go?"

Rhonda didn't say anything.

"Don't you want to help me get set up?"

The girlish excitement had crept back into Olivia's tone, and it almost sounded strange to Rhonda. Old Olivia. Frightened Olivia. The Olivia Rhonda had created.

When Olivia had gotten into the sorority at the University of Arizona, Rhonda had driven straight out with gift bags for the girls in Olivia's rush group. She had Mexican food catered for the swearing in ceremony and bought a new flat-screen for the house. By the time she'd left, Olivia's room had been repainted and wallpapered, and supplied with fresh linens and a new bunk bed. "Your mom is so great!" the girls cheered to Olivia as Rhonda left, which took her a while. She didn't want to leave. Oh, how she had wanted to stay, to relive her college years over again.

"You went all the way to Asia by yourself. You got into NYU by yourself. You don't need me," Rhonda said. She didn't bother trying to sound upbeat. Ultimately, she couldn't. "You'll be fine, dear."

There was a long silence on the other end.

23

Olivia wasn't just fine; she was on a high. Living her dream. At least that's what she'd persistently been telling her mother over the phone for a year and a half. Yes, time had flown. She was about to enter her senior year at NYU and still her mother had yet to come for a visit, as Olivia had suggested on multiple occasions, for a performance piece, a scene reading or, most recently, this summer production workshop she'd gotten involved in. Her mother kept punting, as if it were better (and simply easier) to wait for Olivia's inevitable implosion, her retreat home. Oh, certainly her mother remained positive and upbeat when they spoke, in that comatose state of whatever-you-want-let-me-know-and-I'll-get-it-for-you. But behind the façade Olivia knew that her mother had no real faith in her, probably because Olivia never really had any faith in herself.

Until she had met Marco, that is. And everything changed.

Marco. The name whispered in Olivia's ears now, as she paused at the stage door entrance, always the same pause, that breath of anticipation, before her limbs kicked into gear and she pushed through the door and marched to the dressing room, where she immediately rearranged the costumes for scenes two and five that Sean, the intern, had prepped because he never got it exactly right and she didn't have qualms about telling him so. Gail, the lead, was late again. Olivia gave her some silent treatment about that, and there was some flurry getting her dressed and in queue before Olivia could affix her earpiece and get in position, stage right, where she stood biting the crusted ends of her fingernails.

Here we go, she thought, as the lights dimmed and the opening score blared to a deafening level. While the actors moved into their places, Olivia took a quick peek at the house. Packed. For once. "You're welcome," she mouthed to Ken, her boss, out there hiding in the audience somewhere. He'd have to thank her later for going above and beyond the call of duty. Her duties being anywhere from cleanup to concessions to makeup to props to lights to being an extra for all the female parts and some of the male parts too.

Ken had warned her that the job would not be glamorous. As if she'd been fed with a silver spoon her whole life, *ha*, more like a shovel, he had no idea how unglamorous she was. She'd been lucky to get a spot in Ken's summer series. He'd been her teaching assistant junior year, and, drawn to one of her scripts, or so she liked to think, he asked her to join. If things went well she could workshop her final thesis play here in the fall. She was ecstatic until she actually saw the theater, an old church on the corner of First Avenue and First Street that Ken was using his life savings to reconfigure; the sanctuary would become the stage, the seating was cold metal. The church was nowhere near Broadway, let alone the theater district. In fact, it was so far downtown that they might as well have been in Staten Island.

Their first two plays were flops, the first panned by critics and lasting only two weeks, the second better received, but still no crowds and lasting five weeks. Now, for their last production of the summer, this *Play about the Hooker* (Ken's mom was a hooker, apparently, according to Gail, who knew more about Ken then Olivia liked to know), drastic measures were in order.

She'd set up a Facebook page, sent out tweets and put clips of their show up on YouTube. She'd even stood on the street corner and handed out fliers dressed in fishnet stockings and a fitted leather tank dress, which was rather humiliating. But it had worked, apparently: the house was full. What she wasn't expecting was for that full house, once the play was over, to jump to its feet and whoop and holler, as it was doing now. *Mom?* This was Olivia's first thought, that of her mother out there, cheering so loudly as to make up for everyone else who wasn't cheering, hence the sound of a standing ovation.

No. Olivia looked out again. Her mom was not out there. This was not the result of her mother buying tickets for everyone she remotely knew in order to make sure every seat in the house was filled. No. This was the real deal.

Even Gail and Mitch, the male lead, glanced over at Olivia for confirmation that this was really happening. Then they jumped up from their slumped-over-dead positions to receive the applause with waves and kisses as if it had been this way all their lives. The rest of the actors joined them, a chain link of raised hands, and the din was electric. Olivia could feel it wash all over her, the praise. The applause. She was pretty sure she'd never felt anything like it, because this time it wasn't so much about her as it was about Ken. He'd worked so hard for this. He deserved this more than any of them.

People didn't seem to want to leave. And when at last they did, with all the lights up, the world having returned to its strange, anticlimactic state of repose, Olivia got busy with the postshow wrap-up. She scribbled down all her mental notes from the production onto her notepad—*tell Gail no fidgeting, everyone can see her fidgeting, and Mitch needs to work on his lines, he's stumbling over his lines in Act II, though the audience didn't seem to notice.* Then she got busy helping Sean with the props and marks on the stage, removing some and replacing others, triple checking to make sure everything was exactly where it needed to be for tomorrow night's performance. When she was done and Sean had bolted, she stood on stage and squinted out into the audience, where the one remaining patron sat with his script, taking notes with a penlight.

He didn't notice her standing there. Or wouldn't. It was not like you could miss her. She sometimes wondered if he even liked her. As she began making her way up the wooden plank steps toward where he sat, she could see that sheen of worry on his forehead, and that his eyes were bloodshot. Unshaven, he looked aged, though he was probably only thirty, she guessed. They'd been "friends with benefits" on and off for a year now and she'd yet to find out how old he was. "Too old for you," was always his response.

Her instinct was to put up her hand for a high five, but something told her that that might be premature. She sat down beside him. "Want to go over production notes?"

"Let me guess. Gail is fidgeting, and Mitch flubbed his lines in the second act."

"I'll work with Gail. You work with Mitch."

"You work with Mitch. I'll work with Gail."

Olivia gave him a sidelong glance. Mitch had become more than just a wicked flirt. Was Ken really that unaffected?

"Still, Ken, did you see their response? That was totally awesome."

"Reviews aren't in. Let's not get ahead of ourselves."

"I mean, that at least deserves a drink. Let me buy you a drink."

Ken got out his laptop. "I have to get this budget done for the investors."

"You said we could go over my new ending. Come by later?"

"Leave it with me."

Somewhat deflated, she pulled the script from her back pocket, where it had been living for about a year now. It was her senior thesis play, the one to which he'd been drawn and had been helping her polish. The problem was the ending, this was her umpteenth version of one, and she was surprised to see him flip right to it, as if he just wanted to get it over with.

Some minutes passed.

The muscle in his cheek began pulsating.

"Well?"

He handed it back. "It's good."

She cocked her head. Gave it a few moments. "Okay, now what do you *really* think?" Ken was her harshest critic. He would never say *it's good*, and at first she used to get infuriated. In fact, in the early days, it wouldn't have been uncommon for her to stomp away from his criticism in a fit of tears. But now she craved it, even if it resembled disgust, for he wasn't afraid to say directly what he thought, to the point where if he ever gave her a direct compliment she'd know something was wrong.

"You're sick of it, aren't you?" she said, her face falling flat.

"I said it was good."

"That's what I mean." She stood up. Dead inside, what feedback could do to her sometimes.

"Really, Olivia, this ending is fine. And so was the last ending. And the ending before that."

"You're sick of *me*," she muttered.

"I've told you what I think about puppets, Olivia."

A strangled sigh, for he was right; she knew he was right, and she had tried, so many times, to write the puppets out, but then, there they still were. She took back the script, swallowing her ego. For Ken, back at his spreadsheet, was in no mood. After all, it wasn't *all* about her. "How do they look?" she asked finally, referring to the finances.

"*Hooker* needs a long run or we're not going to survive."

"Oh, but I think *Hooker* is the one," she said, with a resoluteness worthy of her mother, a woman who would do anything, I mean anything, to see the person she loved succeed. If only Ken would turn to Olivia now, look deeply into her eyes and say, "You think so?" Olivia would know that he felt something for her too, something that might be a little bit like love.

"We'll see what *The Voice* has to say," he said.

She said, clearing her throat, "So, you'll stop by later?"

He frowned at his screen. "Shit," he said. And then, to her, "What?"

She said, "Nothing."

"Good, great, well anyway shouldn't you be tweeting . . . or tumbling or whatever?"

"You trying to get rid of me?"

"Yes," he said.

"You could at least lie." With that she turned and bunny-hopped down the stairs, keeping it ridiculous, flippant, as if she weren't serious about him and he need not worry. Passing center stage, she paused to do a Charlie Chaplin routine, refusing to stop until Ken finally said, "Later, Olivia. I'll stop by later." She sucked on her lips, giddy with her imaginations, Ken up there trying so hard not to give into the woman he loved, to not smile at her, but smiling nonetheless.

One last prom queen wave and she was out the door, where her face drew flat again upon sight of Mitch and Gail and some of the other actors lingering in the hallway talking with stragglers, loitering in the lobby on the off chance they might run into an agent or publicist.

"Did he show?" Gail, who had cut Olivia off at the exit, was asking about the critic from the *Village Voice*.

"We'll find out tomorrow."

Mitch came up then and, before he could open his mouth, Olivia said, "I can't host the opening night party, Mitch. Please don't ask me." She'd hosted the last two and, well, who else was going to do it? Who else owned a swanky loft in a doorman building in the West Village? Who else could foot the bill for all the alcohol and pot?

"I've a got a friend from out of town staying with me."

He eyed her with feigned suspicion. "Friend?"

"Family," she assured him.

"I thought you were an orphan."

"Adopted." She dulled her eyes. "I said I was adopted."

"You're not an orphan?" That devilish smile.

"Look. She's Italian, and this is her first time in New York."

"*È bella? Si, io parlo Italiano*," Gail offered.

"She speaks English fine," Olivia said.

Mitch brought his face close to hers. "I can come and translate," he offered demurely. "*Dai, Olivia.*"

She stared from one of them to the other. *Since when had everyone been learning Italian?*

She left.

Outside, the air was so thick she could scoop it up in her hand. Her hair immediately expanded and her thighs stuck together, but she didn't mind. This was her second summer in the city, now officially her favorite time of year, everything hot and sticky, a feast of the walking dead, particularly at this hour, when bars spilled half-naked bodies out into the streets in plumes of smoke and drunken laughter. (Summers in Arizona were spent sequestered indoors.) Three young women were particularly entertaining as they stumbled around in the middle of the avenue trying to hail a cab. When a taxi pulled up and they didn't immediately get into it, Olivia did. The women cursed and bitched, one kicked the door as she closed it, but Olivia didn't flinch. She slid over and gave the driver her address. *Deal with it, ladies.*

Manhattan was the perfect place for her.

She sat back and relaxed, the cab immediately insulating her from the chaos outside, the city now a quiet stream of light. At one point she would have wanted to be ambling with those women, or with women friends in general, but since moving to New York she'd accepted the reality that people were drawn to her money, not her. (Everyone except Ken, that was.) It had been that way before and it was going to be that way now, she'd discovered. So, fine. If someone in the program wanted a party, she'd throw one. It was a way to have people around at least, a community, like the one her mother had had as the mother of a golf protégé, and then the CEO of Knight, Inc., all her parties and fund-raisers, tons of people at the house having a blast. The idea that this was life—wild amounts of fun and friends—was ingrained in Olivia's psyche.

But not one single, real friend, the reality at last sinking in that her mother didn't have one single real friend either. People flocked to her mother because of her money too. It was better to be alone.

And Olivia had grown okay with that. Because she wasn't really alone. Since Asia, she'd had this strange and quietly ridiculous feeling that her life had taken on a mystical quality. As if her feet didn't fully touch the ground any longer. It was Marco, she was sure. He was the reason she'd found the courage to work so furiously upon her return from Hanoi, remaining sequestered inside her sorority house writing that play, then submitting it, as well as a transfer application, to NYU. Marco was the reason she'd gotten in, she was sure.

Marco, her muse, her guardian angel—she didn't expect to see him again. Oh, perhaps at first she had. She'd kept a lookout for him on Skype, or "Evelyn" that was, but the status was never green, and then, one day, the name came up invalid. Olivia imagined him being eaten by wolves in the bowels of one of those grottos. She'd tried to find information about the fable he'd told her, the one depicted in drawings on that cave wall—how and why that woman would leave behind half of her children, and if they ever made their way back. It was the Dragon Prince that inspired her thesis play of the same name, a cross between the *Pied Piper* and *Oedipus the King*. If only she could get past the puppets, past Marco, past the floating pagoda, the luminous lake. . . .

The cab driver honked at a car cutting him off. Olivia sat up, anxious—these thoughts about Marco reawakened suddenly. He'd not told Olivia he had a daughter.

Carlotta was a pretty name, Olivia had thought the first time her mother had said it. "Carlotta is coming to New York, and she needs a place to stay." The way her mother had spoken, it was as if Olivia was supposed to know who Carlotta was. It had only been five days ago; Olivia and Rhonda had been on the phone for half an hour before her mother had coughed up the news just before they were about to hang up. "It's just for a week."

"But I don't even know her."

"You sort of do."

Olivia frowned.

"She's Evelyn's stepdaughter, in a way. So that would make you her . . ." pausing to come up with something, "step-cousin."

Olivia had gone quiet. She couldn't believe her mother had gone to Italy and not told her. And after Olivia had opened her soul to her mother about Asia, and Marco, who was still MIA, according to his daughter. "And she doesn't know anything about him being in Hanoi? Or me being there with him?" There was a long pause. "I thought it was better she didn't."

"Whatever," Olivia had finally agreed, if only to get off the phone. She did not want her mother sensing anything wrong, for Olivia had not been prepared for the way it would hurt to hear of Marco again, even indirectly, starting at the top of her chest and moving down into the depths of her belly.

24

"I still can't believe you walked," Olivia said, gaping at Carlotta's humongous suitcase, secured with tape and bungees. "From Penn Station! Are you crazy?"

Carlotta said something about their team taking the train from Newark Airport, and then dispersing to their respective host families from there.

"You know we have these things here, they're called taxis."

Olivia flashed a wide-eyed smile at the girl, who stared back and said, "You look like your mom."

You look like him.

"Except for the height."

Your eyes, they say everything. "People always say that and then I tell them that I'm adopted and they just stand there looking at me dumb," Olivia said. "Sort of like you are now."

The girl stood clutching a long, leather case and wearing team sweats of a royal blue—a gorgeous doe-eyed giant in olive skin.

"I'm just messing with you," Olivia said.

"You mean you're not adopted?"

Olivia stared at her blankly, and then figured it best to end the conversation there. She grabbed the handle of Carlotta's suitcase, gesturing the girl to follow, and rolled it through the open space—exposed ceilings, cement floors, brick walls—into the one closed space, the bedroom, where the girl paused, as if afraid to enter. "I did that," Olivia said proudly, having followed Carlotta's gaze to the red-rum walls.

"It's a little disconcerting at first. But you'll get used to it."

The girl clutched the case to her breast.

"Is that the sword?"

Carlotta glanced down at the case.

"My mother told me that you were a swordsman or something."

Carlotta bit her lips. "*Fiorettista*," she said, trying not to giggle. "*Fioretto*."

"Huh?"

"You call it a *foil*."

Olivia scrutinized her a moment. "So weird," she said finally.

"What is this weird?"

"You mean *why* is this weird."

Now both of them were lost. "Can I see it?" Olivia asked.

Carlotta, looking relieved, set the case on the bed. She unlocked the hinge and lifted open the lid. Inside, tucked into a lining of blue velvet, lay not one foil but three, long, pencil thin, rubber over the tips, though it was the one in the center that caught Olivia's eye. The grip was different than the others, straight and leather bound, and the steel of the bellguard was honed, worn, riddled with the scars of a thousand battles, it seemed.

"It belonged to my great-grandmother," Carlotta said.

To Olivia's disbelief she recognized the engraving on the bellguard—the crosses over the *R*; it was the same emblem on the letter her mother had received in the mail all those years ago. "What does it mean?" Olivia asked, sitting down and running her fingers over the crest.

Carlotta took the foil into her grip, so quickly and startlingly that Olivia almost fell off the bed. "It means everything," she said. Holding the rubber tip with the fingers of her free hand, she bowed the blade so far Olivia winced for fear it would break.

"Aren't you afraid you're going to, like, kill someone or something?"

"You mean like this?" Carlotta stood, and with one blink, the bed-side candle was split in two. She'd barely moved her arm.

"O-M-G. That's my candle."

"Fencing is not about killing," she said.

"Tell that to my candle." Miraculously, it was still in its same position. "How do you win if you don't kill the other person?"

"You kill them with points." She made a move at the desk chair. "Each touch is a point." The bedframe, the trashcan, the lampshade, "*Touché. Touché. Touché.*"

"Okay, I get it." Olivia stood up.

The girl stood utterly still now, staring at the blade as if it were a being of its own. After another moment, when Olivia delicately suggested they put the thing away, the girl looked at Olivia as if she might not know her. Then she blinked and said, "*Scusami.* Sorry. Sometimes I get very . . . I don't know how you say it . . ."

"Dispossessed."

"*Si*, yes, this is the word."

She put the foil back in the case, and, with the girl on her heels, Olivia took the case and tucked it into a spot on a high shelf in her closet. Then she headed for the bathroom. "I've got a show tonight," she called back, before realizing that the girl was on her heels but a breath away from her. She paused, turned, and said in a much lower voice, "So I need to get ready." Then she went the sink and began applying foundation. "Every night, in fact. I hope my mother explained to you that I would not be around."

"Your mother told me you are an actress. I cannot wait to go to the show. At what time must I be there?"

Olivia stopped what she was doing and stared at the girl through the mirror.

"Be where?"

"Broadway."

"Broadway?"

"Yes. This is the place. I have heard so many things about this place."

It was like they were communicating in parallel universes. "But where are your teammates? Shouldn't you be with them?"

"We will not meet until practice tomorrow. Anyway, I am happy to stay here, with my cousin."

"Step-cousin."

"*Si*, yes, this is what I say, cousin, the famous actress. They are all very jealous. My teammates. But I don't care. They hate me anyway."

Olivia was a little taken aback. "Look," she said. "I don't know what my mother told you, but I'm not an actress."

"No?"

"My mom gets a little confused sometimes."

Now the girl looked confused, and Olivia, sifting through her makeup box, went on. "Some days I'm an actress, some days a writer, some days a costume designer. Hey." Olivia turned to face the girl, whose big brown eyes cut wounds into Olivia's heart. *His* eyes. She applied some green eyeliner to them before the girl could refuse, before she knew what was happening. "You have gorgeous eyes," Olivia told her, standing back to examine her work, not to mention that enviously luscious skin, that natural, alluring beauty that had so knocked Olivia off her feet. She turned the girl to face the mirror. "Sometimes I'm a makeup artist."

The girl seemed awed, if not embarrassed by what she saw. A touch gaudy, but perhaps that had been Olivia's intention.

"But you are an actress, at least sometimes. You said so."

"I suppose. At least that's what I tell my mother so that she will keep sending me money, because everyone knows that actresses need to starve for a while." Olivia picked up an eye pencil, smoky blue, and was much more subtle in her own application. "In fact, I could tell my mother I was running for Congress and she'd send me a dona-tion check. She will believe anything I tell her. It's like she feels guilty about something. About adopting me, I guess. Or for me having to be adopted." Olivia paused in thought. "In fact," she said finally. "She must feel guilty about you too, if she's taken you on as her project. I'm not sure why she just didn't put you up in some fancy hotel."

Carlotta seemed to be registering little of what Olivia was saying. Which was probably why Olivia was saying it, why she was talking so much. It felt good to say things to someone who could only look into the mirror of Olivia's eyes and smile no matter what, like the girl was doing now because she wasn't from Olivia's world. And yet, she reminded herself, in some weird way she was, and all this made Olivia howl with laughter suddenly.

"But what is so funny?"

"You. You're funny." Then she realized the time. "Hey, can you grab those pants and shirt from the bed?"

The girl disappeared and returned, literally in one heartbeat. Olivia took the clothes, and there was an awkward moment when she thought the girl was going to watch her undress. Olivia wasn't just embarrassed by her voluptuous mass of body, she was horrified by it, and she shut the bathroom door, probably too hard. She dressed and reopened it, and still, to her astonishment, the girl was right there. Olivia bit her lip thinking, finally, the puppy she'd always wanted, the one thing in her entire career as a child her parents wouldn't let her have besides that trip to Hanoi she'd taken without asking them.

In the living room, Olivia gave Carlotta the spare keys and showed her how to lock the front door. At this point she wasn't surprised when the girl followed her out of the building and all the way to the park. In fact, it was kind of nice to have some company, but Olivia did have to finally stop and say, "Well? I guess you'll be heading off."

Carlotta smiled uncertainly.

"Are you all right? You look pale."

"I think it is the jet lag."

"You should eat." Olivia pointed down the street to a deli that she frequented, and Carlotta nodded her head as if to say yes, she would go there.

Olivia began walking, but something told her to pause and she did. She glanced back, and the girl, as she'd thought, was still standing there staring after her. Or, perhaps, Olivia followed the girl's gaze into the far distance beyond Olivia, upward; she was staring at the Freedom Tower hovering above the tops of buildings.

September 11. 2001. Certainly, the girl would want to see the Memorial. Who wouldn't, well, besides Olivia that was, who had no desire to be reminded of all those people spiraling in a tumble of ash to their deaths. The worst year of anyone's life, Olivia's life certainly, the year Aunt Evelyn left for Doctors without Borders because she wanted to *do* something; she hadn't died in those towers but they might as well have killed her, and Olivia hated herself for thinking that way but she did. She hated those towers. Fine, she thought resignedly, back to the present, maybe she *should* at least pay her respects at the memorial. She called after the girl now, "Hey, on Monday I have no shows. We can go if you want." Olivia nodded behind her and upward. "You know. To see the fountains," then adding, because she was nervous, "those sunken, depressing, waterfalls of death . . . if this is what you want."

Carlotta's response to this idea was to burst into tears.

Great, Olivia thought, running back to the girl. "Hey, hey . . . what's wrong?" But the girl couldn't speak, she was bawling now. "Sorry. I was being flippant. I can be obnoxious that way. You might want to get used to it. But I didn't mean anything by it." People began staring. When Carlotta could finally speak, one word came from her: "McDonald's."

Olivia frowned. She glanced around as if looking to see if anyone else had heard that. A Big Mac could in no way be the source of such angst.

"I've never been," Carlotta said, between sniffles.

Olivia had to think hard for a moment now—Sixth Avenue. They sped in a cab there even though it was only a few blocks away. She bought Carlotta a Happy Meal and seated her down at a grimy Formica table. The girl immediately devoured the burger—perhaps the tears were simply starvation. Olivia bought her another meal, and only after she'd devoured that was she able to begin telling Olivia, disconcertingly, her troubles, those that had nothing to do with the 9/11 Memorial or the fencing tournament or the third burger she was now consuming, let alone her father or Evelyn, neither having yet been mentioned, conspicuously.

By the time the girl was done speaking, Olivia was struck dumb. Hence the delay, before she finally said, "But why go all the way to Philadelphia to take the test?"

"Because, as I have said, Giorgio has planned to meet me there."

"But why Philadelphia?"

"Because it is halfway between here and Boston, where he is on a foreign exchange for the summer."

Olivia pointed to a drugstore across the street. "We can walk over there right now. You can have your answer in a few minutes."

"But I have promised him that we will take the test together."

Olivia stood up as if she were going to head to the drugstore herself.

"I cannot disappoint him in this way. We are desperately in love."

After a pause, Olivia sat back down. "Did you just use the word *desperately*?"

"You do not use this word?"

"Not out loud, no."

"You think it is too much?"

"I think it makes all the difference in the world."

The girl's eyes lifted.

"We'll get you to Philadelphia."

When Olivia arrived at the theater, late, Ken was running through lines with Gail in the dressing room, which was why Olivia had wanted to do the run-through with Gail. Mitch she could handle, but Gail alone with Ken she could not. One feeling she despised above all others—jealously, she couldn't stand for it, and certainly not in herself—so instead of letting it absorb her, she went and found Mitch asleep on the dead hooker's couch. How he could manage to sleep before a show eluded her. She roused him, what became a game of resistance as he tried to pull her down on the couch. They managed to get through the scene changes. If only she'd not succumbed those few times (times when Ken was being particularly indifferent), because now he seemed to think he had this hold over her, and, well, perhaps he did. *Desperately in love*, Carlotta's words, came reeling back to Olivia's mind.

Certainly, this thing with Mitch was not *desperate love*. But what about Ken? Olivia respected Ken, desperately, and *thought* she might be in love with him. Did that count? Or did that just make her like her mother? But what was the difference between desperate love and regular love? If only Ken would give her a chance to find out, and perhaps she needed to push things along, takeout Chinese, and at his place for once, she decided, could be just the thing. She would suggest it after the show. But then Ken flew into a fit after the show. Mitch had missed a cue, which made Gail fumble her line and Kendra exit stage right prematurely. "Amateur hour is over guys, We've opened." They all stayed afterward to work through the scene until they got it right.

Olivia was exhausted by the time she got home at 1:00 a.m., the bag of leftover McDonald's on the kitchen counter. She brought it with her to the bedroom, scrounging soggy fries from the bottom, pausing at the incongruous sight of Carlotta, clad in pink princess pajama pants, facedown asleep on Olivia's bed, her limbs splayed wide, her rabbit slipper feet dangling off the corners. *Mitch and Ken in here together wouldn't take up this much room*, Olivia thought, nudging the girl, who didn't budge.

Olivia grabbed a blanket and slept on the couch.

When she woke again it was still dark and the girl was dressed and ready to go. "What time is it?" Olivia looked around, sure she was dreaming.

"It's five o'clock."

Yes, she was dreaming. She let her head fall back on the pillow.

"The train leaves at eight."

Olivia turned onto her side. "We have plenty of time. Go back to sleep."

The girl unfolded a street map noisily. "I must get to Penn Station."

Olivia pulled open one eye, then the other. "And I told you I'd get you there." She still couldn't believe she was letting the girl take a train to Philadelphia only to turn around and come back the same day.

"I should be at the station early. I have still to buy my ticket."

You'd think the girl had never traveled before, the way she was studying that map.

"And how will I catch a cab? It is difficult, no?"

"Oh, hell," Olivia sat up and ripped the map from the girl's hands. "It is very simple. You go outside, you raise your hand, when a taxi pulls up you get in and say these words: 'Penn Station.'"

The girl smiled and nodded. She began shoving things into her backpack, and Olivia got the sneaking suspicion that Carlotta had no intention of taking a cab. That she was going to walk to the station like she had walked to Olivia's apartment from the station yesterday. Maybe this was a bad idea, Olivia thought again. "What are you going to tell your coach about missing practice?"

"I will tell him that I am not feeling well," she said, and then went and threw up in the toilet.

Olivia raised a brow, cringing. "I still don't see why Giorgio can't come to New York," she said, when Carlotta was done.

"Please do not worry."

"Hey, like I said, it's none of my business," Olivia said, shoving on her UGG boots, the only brand of shoes she wore year-round because her toes were addicted to the soft fuzzy fur. Without planning to, she followed Carlotta outside into the predawn light, shoving the girl into a cab before she knew what was happening. Then, on second thought, Olivia slid in next to the girl. "Penn Station," she told the cabbie, who sped off while Olivia eyed the girl, as though to say: See? Was that that difficult?

"*Grazie, grazie mille, Olivia. Grazie!*"

Olivia gave her a sidelong glance.

"*Prego*," Carlotta said. "That's how you say *you're welcome* in Italian."

"*Prego*," Olivia said.

"See. You are learning already!"

No traffic this early and it was already hot as hell. They were at the terminal in fewer than ten minutes, sweating. In turn, Penn Station was freezing, and, as always, the pit of the earth, Olivia lamented, helping Carlotta maneuver through the grungy, chaotic mess. She purchased a ticket from the machine for her. They waited an hour—that's how early they were—for the platform to be announced, wolfed down Dunkin Donuts, and then, the mad rush of business travelers to gate twelve! Olivia had no choice but to send Carlotta off by herself into the thick of it. If she could have she would have escorted her to her seat, hell gone with her. She watched the girl shuffle her way onto the escalator, then stand waving at Olivia like a schoolgirl in descent.

25

There was already a crowd of theater people in the lobby when Olivia arrived at her apartment building after the show. A writer from the *Village Voice*, in fact, had been at the opening and had given Ken an off-the-record thumbs-up, and so the opening night party—now the post-opening night party—was back on, especially since Ken had said that he'd drop by. Ken never dropped by unless he knew Olivia was alone. Certainly not for an opening night party, so sure that they were bad luck and the reason why the subsequent nights' shows were notoriously lackluster.

She had ordered cases of beer, wine, and vodka and snacks from the usual places, all of which had been charged to her card and delivered to her apartment via her doorman, whom she would tip handsomely. When he saw Olivia he nodded over at Carlotta, who stood a head taller than everyone else. She was waiting in the corner by the elevators, looking lost.

"But you have a key," Olivia pushed through the others to get to her. "Why didn't you let yourself in?"

"I wasn't sure if I should."

The elevator door opened and Olivia pushed Carlotta in. People filed in after them.

"Who are all these people?"

Olivia looked around her, as if she didn't know, and pressed the button for her floor.

Inside, people knew how to make themselves at home. The stereo switched on, glasses were found. Someone got the Apple TV working and began flipping through a clandestine video clip they'd taken of the show on their phone. Windows were opened, ashtrays began filling, and wine began flowing. Meanwhile, Olivia deposited Carlotta in her bedroom and told her she'd be right back.

She went to the kitchen and quickly moved the snacks from plastic delivery trays to platters and bowls. She poured the ice into a big bucket, lit candles—those few extra lengths she normally wouldn't extend for freeloaders, but Ken, after all, was coming. And perhaps this was the moment he might actually acknowledge that Olivia and he were more, if only slightly more, than "friends with benefits." Some minutes later she was back in her bedroom with two martini glasses and a full shaker. "Sorry about all this," she said, referring to the crowd now forming in her apartment, the din having exploded into the bedroom as she entered.

Olivia shut the door behind her, explaining to Carlotta that the show was going really well, and, for them, it was cause for a celebration. What came next from the girl, unadorned joy at Olivia's news, was entirely unexpected, as if Carlotta's issues were secondary. "I am so happy for you, Olivia!" Her voice rang out to the heavens, it seemed. And the strange thing was that she did seem genuinely happy. The people on the other side of that wall—artists and their friends—usually seemed too self-absorbed and competitive to be genuinely happy for anybody else. This included Olivia. When someone else got the part, it meant you didn't. When someone else got published, it meant you still weren't. Nothing was pure and unadorned. It was all relative to your own situation.

"Okay, enough about me," Olivia said finally. She handed Carlotta an icy glass. "Now, before you say anything. First. Have a sip of this."

She poured from the shaker.

"Maybe just a taste," the girl said. Then, "Wow."

"Be careful, it's strong," Olivia said.

"At home we drink grappa. This is not so different."

Mitch strode into the room just then.

"Thanks for knocking," Olivia said. Behind him, out the door, she could see that Gail had made her grand entrance, bringing some other people Olivia didn't know, all of them laughing and talking low, that secret club of theirs.

Mitch took a sip from Olivia's glass. "Is this the Italian?"

Olivia introduced them. He pulled out a cigarette and offered it to Carlotta, who took it with great relief and indebtedness. He lit it for the girl, while explaining to Olivia that all Europeans smoked, as if he were the expert on the subject.

"We're having a conversation here, Mitch."

He stood there smiling, from one of them to the other. "Oh," he said, after a minute like that, "You want me to leave?"

Olivia tilted her head.

"You're really tall," he said to Carlotta.

"Master of the obvious."

"I'm going now," he said, and yet he didn't move, and Olivia finally had to push him out the door.

"Is he your boyfriend?" Carlotta asked after he was gone.

Olivia let out a skeptical snort. Then she sipped her martini. "Tell me everything."

Carlotta took a long drag from her cigarette. "Giorgio has asked that I marry him."

Olivia's brows knitted together.

"We see the pink stripe." Carlotta exhaled the smoke and stared out after it. "So there is this big problem."

But Olivia was still on what she had said before. "Marry you?"

Carlotta shrugged with resign.

"Mitch would send me down the river." And just as she said it, he pounded on the door.

"Go away," Olivia said.

He was looking for the shaker.

"I am keeping you from your friends," Carlotta said, wiping her eyes.

"They're not my friends."

"Yes. This is what you have said, and for which I am beginning to understand. We are not very different, you and me."

Olivia took the shaker out to Mitch, if only to scan the room for Ken. She knew what Mitch would do if she were pregnant, but Ken? What would he do? And anyway, why was she even asking herself this question? He hadn't even bothered to show up yet. She went back into the room and closed the door.

"I am never getting married," Carlotta told her. "Giorgio does not understand this. I do not know how to explain it to him. He thinks it is because he is from Lazio, that because of my name I cannot marry him, which is partly true but not the real reason."

"Lazio?"

"It is . . . how do you say? A region? Yes, well, it's in the south."

"And this is a problem?"

Carlotta put her hands together in prayer and shook them at the world, "*E cazzo*, my family—my mother's family, anyway—is from the north," at everyone who would never understand. "You are so lucky, Olivia, not to have a name like mine."

"But the monarchy is dead," she said, using Marco's line.

"*Esatto!*" She went to the window to let out the smoke. "Please explain this to *zia*, and *mamma*, God rest her soul. They still expect that I marry to keep the family honor. But I fence to keep the honor. This I have assured them. I will win for my family. I will win everything there is to win. But I will never marry. *Che palle* this marriage business, no?"

"Forget about marriage, let's talk about this thing growing inside you." Olivia took the cigarette from Carlotta's mouth, went to the bathroom and flushed it down the toilet.

"I can't have a baby!" Like the cry of an animal.

Olivia ran back to her. "Okay, calm down."

"You must help me, Olivia."

Help you? I don't even know you. "I suppose telling your *zia* is not an option?"

"*Mah* no!" The walls might have vibrated. She grabbed hold of the cross at her neck. "*Zia* can never know. You must never, ever tell her!"

"Okay, okay. How would I ever get in touch with her, anyway?"

"She does not approve of Giorgio. She does not know that I still see him."

They fell silent for several minutes. Each of them lost in deep thought.

"You know who I wish was here?" Carlotta said finally, looking at Olivia. "Evelyn. I wish Evelyn were here."

Okay that hurt. That cut deep. Olivia had to take a few breaths to recover. It was all she could do not to put her hands over her ears, for she in no way wanted to hear Evelyn's name uttered from the girl's lips, so painful was it for Olivia to know, as her mother hadn't said but might as well have, that Carlotta and Evelyn had become close, and at a time in Olivia's life—adolescence—when she might have needed her aunt the most.

But anyway, in Olivia's mind it was Rhonda, her mother, Carlotta should wish were here. Rhonda would take charge of this situation like nobody's business. No judgments, no lectures, just get it done. This is when it occurred to Olivia that she'd not heard from her mother, not since she'd called Olivia to tell her that Carlotta was coming. No texts, nothing, which was almost absurd, given her mother's need to know everything. But then, Olivia reminded herself, her mother was not herself, hadn't been anything close to herself, in some time.

"But I have you." Carlotta's head was tilted to one side. Her eyes were glossy. "*Cara* Olivia." Water spilled down one side of her cheek. Tears, and Olivia jumped up, as if in shock. Rhonda had taught Olivia about tears: don't have them. Olivia went and got tissues, then she returned and sat next to Carlotta and patted her cheeks and did her best to comfort the girl, which wasn't easy given her size, the way she had to bend far over to rest her head on Olivia's shoulder.

As if the tears had left a hole in her stomach, suddenly Carlotta was starving. They pushed through bodies to get to Olivia's kitchen. "Does it have to be pasta?" Olivia asked, scavenging through cupboards.

"Before a tournament, I must have one kilo, no more, no less."

"Another round, *bellissime*, my beautiful ones?" Mitch squeezed in with the shaker. Carlotta held out her glass. Mitch poured until her glass spilled over, purposely, so that he could make the Shakespearean reference. Olivia put her palm over his mouth so that he could not, and then got distracted by an incoming text.

Meet me. It was Ken.

"Let's order Chinese," Mitch said, taking Olivia's palm from his mouth and draping her arm over his shoulder.

"Order the girl some pasta," Olivia said, pulling her arm back. "If she doesn't eat pasta, she'll die, apparently."

Come here, Olivia texted back.

I'm at the theater.

Olivia groaned, from both annoyance and deep pleasure.

Mitch was trying to convince Carlotta that noodles were the same as pasta, that, in fact, it was the Chinese who'd invented pasta, and Carlotta turned to Olivia here, sipping her martini. "I think I am looking forward to this food from the Chinese. I have never had this food."

Olivia pulled Carlotta off to the side, out of Mitch's earshot. "I've got to go out. But I'll be back soon."

"Will you be here in time for the Chinese food?"

"I don't know." Then, at the girl's doe-eyed look, Olivia added, "Don't worry, Carlotta: everything's going to be okay. It's a free world. No one has to marry anyone if they don't want to."

Carlotta followed her to the door.

"If you need anything, ask Mitch; he knows the drill."

"Drill?"

She left the girl with her martini tilting too far to one side.

Ken was in his usual spot in the darkened theater, no script, no penlight, no laptop; he was just sitting there slumped in his seat, drinking a beer. She sat down next to him, slouched down to his level, and stared where he was staring, face forward, into space.

He handed her his beer and she took a swig. She turned to hand it back, and he leaned in and kissed her. His lips were wet from the beer, sloppy, and it occurred to her that this wasn't his first beer. They kissed again, deeper, harder; he was pulling her onto his lap. But then she pulled back suddenly.

"Sorry," she said, sucking her lower lip.

He sat back and sighed.

"It's just weird."

"What's weird?"

"I don't know. It's just different."

"What's different?"

"What are we doing?"

"We're working our asses off, that's what we're doing."

"I mean us."

There was a pause.

"Olivia . . ."

"I know, forget I said anything." She tucked her hand between his thighs, buried her head in his chest, but the moment was gone. There used to be a surge between them, a connection that ran from him to her and back again, hadn't there? She leaned her chest into his, but he pulled back and reached down for another beer.

"Are you okay?" she asked.

He cracked open the bottle and threw the cap at the stage.

She watched it roll in circles until it stopped. Then she looked back at him. "What happened with the investors?"

"They pulled out."

"Of the fall play?"

"Is there any other?"

It hadn't really been a question. "But did you tell them about the *Village Voice* review?"

"I told them."

Her heart sank.

A minute went by like that.

"Fuck."

"Yep."

"This show's going to be a hit. They don't care?"

"Apparently not."

"Then we'll find other investors."

"Where?" He looked at her, pointedly.

"Where we found the last ones. It's a good script."

"It's a great script. Your best work, Liv."

She gave him a sidelong glance. "Now I know you're drunk."

"I'm serious, Liv. And it's time you got serious too."

"Who says I'm not serious?"

"It's time you took yourself seriously."

Her heart swelled. This must be love, this caring for each other. Carlotta may be against marriage but Olivia certainly was not. In fact, if Ken asked her right now she'd probably say yes. They would get the theater on track together. They'd become a team, a one-plus-one-equals-three kind of team. "Look, Ken," she said.

"Olivia," he said. "I think it's time you went to your parents."

She pulled her head back slightly. "For what?"

"For money, what else?"

"I can't go to my parents," she said, after a pause.

"Why not?"

"Because," she said, flustered. "Just because, that's why."

"You go to them for everything else, why not this?"

"How do you know what I go to them for?"

"Everyone knows, Liv."

"Everyone knows what? What does everyone know?" Her tone pierced the blackened space.

"Oh, come on, Liv. Don't get dramatic."

"No, I want to know. Everyone knows what?"

He went silent. A knowing silence, like he'd known about her all along. That she was like this, like what everyone said about her behind her back.

"Say it."

"That you're rich."

She seethed. When anyone ever said the word *rich* in reference to her, only one other word came to her mind, and it rhymed.

"Olivia," he reached for her chin but she blocked his arm with her elbow. *Rich bitch* is what he had wanted to say, she was sure, she could see it in his eyes, and she was blown away. Literally, shot backward against the wall which she was now sliding slowly down toward the cold, cement floor. A full year she had devoted herself to this man. Had he been stringing her along all this time with this idea of talent? When she stood up again she was unable to feel her legs, or her rage, but they were there. She'd come all this way on her own, and yet nothing had changed. She'd done nothing on her own. She stumbled down the stairs.

26

Sweat dripped from Olivia's forehead. Her limbs were trembling. She was pinned up against a wall while the blades came hurling at her. She could feel the cold, steel-like breath against her skin, and it wouldn't stop. Not until the outline of her was complete, her disproportions locked in, all her asymmetries and inadequacies. When would it stop? When it struck her between the eyes, like the one launching at her now, she woke in a loud gasp, her eyes flying open. She panted and blinked and looked around her, adjusting to the morning light reflecting off the rum walls and Mitch's ass. The sight of him there, facedown, lying naked beside her, startled her.

Her mind rewound, slowly, to the night before. She saw herself stumbling home to a dwindled party, Chinese takeout in the sink, empty wine bottles, cigarette butts, and dirty glasses everywhere. Through the haze she saw Mitch smoking a cigarette while holding onto something, or somebody, out the fire escape window, "Making sure she doesn't fall out," he said.

"I hate people," Olivia said, grabbing the bottle of tequila.

"This one's interesting." Mitch motioned at the girl, which was when Olivia realized it was a girl, hanging out the window retching, not just any girl, but Carlotta. "Oh, shit," Olivia said. Carlotta's leather case was open on the dining room table. "Where the fuck are her foils?"

"Have you seen what she can do with that thing?" Mitch pointed toward a few split apples on the floor, and Olivia thought, *so much for honor*. She crawled past Mitch out the window onto the fire escape, past Carlotta to the railing, where her great-grandmother's namesake dangled perilously between the bars. Olivia brought it back, unsure what to do with it because someone had, accidentally or not, poured wine inside the case. Mitch took the foil from her, and stabbed it into the half-dead floor plant, alongside the two others.

"Thanks," she said.

He helped her get Carlotta into the bathroom, where she continued to throw up and where Olivia and Mitch stood at the doorway trading sips from a tequila bottle while waiting for Carlotta to stop groaning and pass out. When at last she did, Olivia slid a pillow under the girl's head and covered her with a blanket. She was too heavy to move.

"She's pregnant," Olivia said, turning around to find herself in the arms of Mitch, who'd apparently not heard her. "You're beautiful," he said, pulling her close, as if he knew what made her tick, what made any woman tick. And yet she closed her eyes and let his mouth find hers. "You're beautiful," he murmured. The more the words were said, the more you needed to hear them. "Am I?"

"Yes, Olivia."

The less sure you were of them.

"You're beautiful."

Until the words became just what they were. Words he continued to say as they made their way to the bedroom and he began stripping off her clothes and found his way inside of her. "You're beautiful." Said one last time just before Mitch passed out not five minutes later, after the thrusting had grown far too gentle, before he'd even come. And then it still took her a minute to catch up; her eyes had been slammed shut willing her body to come before he did, which was virtually impossible, and then finally it occurred to her he wasn't moving. He'd gone limp inside her. She rolled off him, disgusted at herself and the world, and then passed out too.

It will be humiliating. Sometimes it will feel like you are groveling. Marco had said, though Olivia was pretty sure he wasn't talking about this kind of groveling. Groveling to hear that you're beautiful. Should she grovel her way back into Ken's bed too? All she had to do was hand over some hard cold cash, apparently. Cash her mother would hand her in a nanosecond. All these disgusted thoughts appeared as Olivia stumbled to the bathroom the next morning to pee. It wasn't until she got there that she remembered Carlotta, passed out on the floor. The girl's eyes were closed, her hands a pillow under her face. She looked oddly angelic. Olivia figured on just leaving her there to keep sleeping it off, and then, ever so softly, came these words from the girl's mouth: "The train station."

"Not that again."

"I must meet my team."

There was a pause.

"For what?"

"The tournament."

Her eyes still weren't open.

"Tournament! What tournament? Not *the* tournament." Come to think of it, Carlotta had mentioned it a few times, but not today. Certainly not today.

"It's today."

"Fuck me. What time?" She went over and shook the girl, who groaned back, "The exhibition match is at three o'clock."

Olivia went and got her iPhone. It was twelve thirty. "You'll never make it." She scrolled through her contacts for a car service. "We'll drive you there. You'll have to call your coach."

She put the girl into the shower and turned on the cold water. Carlotta screamed, which was a good sign, and she looked better afterward. Olivia got her dressed, made her drink water, which she proceeded to throw up ten minutes later. Sure enough, of all times, Olivia's mother decides to call. But it wasn't about Carlotta or the match or anything remotely coherent as that. It was gibberish, probably a butt call, and Olivia didn't have time to think about it. She shoved the phone into her back pocket and pulled the girl to her feet. "Come on."

In the car, next to her thousand-pound team duffle with the foil handles poking out from the zipper, Carlotta sat slumped against the window.

"You're not, like, a critical player, are you?"

"I am the best."

Olivia blinked at the girl. Here she was, practically dying, and yet this unwavering confidence. *Sorry, but it's true*, was the look Carlotta returned.

"Well then, you're going to have to suck it up."

She nodded.

Olivia gave her a box of crackers. "Try to get some of these down."

At the Princeton University campus, a security guard directed them to the fencing arena, a massive, multilayered tent, architecturally sleek, modern, shiny new, freezing cold, and already packed with spectators. They found the visiting team locker room and Olivia pushed Carlotta through the swinging double doors.

Olivia went outside to call her mother and found two voicemails waiting for her. One from Ken, which she immediately deleted. The other was from her brother Stevie. Stevie? Something about being worried about their mom, something regarding the foundation, then he cut to the sendoff party for Dad and Brie who were off to Hawaii, and oh, how Olivia could not be bothered . . . . She went back inside, where it felt even colder now, as if they'd switched up the air conditioning to fit the icy sharp, scissoring and slashing dinned atmosphere.

Fencing stations were spread throughout the multi-domed space, where different levels of opponents faced off. She saw Carlotta among none of them as she moved anxiously from one station to the next, but then how could she recognize anyone in those getups? And, by the way, how was the poor girl going to breathe? Just then Olivia spotted her—even in her suit, Carlotta's tall, statuesque figure could not be mistaken—she looked sweaty and pale, and her coach, looking dismayed, was pouring Gatorade down her throat. Olivia pushed her way closer to the front. Carlotta's hair was pulled back severely. Her coach kept wiping her brow.

Carlotta was about to slip on her mask, but just before she did, she gave Olivia a conspiratorial wink, and Olivia, surprised by this, bit her lip.

Carlotta donned her mask and took to the strip. Her opponent approached from the other side, and the two stood still facing each other. There was a moment, just before they whipped their swords to their sides, where Olivia could have sworn she'd seen the girl sway. Then the match began, and Olivia closed her eyes. When she reopened them again Carlotta was deftly and easily maneuvering her opponent backward down the strip, in control from the start. An electronic scoreboard flashed and buzzed, the fencers continually reassumed their starting positions, and Olivia had no idea what was going on. Other than that the number on Carlotta's side of the scoreboard kept going up and up and up. So much for: *Touché. Touché. Touché.* More like: *buzz, buzz, buzz,* along with an errant gasp from the audience. Before Olivia knew it Carlotta was ripping off her mask and approaching her opponent with an outstretched hand. It all felt rather anticlimactic.

Olivia took a seat in the stands. The matches went on like that, Carlotta easily wining each one of them. At one point, hours later, when Olivia might have been dozing, someone poked at her shoulder and she started awake. It was Carlotta. "*Andiamo,*" she said. "We go."

"But shouldn't you ride back with your team?" And then, after more thought, "Forget I asked."

Carlotta showered, got her things, they left.

They boarded the train back to Penn Station, and for the next forty-five minutes Carlotta texted back and forth with *zia* and Grand Master about the matches, all the while explaining to Olivia, "I know you think that I am crazy. That I must always be contacting *zia* and Grand Master. It is just better if they do not worry. If I don't text them they worry. It is too painful to have them worry."

Speaking of which, Olivia remembered her mother's butt call and began wondering what her mother had been doing at the time. How she was doing in general. Not well, according to Stevie. But what did he know? He only called Rhonda when he needed money, Chase too. And then, well, then Olivia flushed of shame. A deep-seated, head-to-toe kind of shame. She was no better than either of them.

No. Not true. Don't let it be true. She *was* better than them. She just needed to hear her mother's voice, her absence having struck a deep chord suddenly, burying itself in Olivia's chest. She missed her mother. The protection she embodied. No matter how much Olivia pretended not to miss her, ever since Asia, following this path toward dreams, accepting this idea of being alone. She'd stepped out of herself. Focused on her pursuits. Had groveled. But in reality, she'd not been alone. She'd had Marco, or his spirit anyway, and when his spirit didn't materialize she replaced him with Ken. Now, who would replace Ken? Would she always be searching for someone to fill this big aching gap of her existence? Love, in its fullest, deepest form?

What made her so unattractive?

The reality was that she didn't want to be alone.

The taxi line in front of Madison Square Garden was painfully long. These thoughts of Olivia's loomed while she and Carlotta shuffled their way forward in a queue that moved so slowly Olivia thought she might crawl out of her skin. The sky hovered low and gray. The buildings appeared bleak and morbid. A jackhammer pounded at her nerves. Her senses. Carlotta's too, her face growing more and more ashen, the high of her fencing win becoming overshadowed as the reality of her situation made its way back to the surface.

"Let's walk," Olivia said finally, pulling the girl out of line.

It felt good to be moving. Walking fast (she so rarely walked, always opting for a taxi), they streamed in and around the crowds barreling out of offices and takeout delis, pulsing their way down Seventh Avenue. The crowds thinned as they got to Fifth, and even more so when they turned on Broadway toward Union Square. By the time they reached the park, at last they could breathe a little. A slight breeze moved the trees and made the air feel lighter. The humidity had let up, a hint of fall, the beginning of things, the distant, homesick sounds of laughter on a playground.

"It's weird," Olivia said finally. "We only just met, but it feels like . . ." She paused, not knowing what, exactly, it felt like.

"I don't want to go," Carlotta said, her return to Rome scheduled for the following evening.

"What are you going to do?" Olivia asked.

"I must prepare now for the Olympic trials."

"I mean, about . . . you know."

Carlotta sighed, long and deep. "I cannot have a baby. It is impossible for me to have a baby. But Giorgio says that if I have an abortion, he will never forgive me."

They held eyes. Then Olivia said, "You realize I'm adopted."

Silence came, followed by a sniffle.

"We wouldn't be standing here talking right now if my birthmother had aborted me."

Carlotta's shoulders dropped. "I am so sorry, Olivia. I know what I want to do is not right." She was palming the cross at her neck again, as if she didn't want it to overhear.

"I just want to make sure this is what you want," Olivia said.

They stopped walking. The girl dropped her bag. Her whole body seemed to sink into itself.

"This is not about honor, Carlotta. Or obligation. It's about *you*, and if this is the right decision for *you*. Not for *zia*, not for Grand Master, not for Giorgio. . . ."

Carlotta, who'd been staring down at her feet, turned and faced Olivia now. She wiped her eyes. "I don't want a baby," she said.

It was late by the time they got back to the loft and, struck with hunger, Olivia went directly to the kitchen to rummage through what was left of the Chinese takeout. "You want some?" she called back to Carlotta who'd headed off to the bedroom to drop her things.

Olivia sucked down some cold noodles while reheating the moo shu pork. She ate directly from the carton while heading for the bedroom, where she found the girl standing motionless, her eyes glued to the sketch of Evelyn that Olivia kept tucked in a far corner of her bookshelf.

"Where did you get this?" Carlotta asked in a grim, almost haunting tone.

Olivia stood still staring at it. It hadn't even occurred to her what it might mean to the girl, who turned to Olivia now, almost accusingly. "It's my father's."

The man who'd remained mysteriously absent from conversation.

"He gave it to me," Olivia said.

Everything about Carlotta was now changed, her face of bitter stone, her eyes full of questions, as Olivia went through her story.

"I have been waiting for my father for three and a half years."

"But he is gone now. And it all feels like a dream. Marco calling me like that. Evelyn's ashes, where we buried them."

"He didn't mention me?"

"He disappeared as if into the mist."

Carlotta settled her eyes back on the drawing, where her gaze proceeded to morph, ever so slowly, from disdain to discern. It was a while before she spoke again. Before she turned and examined Olivia's face as if tracing it with her eyes. "When I first saw you," she said, her voice an octave lower, "you looked so familiar. I thought it was Rhonda you reminded me of, that's who naturally came to my mind, because you were her daughter, and she had made such a strong impression on me in Italy. But now I realize that it wasn't Rhonda you reminded me of at all." Her eyes settled back on the drawing.

"I know," Olivia said, following Carlotta's gaze. "People used to say I looked like my aunt Evelyn."

"Not Evelyn," Carlotta said, turning back to Olivia.

The way she was staring. "What?" Olivia said.

Ruminating. "You tell me that *papá* and Evelyn met before he married my mother."

"Presumably, yes."

"*Quando?* When, exactly, did they meet?"

"I don't know," Olivia responded, flustered. She thought for a second. "Marco said that Evelyn was in Italy visiting a friend. There was a basketball game . . . and then, something about rolling dice."

"*Papá* married *mamma* in 1993. When were you born?"

"1993."

"I doubt he knew."

"Knew what?"

There was a moment of silence before Olivia said, "Look, Carlotta. I see where you're going here, but," she paused. Carlotta had gotten out her phone and was scrolling through photos. "Here," she said, handing Olivia the phone. "I don't have a picture. But this is the painting my father did of her." Olivia, staring at the photo, said, "She's like a million years old."

Carlotta took the phone back, zoomed in on the image with her fingers. "The lip. Look under the lip." Carlotta moved in closer. The sides of their heads were touching. "This . . . mark," she paused, struggling to find the word for what it was. Then she touched Olivia's lower lip with her finger. "This here. You have it."

Olivia narrowed her eyes at the picture. "Who is she?"

The girl responded with a reverence Olivia had not heard from her before. "She is Duchess Irene of Greece and Denmark." Something from another era, times past. "She is my great grandmother. It is in her honor that I fence. *Nonna Irene*, the grandmother of my father."

They held eyes. Carlotta put her hand over her mouth. After a few moments like that, Olivia sat down on the bed. Her chest was moving in and out very deeply, and yet it seemed no air was getting in. "It can't be true," she said, not so much to Carlotta as to herself. "He would have said something to me if it were true."

But Carlotta had not apparently heard Olivia, for her face was breaking out in the most wondrous of wonders. "We're sisters," she said.

"We don't know for sure."

"I have felt this since I arrived."

"Half-sisters." It came out a whisper, as Olivia dug back into the recesses of her mind searching for hints, clues. All the while there was something growing inside her, the seedling of knowledge that had perhaps always been there.

"It can't be."

"Oh, but it can, Olivia. It can."

27

A wave came at her. Oncoming and massive, terrifying, and yet oddly comforting, for there was this sense that she was not alone, that another presence was being pulled into the belly of the great crest along with her. Together they rose, screaming with delight. Or just screaming, and it was here, just before the fall, that Rhonda's eyes jarred open from a sleep that, once again, hadn't felt like sleep. The shades were drawn and the TV was on and tissue lay all over. "Evelyn," Rhonda whispered her sister's name in the darkness. *Tell me what to do now, Evelyn.*

No response came back.

Just a screaming echo in Rhonda's ears, one that settled in her jaw, which she proceeded to massage to no avail. Something, someone, make her jaw stop screaming. No. Not her jaw. Her phone. Her phone was screaming, a muffled scream, buried, somewhere in these tangled sheets. Rhonda had long stopped trying to find it.

"Rhonda?"

It was Lillian, tapping at Rhonda's bedroom door. "Rhonda, are you in there?"

"I'm here."

"Stevie's calling. He wants to know where you are."

"Like I said, I'm here."

"He says they're all waiting."

Rhonda shot up in bed. "Waiting for what?"

"The board meeting is about to start."

After a pause, "Today? Now? Are you sure?"

Her silence meant that she was sure.

Rhonda wrapped a sheet around herself and went and cracked open the door. "Go, Lillian. Go and stall or something. Tell them I'm on my way." With a worried look, Lillian hurried off, and Rhonda went and downed a pill that was supposed to help with the depression and anxiety, but often made her woozy. She was headed for her closet when a searing in her jaw made her go back and grab another pill, this one for the pain. It was her TMJ acting up. Her father had had it bad. For Rhonda it had been a little popping here and there over the years, but never before this explosion of unbearable pain. Two trips to the dentist, another to the chiropractor, two to a specialist, who'd taken one look at her jaw and asked her, point-blank, what trauma she'd endured the past few years, because it was in this time that she'd apparently been grinding her teeth to the bone.

He'd fitted her for a mouth guard but she still needed physical therapy, like, months' worth. He'd given her someone's card, which she'd immediately lost.

In the closet, she grabbed a black pantsuit lying crumpled on the floor, faintly aware this was the same suit she'd worn to the last board meeting. She'd not had it dry-cleaned. To have something dry-cleaned meant to give it a burial. Everything that came back from the dry cleaners (via their delivery service) was heaped on top of the dry-cleaned pile, everything still in wrappers, multiple piles now, stacked waist-high on her closet floor. Unwrapping them didn't occur to her, which is why nothing was on hangers. Nor in drawers. Hadn't been for some time.

She twisted her hair up into a clip, brushed some powder over her jaw to hide the swelling, then hurried to the garage and clicked open the automatic door, which is when a waft of heat engulfed her like napalm. Her body went into a cold sweat adjusting. When had summer unleashed itself? What had happened to spring? Had the cacti even yet bloomed? For she couldn't remember having spotted one flower.

Well, she couldn't take the golf cart in this heat. She'd melt. She'd have to take the Mercedes, a thought that sickened her ever since that time, after a few too many glasses of wine, she'd gotten it into her head that it was time to scratch off the college stickers still so proudly displayed on the back window—Stanford Golf Mom, ha! University of Arizona, ha! University of Dublin, the biggest ha and had that really been *her* idea? This ruse to keep Stevie believing in his dream of playing in the Premier League?

She'd used a razor blade. And now, well, it simply looked like her car had been vandalized.

She started up the engine, set the A/C to blasting, and began to back out. A three-point turn was required, one she could do in her sleep though today she seemed to forget a step, like shifting into drive after she'd backed up the requisite distance. Consequently, when she pressed on the accelerator to pull forward, the car flew even farther backward and drove right over the low stone wall flanking the horseshoe driveway, onto the grass median, missing the saguaro cactus, thank goodness, because Daniel had designed this entire estate to accommodate that poor-looking beast's hundred-year reign in that spot, and smacked right into the For Sale sign. The post cracked, sending the top half timbering over and banging against the base. The sign swung back and forth in a cloud of red dust, with Rhonda sitting there stunned. That sign, it had been there for so long. Two years? Three? Did it matter? She barely even noticed it anymore.

That's how many people had wanted to buy their dream house.

It was Rhonda's purgatory now, where she spent her days in a uniform of yoga pants and an oversize T-shirt, sequestered in her office responding to hundreds of grant requests that came in via email. She wouldn't rest until every last response was sent. She had fired Peggy, the director, who'd been too discerning, and took on the job herself. If you wanted money, there needed to be a good reason why you wouldn't get it. Dreams. Dreams. Dreams—*Come, you dreamers. I will make all your dreams come true.*

She got out of the car, not bothering to examine the damage, for the damage was already done, wasn't it? She went back to the golf cart. But the battery was dead. She tried the second golf cart, which was charged. Lillian. Or, more likely, Daniel, skulking around the property, keeping things from going into complete disarray.

She didn't even golf, Rhonda guffawed, as the cart lurched out of the garage. In fact, she'd hated the sport, she thought, pressing the pedal to the floor as if that could make the cart go faster, at last tipping an imaginary hat to the gate guard, who looked a little confused to see her dressed in a suit, not to mention leaving the community in a golf cart in this heat, not to mention that deranged expression on her face. The most boring, ludicrous sport in the world, besides soccer, that was. She sometimes secretly wondered what sport a child from her own womb might have chosen to play, and then she snapped shut her mind from going there. Why, after all these years, did her mind still go there?

Her hair flew in the beating heat and the air looked like it was melting as she puttered her way up to Stevie's offices just a few miles up the dusty road. Strands of hair were plastered to her face and her pants were stuck to her ass by the time she arrived at the meeting, thirty minutes late.

Knights of the Roundtable! So she referred to them now.

What had originally been such a source of pride for her, back when her two sons sat on either side of her, before Chase moved to Tucson and Stevie had to recuse himself because his investment firm now managed Knight's endowment, back when Daniel participated, in the early days, though he rarely showed up anymore either, certainly not since the divorce, all of Rhonda's pride having been usurped by an impending dread, one now rearing its ugly head in the form of Daniel. Rhonda was surprised to find him seated at the plush conference table, Stevie beside him (everyone else conspicuously missing), the board book open before them, graphs and charts splayed out on the table.

"Let me guess," Rhonda said, taking a seat. "Our averages are down again."

"One might think it was a time for cutting back," Daniel looked up and said.

"Nice to see you Daniel," Rhonda said.

"And yet you've not cut back, Rhonda. You've written numerous foundation checks for . . ." he didn't seem to know where to begin.

"Ark Devices," Rhonda interjected the company's new name, as Chase had coached her. "What are you doing here, Daniel?"

"I have every right to be here, Rhonda."

"You haven't been to a meeting in years."

"That's because I trusted you, Rhonda. You've always been scrupulous."

Rhonda smiled, tightly.

"Why did you fire Peggy?"

Rhonda shot Stevie a glance. He was a straight shooter like his dad. Certainly, he'd been the one to call Daniel about Peggy.

"She was redundant, Daniel." Rhonda grabbed her jaw. Had the pain pill worn off already?

"This isn't funny, Rhonda."

"Like I'm laughing, Daniel."

He stared at her—apparently she was laughing. Albeit silently, her mouth having had screwed up into a ridiculous smile because perhaps it *was* funny, this pain stretching from her jaw down to her neck and arm and settling into her funny bone. Funny as hell.

"And what's all this money you're giving to some museum in Rome?"

She massaged her cheek. "It's called art, Daniel. I'm a patron of the arts."

"Since when do you care about art?"

She wasn't even sure that that question deserved a response.

"Please tell me one single piece of art in that house that you care about. Do you even know where any of it came from? One piece, Rhonda. Name one piece?"

She couldn't, of course.

"So I'll ask it again, since when do you care about art?"

"Let's see," she said, as if she had to think about it. "Our daughter? The one who will soon graduate from NYU in dramatic *arts*? Our daughter who's had a love for drama ever since I can remember? Perhaps that's why I care?"

"By the way, are you going to her fall play?" Daniel asked, diverting the subject because he knew he'd been beaten.

She gasped. "That's months from now, Daniel."

"But you're going."

"Why don't you go?"

After a pause, "I've told you, Rhonda." He clenched his jaw for a moment. "Brie and I are going to Hawaii. We'll be gone for some time. You know we've been planning this for a while. . . ." Rhonda blanked out as he continued, something about some dream of the woman's, something about sailing around the world. No, that couldn't possibly be it. Rhonda blinked. *Everyone had a dream.*

"That's fine if you want to invest in Chase's business, but from now on you must do so out of your personal accounts, not the foundation's."

"What I was going to do, when I received my next royalty payment."

He seemed shocked. "What happened to the money in your investment account?"

She glanced around for her missing accountant, perhaps he could answer the question, or the missing lawyer for that matter, Rhonda didn't need to ask where they'd gone to, she knew she'd been ambushed.

"There's Olivia's loft," she said finally, with no small amount of sarcasm. "Not to mention the monthly maintenance fee. Oh, and Lillian's mother now needs full-time care, and so I bought her an apartment in that wonderful new retirement community. Lillian has done so much for us over the years." She paused here, ceremoniously. "As has the gardener, and the cleaners, who wanted to break away from Clean & Bright and start their own company. As have all the local schools, coaches, teachers, and families that we've come across throughout the years. There are really so many people to help, Daniel."

There was some silence.

"I think you need to step away from the foundation for a while," Daniel said, and Rhonda looked over at Stevie. *You too?*

"Look, Mom," Stevie cleared his throat. "Dad and I have discussed it and we feel that you need to take a break, clear your head."

How many hours I spent under the beating Arizona heat cheering that ball into the net, thinking, please God, someone make a goal? One goal, Rhonda thought.

Stevie glanced at Daniel, who added, "Plus, we're going to need to work some things out with the lawyers, Rhonda, based on this transaction with Chase's company. We can't give grants to for-profit organizations, let alone family members. It's in the bylaws, Rhonda."

Since when had Daniel read the bylaws?

"I don't know what's gotten in to you, Rhonda. This isn't you," Daniel said.

She stood up so abruptly her chair rolled back and hit the wall behind her. "Not me? For heaven's sake, there is no more me. *Me* left me a long time ago. Doesn't anyone get that?"

There was a reverberating silence. Rhonda stood there, ears throbbing, staring into their shocked and mortified faces. Then another spasm gripped her jaw. She grabbed it, and the most beguiling moan escaped her.

"Rhonda?"

Clutching her cheek with one hand, her purse with the other, she ran out of the room. Out of the building. It was so hot the air was melting, the soles of her shoes were burning, and yet she could feel none of it.

"Rhonda." It was Daniel, right behind her, as she was about to slide into the golf cart.

"Where's the Mercedes?"

"At home."

"You can't drive the cart in this heat."

She got in. "Did you want something, Daniel?"

"I tried to warn you, Rhonda. So did Stevie. But you're not answering your phone."

She keyed the electricity on.

"Look, Rhonda. We need to talk."

Normally this was the moment she might brace herself, but underneath the veil of her pain she could only look back at him obtusely. She hated it when people said, "We need to talk," and then paused. If you have something to say, then just say it! Don't pause. For heaven's sake, what was he waiting for?

"You realize that our patents expire next year."

Yes, she was vaguely aware of this.

"And that your royalties will cease."

Yes, she was vaguely aware of this.

"And there won't be any more new patents, since I'm retiring."

Daniel retiring, a thought she'd always secretly abhorred but had never felt compelled to worry about when they were together. The Daniel she knew was always happy to spend his days and nights toiling away in his design studio, free of human contact, particularly that of his wife. And she had liked it that way. She would have been fine to have had it stay that way.

"You need to start planning, Rhonda. Doing . . ." Daniel began, turning away from her. He took a minute to clear his throat. "Something . . ." He cleared it again and turned back finally. Were those tears in his eyes? Rhonda sighed. What the hell had come over everyone?

"I thought I *was* doing something, Daniel."

"I spoke with the accountant, Rhonda. The house is a money pit.

Take what you can get for it and get out. The way you're giving away everything you own, you're going to need the money."

"Maybe I don't want the money. Maybe it was always your money and never mine." She grabbed her jaw again. "Ah, hell shit," she said, as the searing flared. It felt like someone was twisting a knife into her cheek.

"What's wrong with your mouth?"

"It's nothing." She waved it off.

"It doesn't look like nothing."

"My TMJ is acting up."

"Since when have you had TMJ?"

Let's see, ever since I've known you? It was amazing how little he knew about her after twenty years, or how much of herself she'd kept from him. From everyone.

"I still don't understand why you don't go to New York to spend some time with Olivia. It would be good for you."

She gasped, inwardly. Did he actually think he knew what would be good for her? Rhonda could not go to New York. She could not look Olivia in the face ever again with this untold truth between them. Did he have any idea what she'd done? That in her own way, she *had* told Olivia, was telling her in this instant?

"Have a great time in Hawaii, Daniel," she said finally and drove off.

28

She drove with some kind of weird purpose, as if, in fact, she did know where she was going. At some point, when she'd stopped at a light, the sun beating a hole in her brain, she pulled down the visor and a business card fell onto her lap. It was the referral for the physical therapist that the specialist had given her, the one she'd thought she'd lost and what it was doing here she had no idea. The only thing that mattered was that the address listed on it was not far from there, for she could take this pain no longer.

Twenty minutes later she was in a rundown section of town, pulling into a strip mall that consisted of one long, brown, dilapidated adobe structure with multiple doors, establishments that had nothing whatsoever to do with the other—a tire shop, the Dollar Store, a physical therapist, a vegan supermarket, tattoos, and a sign that read, "Healer and Acupuncturist."

Purposely or not, she walked past the physical therapist door and proceeded to the door of the healer and acupuncturist. A dog barked viciously from inside and Rhonda stepped back. Then forward again. She buzzed twice before a man opened it, a rather handsome Asian man wearing jeans, a black dress shirt, and pointed loafers. He was carrying a yapping Yorkshire in his arms, and was murmuring in his native tongue to the little beast trying to settle him. When he looked up again, with discerning eyes, he widened the door to let her in.

Rhonda glanced around, but there was no one else there, seemingly. The space was mostly stark, unadorned, a few rooms separated by cardboard-looking walls left open at the ceiling.

The man sat her down in the waiting area, which consisted of three chairs, no customers, and a water trickling rock formation. He left her with a clipboard of forms to fill out. "Oh, but I'm not a—" she managed to say, before her jaw seared up with pain and she couldn't finish her sentence.

She looked down at the forms. Most of the questions were personal in nature: Was she married, single, or divorced? And if she was married, on a scale of one to ten, how happy was she in her marriage? Happy? Can marriage make someone happy? If the question had said family, Rhonda would have understood, she'd have marked a ten, absolutely, no hesitation. Even with things the way they were today—none of her children having called her for weeks—a ten, still. Always.

Oh, whatever. The question didn't even pertain to her. Apparently, the question about being happy only pertained to those who were married.

Twenty minutes later, her head spinning from all the boxes, the same man came back to retrieve the clipboard. He led Rhonda into one of the cardboard rooms, sat her on a table, put the dog in her arms, and then walked out of the room. She petted the animal's trembling limbs, avoiding its beady eyes and wet nose, and contemplated why she hadn't just left. What kind of pain might bring someone to a place like this?

Thirty minutes later the same man, now wearing a white smock over his clothes, came in with her paperwork, leaned against a table across from her, one leg crossed over the other, and studied her forms.

She glanced behind him out the open door, hoping to see a nurse, receptionist, someone. She wanted to set the dog down, was about to when his sculpted face came at her, abruptly, his eyes piercing with a disconcerting certainty. A few agonizing moments passed like this (could he see into her soul?). Then he asked about the pain. Not *if* there was pain. She hadn't even said anything yet about having pain. Apparently, pain was what he'd read in her eyes.

She mentioned her jaw.

"Where else?" His gaze narrowed skeptically. He felt around her neck and shoulders. His long silky hair brushed against her cheek. She could smell a sweet and sour scent, something he must have had for lunch.

The dog was still trembling in her lap.

He stepped back and studied her. Then he stepped forward again, grabbed her hands. He felt the weight of them, and then flipped them over. It took Rhonda a moment to realize he was examining her palms. Then he let go of her palms, pressed his fingers into her neck, and studied his watch.

"Is it beating?" she asked finally.

He stared off, reading her pulse. Then he stepped back and examined her form again. "You've checked no children." As if he knew she'd lied.

"What?"

He showed her the form, and she looked at it as if it must have been a mistake. Had she really checked no? "I have no biological children," she clarified.

"And this has given you pain."

"I didn't say that."

"You are infertile."

She frowned at him for a moment, a very odd, out-of-body moment. To this day she had never told anybody. Even to Daniel she wouldn't admit it. It was inconclusive, not to mention impossible to believe what one specialist, after seeing dozens, had the nerve to tell her, which was that she had pounded the pavement too much in her youth. Excreted too many endorphins at too early an age, which had left her infertile, what sometimes happened with professional athletes.

"I specialize in infertility," he said.

"I think that ship has sailed," she said.

He was staring intently into her eyes, not so sure.

Five miscarriages by the time she'd received the news, and she'd still kept trying. Even after Olivia came, Rhonda and Daniel still threw all the money they'd had at having a biological baby, and still, nothing. Yes, that ship set sail a long time ago.

He left with the dog so she could change into a gown open at the back. When he returned (without the dog) he had her lay facedown on the table, and soon she felt little pricks along her neck and spine. It didn't hurt, she barely felt anything, and she wondered if along with her mind, her body had gone numb too. All the way down her vertebrae came the little pricks, quickly, efficiently—why was he not focusing on her jaw?—to a spot in her lower back, nowhere near her jaw, and began pushing and probing at whatever he seemed to have found there.

"Your body is ravaged."

"Tell me something I don't already know," she said feebly, thinking about all her old injuries again, in addition to the surgeries, the dozen or so ankle sprains, jammed fingers, bruised knees, all that black and blue. And yet he seemed obsessed with this spot that had nothing to do with any of those areas. Something he didn't like, apparently, for he went and retrieved a small envelope from a drawer. From it he unwrapped a sterilized pin, and, after showing it to her and explaining what he was about to do with it—"I'm going to bleed you"—that it was an ancient Korean healing practice, with her consent, which she immediately gave him, he began jabbing the spot with the pin in quick succession.

When someone says, "I'm going to bleed you," it's usually a good time to say no. And yet, it sounded like exactly what she needed. To bleed. When was the last time she'd bled? Her premature menopause had long come and gone. She couldn't even remember the last time she'd cut her finger. Would the color of her blood even be red?

Jab, jab, jab.

She tried to distract herself by thinking of all the fertility specialists she'd seen in her day, but never anyone like this. Evelyn had tried telling Rhonda it wasn't meant to be, but Rhonda refused to listen. This was not about fate, it was about Rhonda. About making things happen, taking matters into your own hands. There was always an answer to every problem. If you worked hard enough to find it, it was there.

It wasn't meant to be.

Jab, jab, jab. With each jab more regret. Rhonda had never shared her plight to have a biological child with Olivia. She'd not wanted to expose her daughter to any pain. Rhonda bit her lip until the jabbing stopped. He clamped the wound shut and left Rhonda there to "bleed," because bleeding would release toxins and pain, he told her.

Moths began pelting the window searching for light, which meant dusk had arrived. The air conditioner rattled. She lay with her head to one side and let the tears leak down her nose and chin and drop onto the linoleum. She had wanted only happiness for Olivia. Pure, unadorned, which meant avoiding painful truths. The result being that her daughter knew little about her, and probably little about life.

"You need to care about yourself now." It was her friend, back after a long absence, removing the needles and bandaging the pinprick, which had stopped bleeding. She was free of toxins now, she presumed, free to go, the pain in her jaw gone, miraculously. If only in her mind, and perhaps that was the point.

"You will come back tomorrow," he said. "You need much work."

She left there, wondering what had just happened, if it wasn't her sister, in fact, who'd been jamming her with that pin.

You will come back tomorrow. Rhonda peeled out, leaving behind a cloud of dust and noise that could not have gone unnoticed. She would never go back there, that man was a lunatic, it occurred to her as she made the turn onto Cactus Road, when she grasped her jaw again because the pain had come searing back.

She didn't remember driving home. She remembered being hungry, of having a vague idea of stopping at a drive-through, but she didn't stop. Something kept telling her to get home. When she did, she barely even noticed that she'd left the garage door open, something one didn't do in the desert in the dead of summer. She pulled into her garage and parked.

She was losing her mind; she knew this, of course. Had known this for some time. She grabbed her purse, which promptly spilled over, all her useless shit filling the drink holders and sliding between the seats. She gathered what she could, got out of the car, and headed to the mud-room door, still rummaging through her purse to see what was missing, stopping short just before she got there. Her sunglasses were still on so she wasn't sure what it was she was seeing there at her feet that made her go still. A slinky head perched in the air. Was it one of those rubber snakes the boys used to scare her with? She pushed her sunglasses on top of her head. Its tongue was flickering in and out, and for a moment the world stopped spinning. A lifetime passed in a millisecond. Then in one big gasping motion, she leaped through the entrance to the mudroom, slammed the door shut behind her, and used the force of her weight to keep it closed, as if whatever that was—what she probably knew but wasn't ready to acknowledge—might be able to push it open.

Her heart battered at the wood. Was it Rhonda, or was the sky falling down? She leaned in harder, thinking that it must be falling, because here she was, bled of demons, supposedly, and yet what slithered in wait behind this door was a snake, a baby rattler, the worst fucking demon of all.

You lie: you go to hell. The rules were simple.

Fine, okay, you win! But there was still the issue of this snake. Rhonda would have to *do . . . something*, as Daniel had said. She couldn't just leave the snake there. But do what? She should call someone. Stevie? Daniel? No. Stevie already thought she was nuts, and Daniel had dreams to pursue. Perhaps it wasn't a snake at all she'd just seen, but a figment of her imagination. Her mother had gone crazy, after all. Those few times Rhonda had visited her in the hospital near the end, she didn't even recognize her own daughter. She saw bugs crawling up the walls, her arms were levitating, and it was awful. Rhonda couldn't face the idea of ever being like that. No. There was no snake. No. Snake. And, well, time had passed. If it was a snake, certainly it must have slithered back out to wherever it had come from.

She put her ear to the wood, but all she could hear was the hollow pounding of her heart. Did snakes make sound? She took some breaths, trying to relax. Then, ever so slowly, she turned the knob and cracked open the door just wide enough to get a peek and, sure enough, the little beast was not where she had left it, but only because it had slithered right up to the base of the door where it now lay snuggled two inches from Rhonda's feet.

It was trying to get in!

A curdling scream shot through the air as Rhonda yanked the door shut again.

"Mom?"

Rhonda whipped around.

"What the hell, Mom?"

It was Olivia. Oh, thank God. It took Rhonda a moment to speak. "Oh, Olivia."

"What are you doing, Mom?"

She burst into tears and fell into her daughter's arms.

29

Olivia calmed Rhonda down and they called the fire department, the firemen arriving minutes later with a wood box and a long, metal grabbing contraption. With chastising looks, they gave Rhonda the requisite lecture about leaving garage doors open in the desert. She'd been lucky, they told her.

"Ha!" was Rhonda's response.

She was a shaky mess by the time she joined Olivia, drinking a glass of Chardonnay at the kitchen island. Rhonda got down another glass and poured from the bottle. She sat down, and for a minute the two of them just sat there drinking their wine, each in her own thoughts.

"Stevie called me," Olivia said finally.

Rhonda closed her eyes for a moment and nodded.

"He and Dad are worried about you." Olivia's tone was facetious. "'Who worries about Mom?' I asked him. I mean, what is there to worry about?" She looked pointedly at Rhonda.

"Exactly what I said."

"What problem is there you can't fix?" From facetious to sardonic.

"No show tonight?" Rhonda asked.

"I'm taking a break," Olivia said, sipping from her glass.

Rhonda eyed the girl sitting across from her, this woman drinking her wine. "I don't think we've ever shared a glass of wine together."

"No?"

"I've always wondered what this moment would be like."

"Like this, I guess."

Rhonda raised her glass.

Olivia didn't raise hers, so Rhonda reached over and clinked her glass anyway, clumsily, due to the hot glare of the girl's eyes, tunneling, drilling. Knowing. Rhonda braced herself for the blow. The holistic bleeding, the baby rattler: all that was child's play. This was how it would end. Olivia never missed a show, not once since Rhonda had known her. Not one line, one cue, one prop setting or costume change. Even that time when she was playing Annie in *Tom Sawyer* and had a temperature of 101 degrees. It was irresponsible to have her out there, one of the parents had scolded Rhonda afterward, and Rhonda smiled in certain agreement while scoffing under her breath, like it was her choice. Like anything was ever her choice when it came to this girl.

She set her hands flat on the table. "You should know right off, Rhonda." Olivia paused for the word to sink in. *Rhonda.* "I will never, ever, forgive you."

Rhonda didn't say anything.

"For as long as I live."

As if it were all Rhonda's fault.

"Forget about why you chose to lie to me for a moment, Rhonda. Or should I call you Aunt Rhonda." A slight pause. "You sat there and listened to me go on about how I thought that I was in love with him." Her face collapsed into a tangle of sorrow and disbelief. "My father." Her eyes had gone black, and Rhonda averted her gaze to the window, the blaze of white. She felt as if every last crack and fissure in her skin were breaking open.

"God, I hate you."

"I was trying to protect you."

"From what?"

Rhonda took a breath. "What do you want me to tell you?"

"The truth. I want you to tell me the truth."

Rhonda ran her thumb along the stem of her glass. Gazing at it, she said, "Evelyn came home from Italy distraught and pregnant. She wanted an abortion." Then she looked at Olivia. "I wouldn't let her have one."

Olivia looked down. "Maybe it would have been better if you had."

"Olivia, don't say that."

Olivia stood up and paced to the window.

"The idea was that we would raise you together. That someday we'd tell you, when you were older, but then . . ." She paused to collect herself, to detach herself from the words she still couldn't fathom. "Then she died."

Olivia closed her eyes, softly, as if a gentle breeze had met her face. They remained closed, and Rhonda wondered what she was thinking, if she would ever know her daughter as her daughter again, and as strange as this moment was, as awful as it was, some form of release was taking place inside Rhonda, as if the sky were opening up and pouring rain down upon her.

"Does he know?"

A relief so great Rhonda couldn't hear. "What?"

Olivia's eyes were open again, set on Rhonda now. "Does. He. Know."

Rhonda blinked. She shook her head. "I don't know."

"I told Carlotta I would find him; I had an idea where he was and I would go there and confront him."

Rhonda opened her mouth to speak but nothing came out. A long moment passed. Then she got up and left the room. When Rhonda came back, Olivia was back seated in her stool at the kitchen island, her wine glass was empty; she made no note of Rhonda's return, nor of the file folder in Rhonda's hand. "There's no need to search for him," Rhonda said. "I know where he is." She slid the folder onto the counter.

Olivia poured more wine and did not look at the folder.

"I hired a detective."

A shocking, visible stillness on top of what was already stillness.

Olivia, with great care, managed to set the bottle down. Her chest was heaving in and out, pushing and pulling against the heaves of Rhonda's own chest while Olivia slowly and at last reached for the file. Her hands were shaking as she opened the folder, scanned what was there on the first page, and then scanned it again. One more time before staring off for a long moment, the creases in her forehead suddenly deep and many, as if she'd aged a thousand years. She looked back at Rhonda. "Is this right?"

30

O livia drove. Rhonda slept.

Dawn was starting to break. The manmade sprawl was behind them now, before them barren desert, shadows of boulders, scorched earth dusted in orange light. Already the temperature was approaching ninety degrees, but soon the sky would break open and unleash the real heat. Olivia drove fast, as if to stay one beat ahead of it, her eyes glued ahead, to the west, to that speck on the horizon where the road dropped off and everything ended.

An unacknowledged truce, if temporary, left no speaking. Three hours like that, until they came upon a battered old gas station-minimart. Olivia pulled in and she and Rhonda took turns in the single outdoor bathroom while an attendant filled their tank.

Inside, they perused the food options—shriveled hot dogs, soggy pizza—which were not really options at all. They stocked up on chips, waters, and diet Cokes.

"The guy said that there would be nothing until Indio, California," Olivia told Rhonda, who had bought cigarettes and was now leaned up against the car smoking one, her mind far away. Olivia wanted to ask her what the hell she was doing smoking, but then remembered that would involve speaking to her. She should have left Rhonda in Scottsdale to shrivel up and die. Olivia had had no intention of bringing her. But after she'd dusted off and packed up her still mostly unused

M3 for the drive west, her mother lumbered up with her suitcase and tossed it into the trunk. "What do you think you're doing?" Olivia had said.

"I'm going home."

Olivia had not bothered to inquire further. She'd had no intention of giving her mother the satisfaction to think that she cared. If Olivia despised Rhonda for keeping the truth from her, Olivia wouldn't show it, having matured, seemingly, in that very instant she'd discovered her mother to be one of the very best of liars.

On the road again, Rhonda dozing in and out as if recovering from some long-lost sleep, the horizon grew even more barren, more cracked open, if that were possible.

At last, a watery shimmer of low buildings, the beginning of civilization's return, and Olivia pulled off at the first viable exit. Her knuckles were white, and she was sweating. Every joint ached. She couldn't go on and told Rhonda she was going to stop for the night. Rhonda, with her head resting on the window, her eyes soft and open, said that she thought that was a good idea. She seemed almost angelic, which only infuriated Olivia more.

Indio was one of those quirky little towns built for drivers on their way to somewhere else. Kitschy trinket shops filled with Indian silver and turquoise beads, leather goods, and cowboy gear. A par three, mini-golf course, of all things, the main attraction; it came attached to a Super 8, and after checking in, they found a booth at the café adjacent to the ninth green and ordered beers.

Rhonda stared at the faux windmill until their beers came, lukewarm and sweaty. She glanced around, then told Olivia that she and Evelyn had come here once. Absently, she said that they had made this drive, but in the reverse direction.

Olivia picked at the label on her beer. Nothing Rhonda could say at this point would surprise her.

"The three of us did."

This time she looked up.

"You were six weeks old and Evelyn refused to fly with you, so we drove out together, all her things stuffed into the old VW we used to share in high school. Dad was dead by then, and Evelyn had been living with her mother during the pregnancy, which I'm sure was the reason you were born premature—God, I could never stand that woman. We never told her what we were doing, just that Evelyn was putting the baby up for adoption, which her mother, a doctor herself, was all for. She was anti-abortion. But we had always planned that before the birth Evelyn would move to Arizona and live in an apartment near Daniel and me, and then after the birth, she would move in with us. But then, well, you came four weeks early. I flew down, and, when you were strong enough, we drove you back together."

Olivia wanted to put her hands over her ears. *None of it matters. None of it matters. There is only one thing that matters now.*

"I was petrified the car wouldn't make it." A shadow of awe crossed Rhonda's face, as if she was still incredulous that they *had* made it. "No A/C, we couldn't decide if it was better with the windows rolled down or up. You cried the entire way." She shook her head. "God, that drive was miserable."

It was as if the floodgates had opened, and now Olivia was drowning. The café was growing out of focus, the people around them dissolving, the chairs and tables, the plates and forks, Olivia's arms and hands, which were shaking. Olivia should be angry. Screaming with anger. She should reach across the table and slap Rhonda. It was what Rhonda wanted, no doubt expected. But all Olivia could feel was pity, and pitiful.

The heat made for hard sleeping. Olivia awoke before sunrise covered in sweat. She spent a good five minutes rousing Rhonda, who at last startled awake, grabbed Olivia's hand and blinked and looked around until it came to her where they were headed. Olivia pulled her hand back. Her mother's exhale seemed to go on forever.

The coffee was horrible. They took it to go and sped back onto the 5 Freeway, which before long would turn into the 10, which they'd take heading west. Just a few more hours, and it went by quickly. When the 10 turned into the 405, at last, Rhonda roused to life. Olivia couldn't help but notice how her mother looked around and sniffed at the air. How she rolled down her window and lifted her chin to the sun. How she breathed in the air coming at her, the salt and kelp, the oily mist, as if waves were crashing in her mind. Then she turned at Olivia, who'd yet to remove her headphones. *Don't you smell it too?*

Olivia had been listening to Jay-Z and there still wasn't much to see but a dull brown layer of smog.

"That exit, over there," Rhonda said, her first words in hours, and Olivia swerved off the freeway. Olivia hadn't bothered to ask exactly where her mother was taking them. Rhonda seemed to know where she was going. Her eyes were alive with it now, spouting acronyms like "PCH," coordinates like "left at the Shell station," "right over the bridge," "it will be stop and go here," and "watch out for the guy with the surf-board!" Left at the taco stand—the smell of burnt grease—under a quaint walking bridge, through a series of tract homes, tiny A-frame cottages by a bay whose road one followed to get to the beach. Rhonda told Olivia to pull up in front of one of them. They sat there for some time staring at the weatherworn structure, the postage stamp–size front yard. Lawn chairs were stacked against a railing; beach towels fluttered in the ocean breeze.

"She would come to my games drunk," Rhonda said. Her eyes were stony. "I rarely visited her after things got bad. She moved into a sanitarium. I wasn't with her when she died."

Olivia, who knew none of this, remained silent. Rhonda had never spoken about her mother. This being her home, presumably.

"I was eleven the first time she went into rehab. I had to go live with

my father and stepmother and their daughter Evelyn in the godfor-
saken boondocks of landlocked Pasadena. It was a hellish commute
back to the beach, where I played on a number-one-seeded club volleyball team. Neither my father nor my stepmother could drive me back
and forth because they both worked at the hospital 24/7. I was about
to quit, but then Evelyn gave me a printed copy of the bus route. 'You
can't quit,' she said. She was eight at the time. We'd shared a room for all
of two days, and it was as if Evelyn already knew everything about me."

Olivia looked away from Rhonda out the window, beyond the cottage, at the faint glistening of the ocean in the distance. *No. No. No.
She's not going to reel me in with some tragic version of her past. There
were no excuses for what she's done.*

Olivia started the car and they drove off in silence.

"There's a hotel at the other end of the bay," Rhonda said. "Maybe it's
still there."

Olivia made a U-turn as instructed.

"Evelyn and I would stay there sometimes, when we were in college.
I wanted to see my mom but couldn't bear the thought of staying with
her. So Evelyn would meet me at the hotel, and she and I would spend
a few days intermittently at my mother's, the beach, and Surf and Taco.
In the evenings there'd be margaritas on the balcony, perhaps a bar or
two, before crashing back at the hotel. Rhonda pointed at an open-air
shack with a faux thatched roof adorned with a surfboard and a neon
sombrero (Surf and Taco) as their car crawled by, having gotten caught
in a clutter of street traffic, sidewalks filled with lazy, flip-flop-wearing
locals in no hurry to go anywhere. The haze had burned off, the sky
was clear and bright, the swells were brilliant green slits between the
houses.

"Exactly the same," Rhonda said with amazement, when they arrived
at the hotel. In contrast to its quaint, beachy location, the façade was
drab, dank, and mustard-colored, two stories of balconies facing a
parking lot.

"Evelyn and I used to call it the Bates Motel."

A plate of stale cookies sat on a table next to a water cooler in the lobby, which otherwise consisted of a few pieces of drab furniture and a life-size plastic marlin hanging on the wall. But the rooms were clean, Rhonda assured Olivia, when they checked into one with two queens, a small kitchen, and a bathroom. Rhonda fell down on the bed, which caved inwards, and she smiled, as if remembering something. She didn't even unpack, as if suddenly here, in this dump, there was a higher order in which one lived. She'd been freed, and now she was levitating. "I'm going for a swim," she said, rummaging through her suitcase. "It was always the first thing Evelyn and I did."

"Stop doing that," Olivia said. Possibly the first words she'd spoken to Rhonda since they'd left Scottsdale.

Rhonda looked up. "Doing what?"

"Talking about her like that."

"Like what?"

Olivia frowned. Her mother was holding a red, two-piece swimsuit. She couldn't possibly think to walk around in that, and yet, she stripped down right there, to Olivia's horror, not bothering to go into the bathroom like she might normally do. "Mom!" Olivia gasped, turning away.

"Put your suit on," Rhonda said. "And come with me."

Olivia shook her head at the window. Who thought to bring a swimsuit?

Rhonda, wearing nothing but that suit now, grabbed a bathroom towel and walked past Olivia out of the room, heading straight for the beach as if each time a wave pulled back, it pulled her with it.

Olivia trailed her there, not wanting to, but unable to resist the urge. She was of the ocean too now. She was born here, of these women of the sea. She didn't remember the last time she'd seen her mother wear a swimsuit, let alone a two-piece. In fact, she never thought of her mother as having a body, one with curves and sensations. Her mother wasn't a body, she was a force of guts and stamina. A woman of the present not the past.

So where were they now?

When Olivia's feet hit the sand it was scorching, so she ran, passing Rhonda, who remained unaffected, so hardened and chaffed were the soles of her feet—feet that could walk over coals. That was how Olivia had always thought of them.

The stretch of beach was wide, and it took a while to reach the ocean. Once there, Olivia paused unsteadily before the vast body of moving water, for it felt like the ground beneath her was swaying too, her pores drinking it in, the cracks and fissures in her skin closing up in its profound, stupefying presence. But Rhonda kept walking as if there was no water at all. Into the waves, under, while Olivia watched in wonder because, for some reason, she'd always had the impression that her mother hated the beach.

She stood and watched Rhonda for some minutes longer. Then she turned, and headed back to the hotel.

31

When Rhonda arrived back to the room, Olivia was showered, dressed, and finishing the last touches of her makeup in the bathroom. "Is that the dress he bought for you?" Rhonda stood breathless in the bathroom doorway, spent, exhilarated, looking like an entirely different person to Olivia, who had to divert her eyes to hide her disgust—Rhonda's stomach bulging over her bikini bottom, the pockets on her wide thighs, her hair leaking water spots onto her breasts. Put on some clothes, Olivia wanted to say. She barely recognized her mother like this, as if that swim had absolved her in some way. Freed her of guilt, not the mother Olivia knew, not her mother at all.

"That's pretty," Rhonda said, pointing her sandy toe at the string of oddly shaped pearls around Olivia's ankle.

Olivia snapped her makeup bag shut and said nothing.

"Do you want me to go with you?"

"This is about me, Rhonda. Not you." Olivia went to the chair by the door and began strapping on her sandals.

Rhonda sat on the bed, soaking the sheets. "I was thinking," she said. "Screw the Knight Foundation. Arizona. All of it. Let's start our own foundation. Here. Dedicated to Evelyn." She paused to gauge Olivia's reaction.

There was none.

"You could run it. It could be for whatever you wanted, maybe something to do with Doctors without Borders, medical students, or the theater, for that matter. . . ."

Olivia put up her hand.

"I know it's a lot to think about right now, but . . ."

"Please don't, Rhonda."

"Will you at least think about it?"

"Another one of your charities? Really?"

"But this would be different."

"It's just another way for you to placate your guilt."

Rhonda sat up.

"Do you realize that all you ever think about is your money?" She did not give Rhonda a second to respond. "When something's wrong or not right, money is your answer. It's your answer to everything. Let's give money."

Rhonda sighed, inwardly, and reached for her T-shirt.

"What about love? What about honesty? Did you ever think about that for one second, did you ever think about the fact that if you weren't throwing your money around at any charity of the moment you were participating in after 9/11, Evelyn wouldn't have felt so disgusted? Disgusted enough to leave us to go *do something*?"

Olivia paused to catch her breath.

"Do you ever think that if you had acted differently, if you hadn't driven her away, Evelyn might not have been on that street in Italy when she was? That maybe she'd still be alive? Have you ever thought about that?"

"Every day for the last four years," Rhonda said, pulling on her shirt. She looked defeated, stripped of whatever exhilaration she'd brought back with her from the beach. Mission accomplished, Olivia thought, going back to fastening the buckles of her sandals (there were many). She would not let herself feel sorry for Rhonda. Olivia could not back down. No matter what internal struggle Rhonda might be going through, she deserved to be punished for what she'd done.

At last, the final buckle. If only Olivia's hands weren't shaking so hard; the buckle got caught on her anklet and broke the chain. Pearls ricocheted everywhere.

A gasp came from somewhere, Rhonda presumably. There was an unconscious moment. The sound of tinkling beads. The sight of Rhonda on the floor crawling around gathering them up. All this went on in slow motion seemingly, Olivia unable to move. It was a ridiculously pathetic sight. "Stop it, Mom," she said finally.

"Hold on, we'll find them." Rhonda was under the table now. "We can get it fixed."

Olivia got down beside her. "I'll get them, Mom . . . just don't . . ." *Don't touch them.*

Rhonda sat up and bumped her head on the tabletop.

Olivia gasped at her, then had to bite her lip not to laugh, Rhonda there rubbing her head. With her other hand, she passed Olivia the pearls she'd found. "Evelyn didn't leave because of 9/11," she said.

Olivia frowned. "But . . ."

"She came to me and said that she was miserable. That she looked into your eyes and saw him." She paused. "She was already going to leave, even before 9/11."

A breath of wind through the window sent the curtains fluttering.

"Why did you lose touch with her?" Olivia asked. The question had just come to her. "I always thought it was because she was with a married man, but it wasn't just any married man, she was with Marco again. You knew he was my father."

"It was so long ago. . . ."

"You were afraid that she'd come for me, weren't you?"

Rhonda didn't say anything.

"Well, did she? Did she come for me then?" When a solid minute passed and no answer came, Olivia crawled out from under the table, albeit awkwardly, trying not to spill the pearls in her hand, which she then poured into the inside pocket of her purse. She finished fastening her sandal buckle. Placed her toiletries and makeup into her suitcase, zipped it up. She looked around the room with one last sigh. Then she headed for the door.

"Why are you taking your suitcase?"

"I'm not coming back."

Rhonda got up off the floor. "You can't stay with him, Olivia. . . ."

"I'm not going to stay with him, Rhonda. After I see Marco, I'm going to Rome. I have family there, you know." She opened the door. "Don't try to contact me." She walked outside, pausing, momentarily struck by the warmth of the sun.

"She came for you." It was Rhonda, at the doorway behind her. "After Marco's wife died and they moved back to Italy. She called me."

Olivia turned.

"I told her that she'd had her chance to be a mother. I was the one who had raised you. I was your mother." Her eyes receded, ever so slightly. "I told her not to call again."

Olivia scrutinized Rhonda for a long, hard moment, a blade of sunlight distorting her face. For a moment it was Evelyn's face. "Why do I get the feeling that you're lying to me again?" Olivia said, staring into her mother's eyes. "Both of you. Have either of you ever *not* been lying to me?"

"Hate me, Olivia. I'll understand. I do understand. I just can't bear the thought of you hating Evelyn."

"You can't tell me how to feel."

"I'm not lying to you."

Olivia shook her head. "I suppose it doesn't matter either way. Evelyn may have come for me, as you say, but she never wanted me. Not in the beginning, not in the middle, not even in the end. If she had, she would have fought for me."

Rhonda may have tried to say something, but Olivia was already gone, in her heart, in her mind, and now, she was in her car, taking a moment to steady her breath and remind herself that she was not alone. Marco had been lied to, too. Carlotta. They'd all been cheated. Not told they were father and daughter. Sisters. They were in this together now.

We can be a family, Carlotta had said. Ever since New York, it was as if the girl had a direct line into Olivia's soul, the two of them connected now in this unfathomable way. They'd been texting daily since Carlotta flew back to Rome with her team. Texts that went like:

I still can't believe it's true.

I know.

I've always wanted a sister.

Me too.

Life is strange.

Olivia typed the directions to Marco's house into her iPhone. It was a straight shot up Ocean Avenue, and with no traffic her map said she'd be there in twenty minutes. She was hoping it would be more like an hour; all this hurrying, suddenly she needed more time for her emotions to catch up with her actions.

Ocean Avenue turned into a bridge that crossed over a sea of towering cranes and massive container ships. It dropped her off into a suburban sprawl of strip malls, a valley of fast food that ran along the base of hills that looked out over the harbor. She headed up one of the hills, where the homes got nicer, richer with ocean views, and then disappeared altogether.

Toward the top of the hill, through a gate—not just any gate but Angels Gate, the sign read—was an old army barracks that had been redeveloped into an artists' community. Beyond that, a horizon of infinite blue so gripping that Olivia found it hard to keep her foot pressing the gas as she wound farther up the road that seemed carved into the sky. At the very top, everything came to a lofty, weightless lull as she pulled into one of the parking spaces facing the ocean. She turned off the engine and sat for a moment, enveloped by a whispering silence so pure and deep that it felt as if she were not above the ocean but below it.

She took a deep breath and got out.

The pines rustled softly as she wandered around a series of faded-yellow single-story buildings with slanted red roofs. The wind flirted with her bare legs under the dress she'd brought specially to wear, the one he'd bought for her in Hanoi, which was too big for her now. Through some open doors, she got glimpses of artists at work—an old man hunched over a pottery wheel, a young woman in a mask cutting a stone, a couple arguing over the stitch of a dress. Artists working hard at their craft, and she wondered what Marco was doing here among them, if he'd started painting again, learning and growing and creating himself, like Confucius had said.

In one of the clapboard windows stood a painting of a woman walking toward the sea. Next to it was a door marked #15, which was locked. Olivia put her face against the darkened glass. Beyond the painting she could see canvases stacked against the walls, one of them portraying the elephant dance, as if recreated from the cave wall, and she stepped backward, gasping, her heart beating through her chest.

He could be at dinner, she thought hopefully. He wouldn't miss dinner, and she smiled now, remembering the focus and intensity with which food found its way into his mouth, as if it alone sustained him, that spicy fire scorching his soul.

There were some picnic tables in a grassy corner and she went and sat on one. Nearby, a bronzed stick figure stood with arms reaching up to the sky. Otherwise, there didn't seem to be anyone else around. The ocean was windswept. She watched the whitecaps tumble and skid. At some point it got cold, and she wrapped her arms around herself. The wind calmed with the dying sun. The light felt airy, dappled. She pulled out the notebook from her purse finally, the notebook that had started everything, and held it to her chest. She had yet to open it since she'd found it next to the box holding Evelyn's ashes, where Marco had left it for her, wondering if Evelyn had perhaps written a message for her in it, or perhaps she'd finished the story she'd started, the one about the prince and the girl and the circles and the searching, the story of her and Marco. It was always there, the knowledge, right before Olivia's eyes, and yet she hadn't known what she was reading, what Evelyn was trying to tell her, which was that love is an illness that can make you do the most devastating of things.

When she looked up again the sun was sinking into the ocean.

She went back to the studio, but it was still not open. She found the two dressmakers at work two doors down. "Do you know about the painter's studio?" Olivia asked.

The woman, wearing a gauzy white dress, looked up, startled, as if she was not used to seeing people.

"Will he open soon?"

"He opens the studio when he is in the mood," she said, turning back to her stitching. "He's temperamental that way."

Olivia smiled, clandestinely.

"He keeps to himself."

At least she knew she was in the right place, Olivia thought.

"He teaches an art class there," the man added. "In the back of his studio, Tuesday and Thursday nights from eight to ten. He never misses that class."

But as Olivia was leaving she practically ran right into him. He stumbled backward, flustered, though he did not seem surprised to see her once he realized who it was. "Well, hello," he said.

He seemed taller.

"Hello," she said.

There was an awkward silence.

"You didn't call," she said.

"I'm not good with phones," he said. He got out his keys. "Come inside," he said, unlocking the door.

"Did you know?" she said, staying where she was.

He paused for a moment. "I had an idea," he said. "When I met you."

"You didn't say anything."

"I wasn't sure."

"And you're sure now?"

"You're here, aren't you?"

There was a pause.

"Please come in," he said, and she did.

He closed the door behind her. "Would you like something to drink?"

"No thank you."

"Some water?"

"Whiskey?"

They shared a shy smile. "I would have to drum some up."

"Water is fine."

He returned with a glass. "Sit down," he said.

She stayed standing, the glass trembling in her hand. "I thought you were dead. I thought you'd been killed. Or had jumped off the edge of some cliff, all these tragic notions. I tried to put you out of my mind but I couldn't. I had dreams of that wedding parade. Who were the children that princess left behind? And why? I even wrote a play about it."

"How did it go?"

"The father drowns them. He drowns them all."

He narrowed an eye in mock scrutiny. "A Greek tragedy then."

"The truth is, I haven't been able to finish it."

"I see."

"I've been afraid of something nameless since I met you." She paused, breathless. "And now I find out that you've been here all along. Of all places," she put out an arm to encompass *of all places*. "This little seaside dreamscape."

"This is no dream."

"Why here?"

"Because I can't be anywhere else."

"I don't understand."

He looked down, as if it was impossible to explain, and she thought, they would have time. She could wait.

"That night, after I left you, I spent the night in one of the floating villages. Gilles met me, as planned. We drank a parting bottle of whiskey together. The next day he took me by boat to the harbor at Cat Ba, where he had arranged for my ride on a container ship headed for Egypt. I had not been back to Cairo since I left at the age of sixteen, and I wanted to go back. But then, three weeks later, the ship made its first stop at the Port of Long Beach. I did not know it would stop there, I'd put no consideration into the month-long journey, all my thoughts were dedicated to what I thought would be my last and final destination." He paused, staring quietly out the window for a few moments. "Evelyn spoke of this place often," he said, "where she grew up, with great affection. I walked off the ship—literally, right over there." He pointed down at the harbor, underneath the bridge, to where all the ships were that she'd seen on her drive over. "And didn't get back on. I walked into these streets. Walked and walked and my path took me upwards, until I was as high as I could go and I found myself here. I rented a studio. I picked up a brush for the first time since Evelyn's death and I haven't stopped painting since."

He turned to face her, his eyes wild. "Don't you see that it was her?"

Olivia took a step back. *What was her?*

"It was her that brought me here." The way he was staring at Olivia, it was as if he were seeing Evelyn. "Because part of her is here."

I'm here.

He put his hand on the drawing table to stable himself. "That day," he said. "That day you told me about the psychic . . . that you hadn't believed Evelyn was dead because it was too much of a coincidence. Well, I had never believed Evelyn dead, either. How does a living being vanish into thin air?"

"You're not angry at her?"

He didn't seem to understand the question. Olivia paced to the other end of the room, where there was a window that looked out onto the picnic table where she'd been sitting. She wondered if he had seen her from here, if he had watched her for some time. He could have left, but he didn't. "You're not angry at her for not telling you about me?"

He went to the window next to hers. Staring out, he said, "It didn't feel so much like fate. But perhaps that's what it was, running into Evelyn like that, again, after all those years." He turned to face Olivia. "I had come to Bangkok to see about an Italian plate from the 1600s recently discovered in a private collection that belonged to my family. While there, I contracted a mild form of food poisoning, and had gone to the hospital to receive treatment. While waiting for the doctors, I went to find some water that wasn't contaminated, if that was possible, for I was horribly dehydrated. I quickly got lost in the maze of crowded hallways, and as I tried to find my way back, someone grabbed my arm, the soft, frail hand of a woman lying on a gurney pushed up against a wall.

"It had been ten years but there was no question about the feel of her flesh, no question when at last I did look down at the warm hand from where this touch came, both of us soaked to the bone with illness and sweat, she though but a waif of her former self, that it was Evelyn, and so then there was no question why she was there, why I was there, why I existed at all, for this moment, this moment when our paths crossed again."

There was some silence.

"She'd been flown to Bangkok from Myanmar, where she'd contracted malaria."

Olivia pressed her hands together.

"Was it a fluke? Fate? It didn't matter," he said. "That's when I left Italy, my wife, my child. And while we were happy for a time, Evelyn and I, there was always something else. Something that was there when we were together before but had gone missing."

"But she is dead," Olivia said. "She's dead and I'm alive."

His eyes found hers, but she knew that he could not see her, and Olivia's only wish in that moment was that they were back in Hanoi, neither of them knowing anything.

"Carlotta and I, we belong to you."

"I can't give you anything."

"I don't want anything," she lied, pausing, hesitating. "It's Carlotta. She needs you."

A look of alarm, as if he'd been struck. "Is she all right?"

Olivia bit her lips. She'd promised not to say anything about the pregnancy.

He came over and grabbed her shoulders. "Tell me. Is she all right?"

Olivia gasped and stepped back and he let go. That deep-seated anger.

"She's fine. It's just . . ." Olivia paused, unsure; at times he really frightened her. "She misses you."

He turned away, distraught.

Olivia came to him. "I want to help you. How can I help you?"

"Leave me be. Leave me be!"

The walls trembled.

Olivia gasped and ran out.

32

She managed to get in the car, but was shaking so hard she couldn't get the key in the ignition. These past two years, she'd been floating on the coattails of this mystical God that didn't exist. She sped down the hill. Her phone may have buzzed but all she heard was a pounding between her ears.

Down the hill, she didn't know where she was going. Everything felt at once hollow where just an hour ago it had felt full. She began following the ocean. Before long she was driving on a road so bumpy and jarring that she'd be certain it wasn't a road if other cars were not on it. Mansions rose up on golden hills to her right, and to her left, a plunging drop to the sea toward which everything slanted and slid. Olivia leaned right to compensate. But there was no compensating.

At the first opportunity she turned inland, up one winding hill and down another. There were a series of strip malls—flat and dull and depressing. Standstill traffic. She found herself in a turn lane that led onto the 91 Freeway, and suddenly she was speeding along a road ten lanes across with throngs of evening commuters. She merged onto the 110, then the 405, the 22, whatever freeway beckoned, rivers of white light before the shadows of distant hills, a purple veil of twinkling loneliness.

Her phone had been buzzing. It kept buzzing, until at last she retrieved it from her purse to see a series of texts from Carlotta.

Did you find him?

Traffic slowed to a standstill. Olivia texted back, *He wasn't there. When will you see him?*

The detective was wrong. I'll keep looking, Carlotta. I promise.

Olivia couldn't tell her. It was clear Marco wanted nothing to do with them. And she couldn't disappoint the girl who'd already been so disappointed, losing her mother, being abandoned by her father, and now, this unwanted pregnancy. The vision was still fresh in Olivia's mind: Giorgio, who'd taken the train in from Boston the morning after Carlotta's tournament, a sniffling mess, down on one knee before Carlotta begging her to marry him, this was the solution, a man's unwavering devotion. But Carlotta remained resolute about not wanting to get married even though she loved him as much as a person could possibly love anybody. Giorgio, failing to see why Carlotta would refuse him in this way, turned pleadingly to Olivia, who'd been standing there in disbelief—*was he actually down on one knee?*—the three of them frozen in time under the stars and fairies carved into the rotunda of Grand Central station, the world a thriving, hectic mess.

Were there still princes, after all?

Princes, and then Dragon Princes.

We don't need Marco, Carlotta texted back finally. *We have each other now.*

Olivia's heart melted into her chest.

We are waiting for you in Rome. Baci.

Baci meant "kisses," Olivia had learned. *I'm sending you kisses.* It was always how Carlotta ended an exchange, and Olivia hadn't quite gotten used to it, coming from a family where one's feelings weren't shared in any deep and meaningful way. This girl was the opposite, so open about her devotion to the half-sister she never knew she had, whom she had immediately accepted wholeheartedly into her life. As if they'd always been sisters. It was strange, and Olivia blinked at the message again. *Baci.* Never before had she felt this overwhelming sense of responsibility, this obligation to give love back.

Don't have the abortion, Olivia texted before thinking.

After a pause, *che cosa?*

Have the baby. Whether you give it up for adoption or keep it. Whatever you do, just give it a chance.

Olivia knew she was being rash, selfish, overemotional, but she couldn't help it. Evelyn may not have wanted her, Marco may not want her now, but Olivia had to believe that her existence mattered.

What happened, Olivia? What changed?

At least don't do anything until I get there.

After a long pause, *Mah e' troppo tardi, Olivia.*

Olivia let up on the gas.

It's too late.

Her vision blurred slightly.

A minute later, Olivia's car phone rang. She picked it up on speaker.

"Giorgio found the money," Carlotta said. "I had the procedure yesterday."

Olivia didn't respond.

"Please don't be angry with me, Olivia."

She shook her head of it. "I'm not angry." This unbelievable sting in her eyes. "I'm sorry, Carlotta. Of course it's your choice. Just ignore me, I'm just . . ." she paused to swallow. "Tell me how you're feeling. Are you okay?"

After a pause, "Are *you* okay?"

Olivia bit down on her lip. "It's just all this news about Evelyn. And Rhonda, I can't tell when she's lying or telling the truth. I don't know who she is anymore. I just know that I can't be near her right now." She paused and wiped her nose, cleared her throat. "But forget about me. Did everything go okay? How's Giorgio?"

"He won't stop crying. But he's okay. He still insists that I marry him. I tell *zia* I have the flu. I have missed three days of lessons, and Grand Master is out of his mind, so, basically, everything is the same."

They laughed.

"You always make me feel better," Olivia said.

"But when will you arrive in Rome, Olivia?"

Rome. Olivia had almost forgotten about Rome. Where she and Carlotta were going to be a family. But what was family? "I don't know, Carlotta. I don't know where I belong."

"You must come, if only for a little while. So that we can talk about life."

Olivia's car beeped startlingly. She wiped her eyes and caught sight of the dashboard. Her gaslight was on.

"Olivia?"

She swerved the car into the exit lane. "I have to go. I'll call you from the airport."

"But you're not angry with me?"

"I'm not angry with you."

She ended the call and exited the freeway and found a gas station. Full service. Bright lights. An attendant filled her tank. She rested her head on the seatback. Closed her eyes. Opened them. Her journal had fallen out of her purse, and after staring at it absently for a moment, she picked it up and opened it. Most of the pages were blank. Olivia had not written as much as she'd thought. Doodles and scribbles and names of silly crushes. And Evelyn's story, the one with no ending, for Evelyn had not filled in one word, one single, solitary word. The attendant tapped on the window, startling her. She rolled it down and passed him her Gold Visa. He came back and said her card was rejected. She frowned. Never once had she been rejected. Rhonda was methodical about paying her bills on time.

Olivia gave the attendant her black AMEX, technically a card that should never be rejected. It came back rejected and she sat there, stunned. However awful she'd been to Rhonda earlier—the scene now flashing painfully before Olivia's mind—Rhonda would never cut Olivia off. *Would she?* Olivia pressed her head against the seat back, thinking. Then her mind spiraled into emptiness. Draining itself of everything. She stared at the notebook still open on her lap, warped, brown at the edges, exhumed-like. She pictured her tantrum-child self throwing the journal into the trash. She didn't remember what happened next, just that Evelyn had ended up with it. And the only way that could have happened, Olivia realized now, was if Evelyn had gone back into Olivia's room, retrieved the journal from the trash, and taken it with her. *And kept it with her, always. Something of Olivia's. Something to remember her by.*

She reached into her glove compartment for her insurance and registration. The car's pink slip and her passport were in her purse, where she'd stuffed them in the last minutes before leaving Scottsdale. She got out of the car, walked over to the garage, and asked if anyone knew anyone who wanted to buy an M3.

There were smirks.

"No joke."

A mechanic appeared from behind an engine. He blinked at her, then at the car behind her. "What year?"

"Two thousand eleven, five thousand miles, mint condition, sat in my Mom's garage for the past two years."

He considered it. "Leave me your number . . ."

"I need to sell it now."

"Is it hot or something?"

"I'll give you a sick price, but it's got to be cash."

He looked at her. "Let me call a guy."

A guy showed up thirty minutes later and the deal was done. She didn't haggle him. She took the thirty grand he offered her in hundreds, called a cab, and directed the driver to LAX where, after buying her ticket, she made camp on the floor because her flight wasn't boarding for six more hours. Only when she was in her seat and the plane was about to take off did she have the courage to text Carlotta and tell her that she was not coming to Rome. Not just yet.

33

How long had it been since she had seen a man nude, Rhonda wondered.

"Can I help you?" he was saying.

"What?" she looked at him, not the nude man but the instructor. So distracted was she by this specimen of luscious flesh, that she'd not noticed the instructor. He was coming toward her now, wearing jeans and an untucked dress shirt with the sleeves rolled up, looking almost exactly like she thought he'd look, with a three-day scruff, weathered and chiseled.

"Can I help you?" he repeated, a slight accent, Italian she could only assume. She shook her head no.

He looked back at the model Rhonda couldn't take her eyes from, then back at Rhonda, who, though she had no intention of painting, said, "I'd like to learn to paint." *Those muscled limbs, the faint line of fuzz that ran down from his navel.*

"We are full," he said.

She'd come here to find Olivia.

"But you can come back Thursday," he said, after some thought. "We have a spot then."

At last her eyes settled on his, to see if he was seeing her, if there was any sign of recognition though they'd never met. "What should I bring?"

He squinted slightly. "Paint."

She made her way to the taxi grabbing her chest, thinking she might be having a heart attack. And then she realized there was no taxi. It had left. She stood still, evening her breath and staring at the cloud-covered moon, contemplating what had just happened. She'd not intended to see Marco, but after Olivia had left, Rhonda had gone over to her bed and picked up the book her daughter had left behind, accidentally or not, though in this case she would have been Evelyn's daughter, because the book was *Heart of Darkness*. Rhonda had sat back onto her bed and began reading. Sometime later she looked up and realized that it had grown dark outside, and that Olivia had not texted her yet about how her meeting with Marco had gone. The book had been harrowing up to this point, leaving Rhonda feeling slightly panicked. After texting Olivia and getting nothing back, after calling and getting no answer, by 9:00 p.m., Rhonda had not been able to take it any longer. She'd called a taxi and gone to the address she had for Marco. Had she not told the driver to wait?

And now the taxi was gone.

But this was not the force of her present thoughts. The force of her thoughts was that Marco had not recognized her when she had just assumed he would, as she had recognized him, as if they had met even when they hadn't, as if they had in fact been an intimate part of each other's lives because they had in a way, a vision of him, her sister's Italian lover, emblazoned on her mind like some cover of a Harlequin romance.

Rhonda got out her phone and redialed the taxi service. Thirty minutes, they said. She went over to the bench and waited, both lulled and spooked by the quiet serenity of her surroundings, the murmur of crickets, the missing moon. She rested her head on her folded arms. She didn't know she'd fallen asleep until someone tapped her shoulder. She startled, which made Marco startle. He grabbed the cigar from his mouth and frowned, his face aglow in the shadow of a streetlamp. "Are you spending the night here?" His words came with a cloud of smoke.

"Sorry," she said, flustered. "I am waiting for my cab. I must have fallen asleep."

"You do not have a car?"

"It's in the shop."

"You will freeze to death."

"You have no idea how good the ocean air feels."

He put the cigar back in his mouth and puffed. "I must wait with you, I suppose." He glanced at his watch.

"It's not necessary."

He sat down on the bench. "It's not safe here at night."

She watched the smoke fall from his lips and dissolve into the darkness. She got out her cigarettes and put one to her mouth. "You're not from here," she said, after he lit it for her.

"Part of me is."

"And the other part?"

He took a long puff. "How did you hear of my class?"

"A friend . . . of a friend. A student of yours, I do not remember her name." And then quickly redirecting, "How long have you had the studio?"

"A few years now."

"It's beautiful here."

"It was by accident that I found it."

Headlights moved through the trees. Her cab. She got up.

"See you Thursday," he said, and she looked at him. "Yes. Thursday." She climbed inside the car. She'd forgotten about Thursday.

The cab drove off. She looked behind her just in time to see him disappear around a bend.

Kurtz was less elusive in the movie Rhonda had seen than in Conrad's book, she grumbled now, lying in bed at 2:00 a.m., unable to sleep. It was hard to decipher when Kurtz was myth versus reality. Frustrated, every so often she'd slap the book down and stare at the ceiling. Why couldn't Olivia just text her? Had she made her flight to Rome? One text? Was that too much for a mother to ask, even a lying mother like her? Apparently, yes. Rhonda picked up the book again. The night went on like that. She wanted to get to the end, which she could never seem to get to. After a while she kept succumbing to sleep, finally awoken by a band of light searing her brain, sunlight streaming through a crack in the hotel door someone had left open. Rhonda certainly had not left it open. Or had she? After that bottle of wine, who knew?

Olivia! Rhonda sat up suddenly in bed. Olivia had come back. Her heart pounded with the certainty. She looked around. No signs of her. Rhonda went to the bathroom. Nothing. Her heart sank. *Don't contact me*, Olivia had said. Would Rhonda ever hear from Olivia again? Had she even made it to the airport, or had Marco tied her up and stuffed her into a closet? He was half mad, wasn't he? Or was she the one going crazy?

Rhonda went and got the book and threw it into the trash. Olivia was in Rome. Or she would be in a few hours, and Rhonda took some breaths to calm her heart. Isabella would be there to take care of her. Kind, sweet Isabella. Not to mention Carlotta, that fierce, fencing, big-hearted girl—perhaps Rome would be Olivia's answer. Perhaps there she would finally find what she'd always been looking for.

Rhonda was late for class, not to mention discombobulated after the credit card debacle. She'd stopped off at the art store in Torrance, but when she'd slapped down her credit card on the counter to pay for her overabundance of supplies, it was denied. It took her a minute to process what the cashier had said. Then she got out another credit card, and another.

She'd called her accountant.

"I left you ten messages, Rhonda. You didn't return my calls."

"I was traveling. And I thought you were going to harass me about the house. I told you to just sell it, finally, like Daniel wants. Lower the price, do whatever you have to," she'd cried out suddenly. "I don't care. I want the monstrosity gone!" The cashier had startled, and Rhonda flashed him a pained smile.

"It's a bit late, Rhonda. The family from Vermont pulled out of escrow. They found something else."

"Then find a new family from Vermont. Meanwhile, can you please move some money around, whatever it is you do to get money into my account?"

"There's no money to transfer. You don't get another royalty payment for another two weeks."

"I have a thousand dollars in my bank account."

"I can call Daniel."

"Fuck Daniel," she'd said, and hung up.

The cashier had looked at her. She'd looked at the pile of goods splayed out on the counter, picked out a drawing pencil, and paid for that with cash.

Now she was seated before a clean, white canvas propped up on an easel with nothing to paint it with. Beside her was a large, middle-aged woman painting a forest of some kind, various shades of fuzzy greens and browns, maybe not a forest, maybe something else.

"I work down on the docks," the woman said, sitting back and scrutinizing her progress. "This is what I see all day."

Rhonda allowed her eyes to relax, and soon, the mossy hull of a ship appeared in her vision, gliding along the water. "It's incredible."

"They sell like gangbusters."

"Then why are you here?"

The woman nodded in the direction of Marco. "I think he's why all the women are here."

Rhonda counted four women and two men, one of whom sat beside her, music thumping from his earphones, stroking wildly at the canvas. It was sort of alarming the way he was going at it.

"No model today?" she asked Marco when he passed by.

"I didn't think you were ready."

"Probably not."

She pulled out her pencil. "Where do I start?"

"Where are your paints?"

I was supposed to bring paint?

"Paint is usually a good thing to have. Especially when you're in a painting class."

She tilted her head at the canvas. "I like the canvas the way it is now—clean, untainted." An attempt at levity, which he ignored.

"I have all my new students start with a self-portrait."

She glanced over at the thumper's canvas—a black bowl was coming to life. Or was it a black hole? Marco turned to observe it for a moment. The guy gave a satisfied nod to Marco, who then turned to Rhonda and said, "We all see ourselves differently."

"I've never painted before," Rhonda admitted. "But when I was a kid I liked to draw."

"My students are of all levels. We each work at our own pace."

"Wouldn't it be easier if I had a picture of myself?"

"The picture is in your mind," he said.

"A mirror?"

"No mirror." He walked off. Then came back with a board of paints and a brush. "No pencil." He took it from her. "Just paint."

It turned out to be easy, herself appearing, first in the sand, then the waves, the sky, the sun. Rhonda, in an impressionistic splattering of greens, blues, and yellows. Sometimes clouds. A seagull. A sailboat. Figures, people. Limbs. Every once in a while, she'd glance over at the black bowl, or hole, which was growing bigger, more hollow. "A vortex," she said to him, and he nodded to the music.

Marco appeared over her shoulder sometime later. "I don't see you," he said.

She tilted her head at it. "I'm there."

He took the canvas away and replaced it with a new one. "Start again."

After class Rhonda lingered, pretending to be looking for something in her bag. By the time she left, hers was the last car in the lot, a rental she would now have to keep until she got her accounts settled and could pay off the bill, for she was not going to call Daniel. She'd wait out the two weeks until her royalty payment came through, the royalties on the patents that were set to expire in a matter of months. A reality she needed to face soon. Someday. Until then she'd sit here in this driver's seat of the car she couldn't afford and let time pass, contemplating this idea of following Marco, assuming that he would leave the building at some point, but she was starting to wonder. Time was passing by. Then she spotted him at the cliff, lighting his cigar with what looked like a small blowtorch. He stood smoking and looking out at the ocean.

Someday is now, she told herself, getting out of her car.

He did not seem surprised when she walked up.

The wind had died. The moon was veiled in a charcoal fog. He lit her cigarette, and they smoked in silence.

"That painting in the window of your studio . . . I'd like to buy it from you."

His eyes pinched slightly. "It's not for sale," he said, puffing on his cigar.

"Why not?"

"My work is not for sale," he glared pointedly at her and she waved smoke away from her face as if to say, *I wasn't really serious*. "It's okay," she said, and then feebly, "I don't have the money anyway."

He looked at her strangely.

"In fact, I need to find a job."

"Yes, well, isn't that the way of the world."

"So they say. It's been a while since I've had to, well, try."

"What do you do?"

She looked at him and almost laughed. She could not recall the last time she was asked that question. Everyone knew what she did. She was Rhonda, a woman to be reckoned with. Fixer, maker of dreams, that's who she was.

Who she *had* been.

"That's the problem. Things sort of just came to me."

"You mean money?"

"Yes, I suppose that's what I mean."

"And what did you do with your money?"

"I gave it away."

"I see. Then what are you looking to do?"

She looked at him. Now that the question had been put out there, it was like she'd been waiting for it all her life. She knew exactly the answer. It was so clear in her mind for once that she felt swept away, gliding in some dream, so weightless that she forgot to even answer his question, or what his question was.

"I'm going inside now." He was putting out his cigar.

Her heart jumped. *I could just ask him,* she thought, *ask him if he'd seen Olivia.*

"Can I presume you won't be following me?"

Rhonda stamped out her cigarette. "You can presume so, yes." And then, as he walked back toward the building from whence they came, she called out to him, "Do you live here?"

"These are commercial studios," he said.

"No one lives here?"

"It would be illegal," he said, and continued walking.

At the next class, Rhonda tried to picture the shape of her own face. It was the most difficult part. An oval? Circle? Box? A sphere morphed hastily out from the brush, and she quickly moved on to the hair. Always long, a ponytail, a streak of sun-washed brown dangling down her back.

"You think I come here to learn?"

Rhonda looked up.

The woman was glancing suggestively at Marco.

Rhonda smiled furtively and continued working, though she couldn't help keeping an eye on his movements. He wasn't complementary with his students; every once in a while he'd burst into some kind of passionate diatribe about something he'd see on a canvas. He frustrated easily, it seemed.

"There are rumors going around." The woman had leaned in, Rhonda now her confidante, apparently.

"Witness protection program," the guy to her right leaned over and offered. His earphones were off, and Rhonda hadn't realized he'd been listening.

"Someone told me he's a prince."

"He's Asian."

"Thai."

"European, for sure."

"He lives over the studio and keeps to himself."

"His wife died."

Rhonda went on with her work as if it was none of her business. Marco came by a few times to observe. He said little, and his proximity made her nervous. He smelled like sweat and tears. With him there, she was forced to stop and actually see her progress, this version of herself. One eye was lower than the other, the mouth sideways, the nose disjointed, her face as if seen through a kaleidoscope.

"The hair is interesting," he said.

"It's out of proportion," she said.

"That's the point," he said. "Now we'll learn proportion. Balance. Perception. Depth."

"Are we still talking about painting?"

He gave her a sidelong glance.

"Is this where I find my inner self?"

"The mouth," he said. His eyes hadn't left the canvas.

She looked at the mouth—a slash, a straight line.

"I like it," he said. One more penetrating gaze, and he walked off.

"He sells prints at the street market on Saturdays," the woman told Rhonda as she was packing up her things at the end of class. "In case you wanted to take a closer look."

That Saturday Rhonda drove around town looking for this street fair that ended up being down by the docks. After she parked, she wandered around the stalls for a while, finally spotting him seated on a folding chair under a tent, reading a book. Framed prints of all kinds hung against makeshift walls. There were even more of them stacked in bins, unframed.

"You again," he said.

"I'm not stalking you," she said, walking up to one of the bins and flipping through the prints, maps mostly, ancient ruins. "I thought you said your work was not for sale."

"This isn't my work."

"Oh."

"It's my livelihood."

"Maps?"

"Antique prints. The work of others recreated over and over."

She paused on one print. Unlike the others this one was bright with color, an Asian theme—elephants and animals in a parade of dance and song, and Rhonda gazed at it for a long minute. A wedding parade, and it struck her, and with some force, that this was the cave he had taken Olivia to, the one she'd described in her half-delusional state, the cave that Rhonda would not have believed existed if not for having seen some crude version of the drawing inside one of Evelyn's journals, where she had written about having seen the carving in a cave on some mystical island, and that, some day, she'd take Marco there, if only in her dreams.

She asked him how much.

"I thought you didn't have any money."

"I think I must buy this for someone I know. I think she would like this very much."

He showed her the price tag.

"Jesus."

"It's one of the first runs. It's a collector's item."

"Collectors come here?"

"They'll show up anywhere."

Water the color of jade. Elephants flanked in jewels, gold, and silks carried a bride while the groom followed on foot among birds, flowers, and temples. In the periphery other scenes of domesticity played out, scenes within scenes. There was so much to discover, this world, but only if you chose to see it, if you took the time to see it, as her sister had done.

"Where is this place?"

"It's not so much a place as an idea, a symbol. A fable, actually."

Why were her knees buckling? Had he shown Olivia this print when she came to see him? What had he said to her? He remained entirely unreadable. She'd never met someone so unreadable. As unreadable as her.

He cleared off a chair to indicate that she should sit down.

She stayed where she was, still gripping the print. "Please tell it to me."

"The fable," she added, and while he told her the story of the Dragon Prince, and the woman who left half her children, it was as if she were following along with Evelyn's scribbles, which were morphing into Olivia's words—all of their voices together. As if they'd all been together, as it was perhaps intended.

"But it is a place?"

"Yes."

"And you've been to it?"

After a pause, "Yes."

He narrowed his eyes then, perhaps sensing a sudden stillness in her. He was looking at her cautiously now, as if he'd given away something he shouldn't have. But then he seemed to shrug it off, and Rhonda thought that perhaps he'd realized that she was no one of consequence, that she hadn't been anyone of consequence in a very long time.

He pulled out two beers from his cooler, twisted off the caps, and handed her one.

A man came in, perused the prints for a while, left.

"Hungry?" he asked.

"Starving."

"Hold on." He got up and walked off.

Five minutes later he was back with two tamales from a Mexican woman who sold them illegally from a shopping cart she never kept in the same location for more than a few minutes. "One never knows exactly where to find her," Marco told Rhonda, handing her one. She bit into it—spicy as hell. "Oh, my God," she said.

"I know, right?" he said.

34

They began with still life, something Rhonda would have thought pointless years ago. Still life was dull. Still life was boring.

"I want to paint portraits."

"You'll start with this vase."

There was something about Marco. He was the kind of man, when he spoke, you listened, his tone disarming at times, and yet there was always that tinge of irony. Sometimes she had to remind herself of the game she was playing, she'd have to kick herself for almost blowing it, for saying something he might recognize about her and Evelyn's shared past.

She focused in on the vase, and out of everything else—what went against every fiber of her being. The self-indulgence of it, the purposelessness, she wasn't helping anybody. Nobody was being helped. But in this moment there was nobody, just this rim that she couldn't seem to shade right, the shaft of light on the base looked more like a splotch, the rich texture of cobalt seemed like it was melting.

The next thing she knew class was over and she felt cleansed, as if she'd been to another place entirely. Even the woman beside her looked different. More like a talking head, something about an awful divorce, and this online dating service she'd joined. The men were horrid. But what else was she going to do? She couldn't be alone. Could she?

She and Marco were outside having what was now their customary postclass smoke. "I had a dream last night that I was being chased by elephants."

He looked at her. Was she making a joke?

Yes. She was. "Seriously," she said, "I can't get that wedding parade out of my mind. It's . . ." she couldn't find a way to describe what she was feeling.

"Playful," he said.

"That's it," she said. "How life should be."

"It's a moment," he said.

He was peering at her now. "You remind me of someone."

"Are you married?" she asked, and he looked off suddenly. He took a puff from his cigar. Smoke filled the air. "I loved a woman once," he said.

When he did not go on, she said, "I'm sorry."

"It feels like a long time ago."

She inhaled smoke, trying to keep her hands from shaking. When she could speak again, she said, "There was someone I loved once too." She looked down the hillside, at the road that edged the water.

"It is the fate of all of us, I suppose."

"To love someone?"

"To lose someone. Someone we love."

She looked off. "People say that grief must be shared. But I think they're wrong. No one understands."

"Grief is between you and your maker."

She noticed the cross around his neck. "Do you believe in God?"

He smirked. "The Man is part of my fiber. The reason why I have made so many mistakes. . . ."

"And yet . . ."

"And yet, I have never had the courage to turn away."

She asked him if he had children.

"All these questions."

"Sorry." And then, "Well?"

"Yes. And you?"

"No children," she said. It wasn't a complete lie. She didn't have biological children. And her acquired children wanted nothing to do with her. "My husband and I decided that we didn't need children." She paused, cautiously. "We were happy together, content to go it alone." In the back of her mind was something Evelyn had told her, when she'd come to Rhonda wanting the abortion. The child would be the end of her and Marco. The child would tear them apart. "But you already are apart!" It would come between anything they had ever had. It was so contrary to Rhonda's beliefs back then, her beliefs now. It defied logic, for a child was the ultimate consummation of love, what sealed the marriage and, without a child, well . . .

"And?"

She felt his eyes on her.

"How did that work out for you?"

"Not well," she said, meeting his gaze with a fleeting smile. A long moment went by. "It's been a long time since I've been happy."

She held still for his reaction. A flinch, a shift, but there was nothing. In fact, everything about him said that he understood. Perhaps he'd seen something in her eyes that mirrored his own, which was that neither of them would be happy again. Not in the true sense, anyway.

"Do you want to get something to eat?" she asked. It came out desperate, a surprise to them both. "Just something quick, or whatever. Or not. We don't have to." She'd switched her tone to upbeat and casual, though it was too late. It was as if he'd seen right through her and perhaps he had. He was walking away.

She looked down.

"You coming?" he said.

She looked up. He'd turned around and was waiting.

She ran to catch up with him.

Above his studio was a small room with a bath and a half kitchen.

"I thought you said . . ."

"Nobody knows."

He pulled a pot from a nail on the wall and set it on the burner. "I made Kushari last night. I hope you don't mind."

She couldn't possibly pronounce it.

"Don't worry, you'll like it."

He pulled out a variety of Tupperware containers from the half fridge and began pulling off the lids. Rice, chickpeas, lentils, caramelized onions: he took big spoonfuls from each container and added them to the pot, mixing in red wine and different, colored spices from Ziploc bags. "Traditionally, you're supposed to add pasta and tomatoes," he said. "But, for me, an Italian, there can be no mixing." As he focused on what he was doing, Rhonda glanced idly about looking for signs, a lost pearl perhaps, something Olivia may have left behind. Some indication that she had been here. But there was none, the place was sparse and meticulous and absent of memento. And yet, this pungency filled her lungs, this hazy veil of desperation. Magnetism. Her eyes on him again, so methodical and intent about what he was doing. Those long graceful limbs and pensive, brooding features.

He cleaned and put away everything right after he used it. The problem was that he had only one fork and one plate. So he gave her the fork and served her with the plate, and he ate the rest directly out of the pan with chopsticks, ripping off hunks of bread for both of them. "You don't mind, do you?"

She shook her head.

He devoured the Kushari and it was difficult not to watch him. They did not speak.

For her part, an explosion of flavors.

"Is that licorice?"

"Anise."

She didn't ask what anise was, but apparently it tasted like licorice.

They ate seated on the floor in front of the coffee table, something she and Evelyn used to do when they were kids.

"This would have been barbaric in my world," he said, about the lack of chairs. "But one makes certain compromises."

"Yes, one does," she agreed, sucking on her lips, and not because her mouth was burning from whatever spices he'd added—cayenne, ginger, cinnamon, mustard seed— but because she was smiling, secretly, for he had no idea that she understood why a man like him would find comfort eating seated on a floor before a coffee table.

He poured red wine from a bottle with no label. It was dry, and, not surprisingly, much better than the cheap liquor store bottles she'd been drinking in her hotel.

"Is this an Indian dish?"

"Egyptian."

She took another tentative bite.

"You don't like it?"

After a pause. "It's interesting."

"I ate it often when I was growing up."

She looked at him, confused.

"I grew up in Egypt."

This surprised her. "I thought you said you were Italian."

"Half Italian. Half Greek." He was wiping his plate clean with his bread. When he was done, Rhonda thought that he might not even need to wash it.

"How did you end up in Egypt?"

"Oh, it's a long, sordid, and very uninteresting story."

"I doubt that."

"Trust me."

"Fine. I don't need to know. But it must have been strange. What was it like? Growing up there?"

"Besides the fact that we were discriminated against, most of the time . . ." he paused, narrowed his eyes in thought. Then he seemed to put that thought, whatever it was, behind him because suddenly he softened, a distant smile touching his lips. "Summers. That's what I'll remember always, with great fondness, living with my grandmother. Old but never frail, people were afraid of her but not me, she could never stand airs, or her sons. But me, I could do no wrong. Whatever I wanted, if it was to run around in the streets all day barefoot like an urchin, then so be it."

He seemed to lose his train of thought.

"Is that where your children are?"

He looked at her, as if waking from a dream.

"I moved to Rome when I was sixteen." He set down his plate.

"Do you miss it?" And when he didn't answer, she added, "Rome."

"No."

"Is it where she died?"

He pulled the napkin out from his collar. "I never said she died."

Rhonda thought he might get up and walk out. "Sorry . . . I just assumed."

"Near there," he added reluctantly, pouring more wine.

"Will you go back?"

"If I go back, I can't return."

She frowned.

"My visa is no longer valid."

"Oh."

"I am here on borrowed time."

"Isn't this the part where you find someone to marry?"

He looked at her straight in the eye. "I am already married."

"Oh. I see."

He grabbed his wine glass but did not drink from it. The vein appeared on his forehead. He was growing uncomfortable, if not annoyed, she could tell, at the circular futility of their discussion. As for her, she could play the game all night, and was about to probe more because she knew that he was not married but in his dreams. But then, perhaps it was the wine, the dense weight of the first home-cooked meal she'd had in a while, she felt comatose suddenly, as if she'd been drugged. Dizzy. Something strange was happening.

"Are you all right?"

"I don't know," she said.

"You are tired."

She stood up. "I should be going."

"Can you drive?"

"It was wonderful. The Kush . . ."

"Kushari."

"Yes. That. I have been living off of ramen noodles."

He seemed shocked by this. "You cannot eat in this way. It is not healthy. What is wrong with you?"

She blushed, profusely. *Was he actually worried?*

He went somewhere. She got up, which wasn't so easy. He returned with the print. "Take it, if you want."

"But I can't pay for it."

He waved it off. "Don't worry. It's a knockoff."

There was a pause. "You lied?"

"Yes."

"Do you lie to everyone?"

"Only you."

She bit her lip. She slid the print under her arm. She wasn't going to argue. She left.

35

Rhonda was unable to sleep that night.

The strangeness lingered.

It was hard to imagine that Olivia had not called Rhonda by now, demanding to know why her credit cards were not working. Had she come to the rash, illogical conclusion that Rhonda had cut her off? And how was Olivia paying for herself?

Rhonda switched on the light and began texting Olivia, assuring her that her mother had not cut her off, that there had been this little mix-up with the accounts, etc., that she was working it out, that it was temporary—but it became too cumbersome to text so she deleted it and, instead, decided to call. But when she got Olivia's voicemail, she hung up. Something inside her told her to stop. Just stop. Perhaps it was better to have Olivia far away. Rhonda didn't know what to do for the girl anymore. There was nothing she could do for her, except perhaps to cut her off. Perhaps their present financial situation was Rhonda's only chance at tough love. Perhaps it was what both of them needed.

Because they weren't that different, Olivia and her.

Both of them had been spoiled.

She lay there like this until dawn broke, the caw of seagulls beckoned, and the thick stench of kelp aroused her senses. She could almost taste the salt on her lips.

What day was it? She checked her phone, though she probably didn't need to. The fog outside her window told her everything: it was early September, still too early for first semester classes to begin at UCLA, but not for double days. She threw on sweats and flip-flops and climbed into her rental car as if by rote, headed in the direction of campus, her headlights on, wiping the fog from her windows, praying she wouldn't get sideswiped from an oncoming car, unable to see but ten feet in front of her. Along the ocean, past the oil pumps, she cruised by the three-story house she and a few other select teammates had been afforded as part of their full rides. Though it didn't seem as huge as she remembered, weather-worn, plastic toys littering the front yard.

She shivered, a deep arctic chill. The car heater had yet to kick in. She rubbed her hands together at a red light, ensconced in the aura of so many half-awake mornings just like this one, racing her car to campus and getting her butt to the training room, so that she could get iced and taped in time to make 7:00 a.m. warm-ups.

She parked in the visitors' parking, Lot D, not her usual spot. Her usual spot was in Lot A, front-row faculty parking—a special sticker that came with her university-issued SUV. Now, it might take her a good fifteen minutes to walk through campus to get to the athletic facility, but no matter how massive and sprawling the campus was, Rhonda could navigate it blindfolded. She made a pilgrimage through the quad, a school of twenty thousand and still, never fewer than a dozen people used to nod in her direction. High-fives all around. Great game last night, Stevenson.

This morning, it was eerily empty.

At last she came upon the athletic facility which sat on the west end of campus, her heart beating with anticipation, which was when it occurred to her to ask herself why she'd come here, for what purpose other than to sit and breathe in the aura of what had essentially been her home for four years. Only now, when she did arrive, she discovered that that aura had been demolished.

A gigantic, multilayered glass-and-steel structure had taken the place of the facility. Bright, pristine, an architectural extravaganza that reminded her of the Denver airport. After recovering from the shock, and then discovering that all the entrance doors had key codes, she wasn't sure what to do. She hovered, and when a couple of girls in sweats and flip-flops not unlike hers went in, Rhonda strode in right behind them as if full of purpose, following them all the way down the hall and into the locker room, smiling as if she knew what she was doing, because, well, even now, she did.

These things didn't ever leave you.

Even if the lockers were no longer metal but washed wood. Punch keys, no padlocks, and instead of benches each member had her own personal cubicle. Steam rooms, private showers, the towels were ridiculously soft. But if the look and feel was different, the sounds were familiar, the smells. Through the far double doors she could hear the din of practice starting, the squeaks and grunts of those first few laps, the aroma of sweat and funk, that sleepy energy in the air.

Memories don't go down with buildings.

This was the first time in twenty-two years that she'd been back.

Memories make up the core of who you are, she thought.

She waited until the locker room cleared out, until she heard the sounds of flailing bodies, a sign that warm-ups had ended and the real practice had begun, before entering the gym so that the coaches would be too distracted to notice her. Practices were never for public consumption, in her day, anyway. She took a seat in the partially open stands whose seats were, if she was not mistaken, electrically warmed cushions, and sat unmoving, perfectly still, watching. She could sit here, in this manner, all day, but then, about twenty minutes into the session, an assistant coach came over, as Rhonda knew he would, and asked if he could help her.

No, she wasn't a recruiter.

No, she wasn't someone's family or friend.

No, she wasn't from the press.

She nodded upwards, toward the rafters, where an All-American jersey hung with the name Stevenson on it, and he said, "Hey! Cool." He was half her age, and certainly didn't remember what contribution she'd ever made. Class of '83. They'd won everything, and three of them went on to play in the Olympics. . . .

He shook her hand. "Want to meet the team?"

She said, "I just want to sit here and watch, if that's okay."

"Of course," he said, heading back and rejoining the practice. There were some whispers and nods and even a wave or two from a few of the players, those who had the good graces to pretend they knew who she was, for a moment, anyway, before getting back to their drills.

Rhonda smiled wistfully back. These girls, the young and thriving, the bold and the glorious, and Rhonda, who'd planned on staying only a short while, stayed for the entire practice, dialed in, strategizing under her breath, anticipating plays, analyzing each player, their strengths and weaknesses, planning their rotations. A captain she would always be.

She glanced at her watch. It was 10:00 a.m. The girls were winding down, finishing their last volleyball scrimmage, after which they'd shower, head to the dining hall for breakfast, go back to their rooms and sleep for a couple hours, and then be back in the gym by one o'clock to do it all over again.

She stood up, which was not easy; her butt had fallen asleep.

She headed for the exit doors, pausing for one last peek upwards, she couldn't help herself; the best four years of her life were lived in that jersey hanging up there. It was a truth she'd never been afraid to admit, if only to herself, and just then a ball whacked her directly between the shoulder blades. It hit hard, and almost knocked her flat on her face. Luckily, she managed to stay upright, and after standing there stunned for a long, pounding moment, she turned around. It had been an errant spike, no doubt, though the rally played on as if nothing had happened, and Rhonda walked out of the gym, unnoticed.

She headed back through campus, telling herself to laugh it off. But, in reality, it stung like hell. She could feel the perfect red circle forming on her back now, the bull's-eye of her humiliation. She supposed she deserved that. She got a vision of herself climbing the rafters to get the jersey down, and then setting it afire. She was staring down at her feet, smirking at the idea when, all of the sudden, she looked up and thought she might be lost. She was smack in front of the education building, which stood on the south side of campus, the complete opposite direction of Lot D.

She had been here once before, a million years ago, to enroll in the postgrad teaching program, which she'd never done. It had been an ideal so entangled with her and Bill's future that when that future ended, so did her ideal. She thought of all the money she'd donated to programs in support of coaches and teachers throughout the years—but had never actually done anything about it herself. Like becoming a teacher, or a coach. Like making the difference herself.

She went inside, and came out with a brochure for the teaching program and an appointment with a counselor for the following week. Apparently, according to the brochure, if she enrolled for this fall, in one year she could have her own classroom. And once she had her classroom, she could apply for a coaching position. She squinted up at the sun, which had broken through the clouds, dissipating the fog and soothing the bruise on her back. All around her: life, the campus now pulsing with it—early registration, orientation—a group of freshman being led around with their parents, parents younger than Rhonda, she couldn't help but notice.

She spent some time at the college bookstore. Bought a baseball hat. She drove around. She sat on the beach and watched the surfers. Then she went to the Mexican dive down in Santa Monica where she and her teammates used to hang out at. To find it still standing was not so miraculous, she supposed, though slightly disconcerting. *People who grow up at the beach never leave the beach.* That went for dive owners too.

What was surprising was to find her old teammate, Lea, behind the bar, now the dive owner. Short, stocky, with that golden, ageless Hawaiian skin: there was no question it was her. If Rhonda played wide receiver, then Lea was her quarterback. Her setter, the girl who made Rhonda look better than she was. They'd become best friends the moment they met, they the team troublemakers, the rabble-rousers— "Work hard, play hard" their motto—and they laughed about it now, once Lea recognized that it was her friend and her mouth fell open; they laughed until they cried.

"You've been in town for how long and are just coming to see me now?"

"I thought you went back to Hawaii."

Lea was divorced as well. No kids.

"I was sorry to hear about Evelyn."

Rhonda nodded, understanding that it was something Lea had to say, something everyone Rhonda encountered from her past had to say. Evelyn had come to a lot of the games. Everyone knew her, loved her. Lea poured them each a tequila shot. They raised their glasses. "For Evelyn," they said, because Evelyn would have wanted that. But Lea wasn't stupid, she quickly changed the subject.

"Did you hear about Carston?"

"No."

"She's coaching the U1 team at USC."

Rhonda nodded. "No surprise there. And Phillips? What happened to her?"

Lea motioned her hand as if she were tipping a glass to her lips.

Rhonda raised her own glass, indicating that it was empty.

Lea poured more. "You missed some crazy reunions."

"I wanted to come."

Raising a brow, "You fell off the face of the earth."

"I moved to Arizona."

"She who hates the desert."

"Yeah, I probably should have thought of that. You seeing anyone?"

Lea smirked. "A variety of first dates, first drinks, coffees—a guy sees my profile online and thinks I'm all *Hawaii Five-O*. The first thing they ask me is if I surf. Then I tell them I'm half Japanese." She cocked her head. "I rarely get calls for the second date."

"I saw Bill," Rhonda said.

Lea shot her a look.

"Believe it," Rhonda said, taking Lea through the story. It felt good to talk about it with someone who knew what she and Bill had been about. Lea, like everyone, didn't know what exactly had happened, just that, suddenly, Bill was in Italy, and married.

"He got her pregnant."

"The lout."

"I wonder if I was ever in love with him."

Lea contemplated that for a moment.

"If I've ever been in love at all."

More shots. They went back and forth with their memories, until it occurred to Rhonda that the shots might not be a good idea. They had another just to make sure, and then they talked about all the other things they always used to talk about, endlessly, and it felt good, as if no time had passed at all between them, between Rhonda and this place and these waves and this warmth.

After Rhonda left, buzzed and out of sorts, on a whim she decided to stop by Marco's studio. It was a dumb idea, especially given the look on his face when he saw her through the glass door. He came over to let her in and got a whiff of her breath. "I can't believe you drove."

"I'm not drunk," she assured him.

He went back to his desk where he'd been sifting through some prints and did not respond.

She came over and picked one up. "What's this?"

He carefully removed it from her hands. "I take it you haven't been to Italy."

A guffaw escaped her. "I've been to Italy."

"Then you should know what this is."

"I didn't see many sights," she said dryly. "Is it valuable?"

"These are first runs. So, yes."

"Okay, now I remember this place," she said, picking up the print again. She and Evelyn had gone to the Pantheon the morning of their arrival, killing time before they could check into their hotel (and before Rhonda headed off for her fateful surprise visit to Bill), meandering down some cobbled side street, in a state of jet-lagged stupor, when suddenly they came upon it. That brooding dome, as if someone had misplaced it.

The crowds had yet to gather. They went inside. It was very peaceful, they both immediately felt it. Evelyn went and stood in a shaft of light that was streaming through the big hole at the dome's center. The picture so indelible in Rhonda's mind, her sister standing there with her head dropped back, eyes closed, arms out, as if giving in to whatever it was she was feeling—*come, take me.*

Marco took the print from Rhonda, again.

She opened her eyes, unaware that they'd been closed.

"Please, sit down," he said, sarcastically, because she'd already done so, right there on the sofa chair, and rather indelicately.

"You're right. I'm drunk."

"Really," he said dryly.

"I went out with a friend from college. A girl," she quickly felt the need to add for reasons unknown to her. "Tequila was always our vice." She hiccupped. He frowned, then went away somewhere and returned with a glass of water.

"Nothing changes," she said, taking a sip.

He got busy with his prints again.

"People, relationships. I haven't seen Lea in twenty-some years, and it will always be the same. We'll always be in college."

She wasn't sure he was listening. "Did you go to college?"

"I attended private boarding schools in Egypt," he said, without looking up. "And after moving to Rome went to university there, where I shared classes with thousands of other students, and learned little from the experience."

"College was the best four years of my life," she assured him, pointing at the new Bruins baseball cap on her head, which was pounding.

"The best four years of your life should be the four years ahead of you." He still hadn't looked up.

"Oh, please," she scoffed. "Can you, of all people, really say that?"

He didn't respond.

"Well, I'm not going to pretend."

"Then why are you here?" he asked.

"Because I know you feel the same way."

"And what way is that?"

"That the good years are behind you." The room was swirling.

"You're wrong," he said.

"Then why aren't you with your children?"

"What do children have to do with this?"

She wasn't exactly sure anymore.

"My children are grown," he said. "They're living their lives."

"So you just write them off?"

A tiny vein began pulsing along his temple. She worried it might burst. "Let's change the subject," she said.

"Good idea."

He shuffled some papers. He went somewhere, came back.

"Guess what?" she said.

He wasn't in the mood to guess what, so she told him. "I'm going to be a teacher."

A bottle cracked open. "I thought the best years of your life were over."

"Well, it's not like I'm going to curl up into a ball and die," which was exactly what she was doing now, in the chair, except for the dying. "No, you're right," she slurred. "I'm so tired of looking to the past. I want to look to the future. It's just a start. I mean, I'm sure we're just kidding ourselves," she paused for his reassurance, which didn't come. "Anyway, Lea coaches in a club league and she thinks there might be a spot for me." She paused, because she'd not admitted this out loud in over two decades. "I've always wanted to coach." With that came an uncontrollable giggle.

"You were an athlete?" Finally, something she'd said that interested him.

"What did you think I was? A painter?" Another giggle.

"What sport?" he wanted to know.

"Fencing," came from her. "Oops, I meant volleyball," she corrected, and something went quiet. Everything but him, perfectly still now, was spinning around her.

She didn't remember anything after that.

36

Rhonda woke the next morning in the bed in her hotel room, naked from the waist down. The Bruins cap sat perched on the lampshade, her shoes lay in kicked-off positions across the room. She thought, hard and long, about how she'd gotten here, but little came to her, other than the fact that there was a reason she didn't drink tequila anymore. She didn't want to know how she'd gotten here.

Marco. What had she said to him, and what the hell had happened to her pants?

She threw off the covers and went to the window. Her car was in the lot. He must have driven her home, she thought, with a rush of blood to her face. She moaned, for longer than she would have thought possible, and then she went and found her cell, which was buried in her sheets.

She began scrolling through her emails, if only as a distraction from the memories, which were slowly filtering back. There was an email from Isabella regarding Knight's sponsorship of Carlotta's upcoming fencing season. Then an email from the new executive director Stevie had hired to run the fund, saying that she'd canceled the fencing sponsorship for this year. Along with a list of all the other projects she was cutting. *Fine*, Rhonda thought, *I'll use my own money for Carlotta's sponsorship*. Rhonda called her accountant. Had the transfer come through yet?

"I was going to talk with you about this. I think your best option at this point is to file for bankruptcy."

She was about to say something. . . .

"It's not as bad as it sounds, Rhonda. The government will take ownership of your house and sell it at estate prices. Which will be a steal for them, but still plenty of cash for you. They'll sell off everything, including Olivia's New York loft. It will all be taken care of."

"Do it," she said.

He'd not expected that answer. "We should meet and discuss this in more depth, Rhonda. Let's not do anything rash."

"I said do it."

"Chase and Stevie will have a say, I'm sure. Olivia . . ."

"This is not theirs to say."

"It's their inheritance."

"I've given them their inheritance. I've given them everything I have."

"You'll need to come back and sign some papers."

"Send me the papers. I'm not coming back."

There was a pause.

"You'll still need to come to court, once we have a date."

"Whatever, fine. You know where to reach me."

She hung up. Bankruptcy. She stood still and thought. It almost sounded glamorous.

She wrote back to Isabella and told her that she was sorry but there would be no contribution this year. But, not to worry, she knew where to find Carlotta's new sponsor. . . . Her own finances were in disarray, and the truth of the matter was, she was broke. It felt good to say it out loud, which she did now. "I'm broke." Or broken. She let out a wicked laugh and continued typing. Feel free to announce to the world that I'm broken. Please tell Carlotta to let Olivia know that her mother is broke. That she didn't cut her off, that, in fact, they were now both cut off unless Olivia wanted to call her father, if she hadn't already.

Her father in this scenario being Daniel, not Marco. It occurred to

Rhonda to wonder if Isabella knew the truth about Olivia, if Carlotta had told her and it was all out in the open now, though Isabella had made no reference to it in her email to Rhonda.

There was a knock at her door. She went still, listening to her heart pound. Then she went for the door, at which point she realized she had on no pants. She threw on some shorts that lay within arm's reach, and when at last she opened the door Marco was there, holding two cups of coffee and a brown paper bag, looking haggard, a mess.

"You brought me home."

As if he might not know.

She widened the door to let him through.

He set the bag and coffees on the table strewn with week-old newspapers, an empty bottle of wine, and half-eaten cups of ramen noodles, which he eyed conspicuously.

Her clothes were everywhere but inside the drawers, both queen beds were unmade, and her dirty laundry was piled on the floor by the window.

"It's a mess," she said. And then, sighing, "I'm a mess."

"Evelyn said you were a slob."

They held eyes for a moment, until Rhonda gave in and exhaled, "I don't know if I'd go that far." She paced around nervously, picking up undergarments from the floor and the chair.

"Mind you, Evelyn said it in the most endearing manner."

"I bet." The pile of clothes in her arms was getting bigger. "What time did you bring me home?"

"Two."

"And you've been . . ."

"Walking."

"All night?"

"Yes."

She sat down on the bed holding the clothes.

He said, "So this was what? Some sort of test?"

Avoiding his gaze, "It wasn't planned. I came to your studio looking for Olivia, and then . . ." She looked at him, full of abandon. "How did you figure it out?"

"Evelyn had a Bruins cap also. But hers was old, worn; she never traveled without it."

Rhonda nodded at the floor, *my* cap, she didn't say. She had always wondered where it had gone.

"She had a sister who played volleyball in the Olympics." His voice rose. "For heaven's sake, I used to sit on the rocks and watch Evelyn and Carlotta pass back and forth that volleyball for hours!" His eyes grew dark and distant. These were things he did not want to remember. "I want to know why you did this to me."

"I don't know!" she cried into the reverberating silence.

It took a moment for it to settle.

"Curiosity?" She offered meekly. "Loneliness?" She let go of the clothes she'd been holding, watched them trickle to the floor. "Maybe I just wanted to be someone else for a while."

A shadow came over the room. "All I wanted was to be left alone," he said. He began pacing. "I have nothing to give anyone." He'd paused as he said it, as if even he didn't seem so sure anymore.

"Is this what you told Olivia?"

His silence meant yes.

"You know she changed her life for you. After Hanoi, she enrolled at NYU. She finally followed through on something all on her own—this, after I spent her entire life screwing her up." She took a breath. "And it was all because of you."

"I told her to move on."

After a pause, "That's what you told her!" Tears came to her eyes. "At some point, Marco, you're going to realize that there is nowhere to move on to."

He slammed opened the hotel room door and paced out into the parking lot.

After a stunned moment she went to the window, her eyes following his movements. He was praying to the sky it seemed, in Italian, berating her, she presumed, him, the world, Evelyn, in that angry, gesticulating, frustratingly endearing tongue of his. He didn't stop for some time and, after a while, she had to bite her lips to keep from smiling at the half-deranged demeanor she'd managed to elicit from him, impressed that she could rile someone into such a state and, equally, that she could be so riled . . . so incensed . . . and perhaps she was falling in love with him. A thought that struck her with no small amount of alarm. She couldn't possibly, and yet . . . she went over to the bag he'd brought and opened it. Her heart moved into her throat. *Bagels. You brought me bagels.*

He paced back into the room suddenly and she gasped, caught gripping the bag. He looked at the bag, then at her standing there biting her lips. "You can't hate me that much if you brought me bagels," she said.

"I wouldn't have let Evelyn do it," he said. "If I had known. If I had been in on the decision, I wouldn't have let her give the child away."

"But would you have married her? Would you have broken your ties with your wife, your family obligations, if you had known?"

He couldn't answer.

"She was petrified that you would. And that you'd regret it, and her, forever."

He gazed, as if through her, for a long moment. "Let's walk," he said.

She said, "If only I could find my pants."

He pointed over to the chair, where they lay perfectly folded.

She blinked at them, a drunken flash from last night. "You didn't . . ."

He frowned, and shook his head no.

The sea glistened down the short block to the beach. They carried their shoes across the sand to the shore, and then walked along it, the sun rising on their backs and the water tugging at their feet.

They walked without talking. She watched her feet dig into the sand, each footprint a cascade of iridescence, a pounding echo in her mind, as if she could hear beneath the shore's surface, where all the baby crabs had scurried through bubbly sinkholes, running from her, this giant stomper, this invader of natural earth.

"Can we sit?" she asked finally.

They sat down facing the ocean. She hugged her knees to her chest. He braced his arms behind him.

"I don't even remember what exactly happened between Evelyn and me," Rhonda said finally, staring at the waves. "How do two people once so close fall out of contact for six years?" She looked at him. "How is that possible?"

It was a rhetorical question.

"One week turns into two, then three, then a year has passed. You're thinking of her constantly, arguing with her in your mind, laughing with her in your heart. Soon enough those six years have passed and you're getting a letter telling you that the world as you know it has ended." She grabbed a nearby shell and flung it at the waves.

"We fought the day she died," he said.

Rhonda went still. Until this day, she had not wanted to know.

"About the risotto, of all things."

She glanced at him. His eyes were glossy, as if he were outside of himself now, staring down at the two of them, not at himself and Rhonda, but at himself and Evelyn, in that tiny kitchen in their cottage by the sea. "She hated when I put butter in the risotto. She would always say that I was a tyrant in the kitchen, and I was. I was that day. That day she ran out to get fresh air in the guise of fresh bread and didn't come back."

He sat forward and rested his elbows on his knees.

"It was Evelyn who insisted that we move back to Italy, when my wife became ill, to care for Carlotta. She wanted Carlotta and I to remain close. And those were the best times really. But I also think they were the times that brought Evelyn great sorrow. That they reminded her of her own childhood in some way."

"We were a family," Rhonda said. "Evelyn, Olivia and I. For a while anyway."

"Was he good to her? Your ex-husband."

"As good as he could be. He was not a passionate man, and Olivia has such passion, such desire. I think he felt uncomfortable around her and she sensed it." Rhonda turned and found his eyes. "Evelyn never told you about Olivia?"

"She told me about her *niece*, Olivia," he said. "But when Olivia arrived in Hanoi, I knew." His eyes grew luminous, a deep, aching nostalgia.

Rhonda placed her finger on an imaginary spot just below her lower lip.

"The mark of royalty."

"The woman in the painting."

He looked at her strangely.

"I was at the cottage. I went for Evelyn's things."

"My studio?"

She smiled. "You left it unlocked."

"And you found her notebooks?"

"I burned them. She told me to and I did."

He peered at her, curiously. "You're more courageous than I thought."

"I'm glad you see it that way. Olivia might not."

"Those were Evelyn's private thoughts. They should remain private."

"Olivia went to Rome," she said, because it seemed like that's what his eyes were asking, and he nodded. "Isabella will take care of her."

"And Carlotta," she said.

A softness came over him, envisioning his daughters together, perhaps, Rhonda liked to believe. Then he got to his feet. Wiped the sand from his pants. He said that he should be going.

Don't go.

It was Sunday, he said. He had passed by a church earlier, and he wanted to go there.

When she asked if she could go with him, he said, "I don't want to ruin any more lives."

She held out her hand, and he helped her to her feet.

37

When she told him what she wanted, he didn't seem shocked. Though his lips parted ever so slightly. As if slipped open by a finger. This was how it was to be.

She had waited for him outside of the church, the ocean pouring off her, having gone back to the hotel for her swimsuit, then back to the ocean, back into her beginning, cleansing herself, preparing this deepest part of herself.

But there was nothing that could prepare her. There were only his eyes, tunneling, digging, as if he were starting from the inside of her, and clawing his way out.

From where he stood at the edge of the bed.

Devouring her with his eyes.

Then his mouth.

The sheets were on the floor. The pillows.

"Think of it as an exorcism," she had said.

His body.

He grabbed her legs, and pulled her toward him. She pressed her hand on his pelvis, to stay the thrusts.

And then she let go.

Would he hurt her, she might have wondered at one point, if his eyes hadn't wept of such sadness, such hope? If his skin didn't breathe like the Earth itself? This was as much for him as it was for her.

Would he eat her alive?

It took her a long time to come. And when at last she did, this explosion of longing came streaming from her eyes. She had never come before, she was sure of this now, cracked open, everything wiped out. She bit the back of her hand. Her upper arm pushed against her brow, pressing hard against the blinding white.

When he came, after her, she'd never felt such an overwhelming sense of—strangely, unexpectedly—compassion. For what, exactly, would remain the deepest mystery of her life. Human nature, perhaps. The baseness of it. The sum of all she was.

The bagels were ripped into pieces, gone.

She'd powered down her phone.

It wasn't strange.

For the first time in her life, she wasn't embarrassed.

She wasn't ashamed.

She rested her face into the hollow of his navel. She didn't think of Evelyn. She didn't think of anything, but the rise and fall of his chest.

They swam in the ocean. He hopped up and down. It was cold, he said.

She said, "It's perfect."

He jumped in and screamed.

They fell into the waves.

Thirty-six hours later, he left to go teach his class.

She glided about in a daze. Coffee. Wine. She needed a drink.

Instead she turned on her phone, by rote.

In her email there was a response from Carlotta on behalf of Isabella, who was trying to clarify what she felt might have been lost in translation. Her aunt was sorry about the difficulties Rhonda was having. Certainly she was not to worry about the sponsorship. Carlotta was happy to announce that she would be on her way to the Olympics next June! A position she would not be in if not for Rhonda's support the last two years. And while Carlotta had offers from multiple sponsors now, she would always think of Rhonda as her mentor, her American idol. More importantly though, she had to confess that Olivia was not in Rome. She'd never come to Rome, as the two girls had planned.

Call me on Skype, Rhonda texted Carlotta. *I'll be waiting.*

Her Skype rang within the hour. "I wanted Olivia to come," Carlotta assured Rhonda. "I asked her to come. And at one point she was going to come. But then, at the last minute, she called and said that she was not coming."

"But where did she go?"

The girl stayed silent.

"She didn't tell you?"

Carlotta bent down to grab something on the floor, presumably, disappearing from the screen momentarily. When she sat back up she said, "You look different."

"Carlotta," Rhonda said sternly.

"I'll text her now."

Rhonda watched her do so, noting that the girl didn't seem too concerned, which meant that if she did know where Olivia was, she was safe.

"There," she said. "I have texted her to call me."

"Let's wait and see if she does," Rhonda said.

After a few moments of waiting, Carlotta idly asked Rhonda when she was coming to visit them in Rome. They were always waiting for her to come. Especially Giuseppe, she added, smiling wryly.

"Oh, please," Rhonda moaned.

The girl giggled. "If Olivia is my half-sister, what does that make you?"

"Your friend," she said, and a smile exploded on Carlotta's face.

Rhonda agreed to hang up if Carlotta promised to text her when she heard back from Olivia. Afterward, Rhonda tried texting Olivia herself again, but to no avail.

"She's gone." She'd driven over to Marco's and interrupted him in the middle of his class. He pulled her off to the side. "She's not in Rome," Rhonda said, sliding her laptop out of her purse. He moved her into the front gallery. "Calm down. Who's gone?"

"All this time . . ." She moved aside some prints and set her laptop on his desk. "I thought she was in Italy with Isabella. Being cuddled and coddled and fed and looked after in all those ways that I never could do. And now I find out that she's not there. That she never went there." She logged in and opened Skype. She dialed Carlotta, who answered right away. Rhonda turned the screen to face Marco and said, "Talk to your daughter. Tell her you love her or something. Speak to her in that native tongue of yours, and get her to tell you where Olivia is. I know she knows where she is."

He stared at the screen, motionless.

"She's not going to bite you."

"*Papà*," Carlotta said carefully. "*Sei in America*?" Her voice was full of hurt and accusation, and Rhonda backed off slowly, watching him intently, waiting for the moment, this moment, when his shoulders softened and his eyes dampened. He exhaled, deeply, and at last they did begin speaking to one another, father and daughter, slowly at first, tentatively, hand gestures in lieu of words. Laughter, and then their sentences blended, overlapped in a language beyond the language; at one point it seemed as if they were arguing, but who knew. Theirs was an exchange so fluid and organic, it was if they'd not been apart for one day.

Rhonda felt transcended. All of them, they were but just a touch away from each other. One reach. One touch of a phone. One call to break the silence of a thousand years. One call to stop someone from showing up on your doorstep, dead.

"Olivia's in Hanoi," he said, after hanging up. He was still blinking at the screen. "She's okay," he added. "According to Carlotta."

It took a minute for the relief to settle in. Not that Olivia was okay, but a relief born from knowing that Olivia would never again feel alone in this world. She had Carlotta now, a direct line, soul to soul. And it didn't always happen between sisters, but when it did it was like a gift, the greatest gift Rhonda could ever have given to Olivia, right there at her fingertips, something she should have given her a long time ago.

"She's working at the clinic."

"Where Evelyn worked?"

"I'll make some calls," he said.

"No don't," she said, grabbing his arm suddenly.

"I know someone," he said. "It's no problem."

Rhonda loosened her grip but couldn't let go. The warmth of his arm radiated into her hand and up her arm, chest and neck, everything still raw to the touch. She brushed her hand against his cheek, along his temple. "She'll find her own way."

Epilogue

The day felt softer, a lighter shade of gray. This was her third time back to the base of the upper sanctum. It was dizzying enough to traverse to this point, a labyrinth of stone stairs and corridors and courtyards in this valley of the gods, but it was this pinnacle she was after, the highest of the five lotus-shaped towers, where the Buddha sat in meditation, where once only kings and monks had wandered.

One hundred and ten steps, it was a seventy-degree vertical climb, according to the guidebook. Formidable, but not to be missed, it said. On her first attempt she'd made it up only ten steps before her heart started hammering so hard she'd had to crawl back down. On her second attempt, the following day, as she came upon the stairs, a monsoon blew in from nowhere. She took cover under the arch between two towering stone tigers and watched the rain come down in sheets. Her sandaled feet sunk into puddles, her fingers were prunes. The rain passed through quickly, but she was too sodden to attempt the climb after that.

And now she was back, a third time, scaling the steps, while her guide, Deng, stood against a far wall smoking a cigarette with the other guides, all of whom were watching her with amusement.

It would be recommended that she walk up sideways, he'd said. She was climbing up sideways now, and it was working better. There wasn't a feeling of freefalling backward, it was more like dragging her body along the floor, she kept telling herself. There were no ropes or hand-rails. Don't look down, another suggestion from Deng. Whatever you do, don't look down.

She wasn't the only one. There was a line of people clambering to the top, where they said the views of the stoned universe were beyond majestic, where she would light a candle and make her offering to the bronzed statue of a fat, bald, bemused man seated with his hands folded in his lap, the enlightened one, so she'd been told. Enlightened or not, either way, it didn't matter. Olivia was here only to see and feel and perhaps understand. She didn't know what the future would hold. She just knew that she couldn't write anything more until she had lived. Traveled. Journeyed. To the places her mother might have been—Myanmar, Mae Hong Son, Kampong Cham, others, many others on this unknown trail her mother had left her. Olivia would go to these places. She would touch the soil and lie down on the earth where her mother might have lain.

From Cambodia, Olivia would go to Chiang Mai and then Laos, then back to base camp, Hanoi, where she would renew her visa at the immigration office. This would give her another three months in Vietnam, her third trip out and back. She had not planned on this con-tinuous cycle of returning. She had not planned on anything, really, when she'd first arrived in Hanoi nine months ago, other than to find her way back to the Sofitel, check in, and, well, just be here, there, everywhere, her mother might have been.

Miraculously, the bicycle taxi driver who had driven her and Marco around was waiting in a long line of others outside the hotel; he'd come running up to her with that big toothless grin on his shriveled-up face as if he'd been waiting in that spot for her, knowing all along that she would return.

She'd climbed in his cart, and from there, they'd retraced her and Marco's steps—the puppet theater, Confucius, the bridge over the float-ing pagoda—to the thatched house by the lake. Sue had been out front, doing her fruitless sweeping. And Marco's driver Toni was working in the garden. The house had been rented to a British couple, visiting teachers at the university, but after Toni and Sue introduced Olivia to them, they said she could rent the hut where Marco had slept for a small fee.

She'd gone and found the clinic where Evelyn had worked, the place that gave out smiles; she'd been curious, wondering, looking for something to do. No one remembered Evelyn, turnover was too frequent to remember those who came and left, but they pulled Olivia into the fold anyway, unexpectedly, the place chaotic, overextended, in need of any help it could get. It wasn't money they needed. People gave boatloads of money. Smiles were the easiest cause to sell, and Westerners clamored all over each other to write checks. What they needed were hands, caretakers for the children, help for their families with travel logistics, arrangements for adoptions, and places to stay. Food. They came to Hanoi with nothing.

She organized trips to the puppet theater for the children and their new parents, and watched their faces twist and turn in all kinds of expressions, as hers had that first time, at the strange delight of it all.

With Toni's help she made a puppet theater of her own. She wrote scripts for the children to perform for their parents and the staff, and afterward they would all hold hands and bow to standing ovations. They'd play all sorts of silly games, Olivia consumed by their warmth and laughter. She couldn't help but feel loved, needed in a way she had never felt before, the actress in her, perhaps, always craving the spotlight.

A month after Olivia had arrived in Hanoi, Gilles came by with a package for her. He was taller than she remembered, she thought, when he leaned over and kissed her hand. "I think you are even more beautiful than I remember."

She hadn't been expecting a visitor and had yet to shower that morning, or wash her face. She wore a tank shirt underneath a sarong that she still couldn't quite wrap correctly. She'd cut her hair short. And yet, for perhaps the very first time, Olivia did feel beautiful.

In the package was a print of the wedding parade, and an explanation from Rhonda how it had come into her possession. With the print came a new notebook, the cover clean, unblemished. It cracked when Olivia had opened it. Inside, a blank slate of someone's future.

At the top, for a date, Olivia had written, "Today." Below that. "I met Gilles again. He handed me a package like our fate had long been sealed. And I thought of those dice rolling, as Marco had once said."

Author's Note

Thanks to the artists' community at Angels Gate, who by inspiring my mother inspired certain scenes in the book. To my editors Sally Arteseros and Jorden Rosenfeld for pushing me in directions I might not have taken. To my 92Y classmates and teacher Sandra Newman for feedback on early chapters, and for sharing their wildly talented work. To Giuliana, as always, for the Italian perspective. To Francesco for everything. And finally to Spark Press for taking me on as part of their mission to support and inspire the work of independent women authors.

NY, 2016

About the Author

© Ron Goodman

Jackie received her MBA from U.C. Berkeley and spent eight years in the fast track of consulting before coming to terms with what was important to her in life (marrying an Italian didn't hurt!); she began writing and hasn't stopped since.

A native of Southern California, she spends a lot of her time in places not her own. As the youngest of four children, she carries with her a strong sense of family to these places, often foreign, and writes about belonging (or not belonging), loss, and love. She lives in New York with her husband. *The Absence of Evelyn* is her third book.

SELECTED TITLES FROM SPARKPRESS

SparkPress is an independent boutique publisher delivering
high-quality, entertaining, and engaging content that enhances
readers' lives, with a special focus on female-driven work.
Visit us at www.gosparkpress.com

Forks, Knives, and Spoons, by Leah DeCesare
$16.95, 978-1-943006-10-6

There are three kinds of guys: forks, knives, and spoons. Beginning in 1988, Amy York takes this lesson to college, analyzes it with her friends through romances and heartbreaks, and along the way, learns to believe in herself without tying her value to men.

The Half-Life of Remorse, by Grant Jarrett
$16.95, 978-1-943006-14-4

Two tattered mendicants, Sam and Chic, meet on the streets, both unaware that their paths crossed years before. Meanwhile, Sam's daughter Claire, who Sam doesn't even know is alive, is still unable to give up hope that her vanished father might someday reappear. When these three lives converge thirty years after the brutal crime that shattered their lives, the puzzle of the past gradually falls together—but the truth commands a high price.

The Year of Necessary Lies, by Kris Radish
$17, 978-1-94071-651-0

A great-granddaughter discovers her ancestor's secrets—inspirational forays into forbidden love and the Florida Everglades at the turn of the last century.

Gridley Girls, by Meredith First
$17, 978-1-940716-97-8

From the moment Meg Monahan became a peer counselor in high school, she has been keeping her friend's secrets. Flash forward to adulthood when Meg is a recruiter for the world's hippest, most paranoid high-tech company, and now she is paid to keep secrets. When sudden tragedy strikes just before Meg hosts the wedding of her childhood BFF, the women are forced to face their past—and their secrets—in order to move on to their future.

About SparkPress

SparkPress is an independent, hybrid imprint focused on merging the best of the traditional publishing model with new and innovative strategies. We deliver high-quality, entertaining, and engaging content that enhances readers' lives. We are proud to bring to market a list of *New York Times* best-selling, award-winning, and debut authors who represent a wide array of genres, as well as our established, industry-wide reputation for creative, results-driven success in working with authors. SparkPress, a BookSparks imprint, is a division of SparkPoint Studio LLC.

Learn more at GoSparkPress.com